Crash Landing

Crash Landing

A Novel

Annie McQuaid

AVON

An Imprint of HarperCollinsPublishers

HarperCollins books may be purchased for educational, business, or sales promotional use. For information, please email the Special Markets Department at SPsales@harpercollins.com.

Avon, Avon & logo, and Avon Books & logo are registered trademarks of HarperCollins Publishers in the United States of America and other countries.

FIRST EDITION

Interior text design by Diahann Sturge-Campbell

Line art sketch drawing © Muhammad_Zulfan/Shutterstock

Library of Congress Cataloging-in-Publication Data has been applied for.

ISBN 978-0-06-337486-7

25 26 27 28 29 LBC 5 4 3 2 1

To Mom and Dad,
for nurturing my creativity and always believing in me

Chapter One

Now

Humidity hung in the air, thick as soup, but Piper didn't mind. Rolling down the car window, she welcomed the last whisper of Georgia sunshine, the mild spring breeze succumbing under the weight of summer's impending fury. In the driver's seat, Tag frowned and jacked the AC up to its highest setting.

Pulling into the parking lot of her apartment building, Tag got out of the slick two-seater Porsche, walked around, and opened Piper's door—the terminal gentleman. Tonight marked their twelfth date in as many weeks. This time they'd celebrated completing their second year of medical school by dining at Tag's favorite restaurant, the Capital Grille, featuring an overpriced menu with dishes that reeked of garlic and left Piper hungry.

"We should continue the evening and open up that bottle of merlot I brought over last week," he said, helping her out of the car.

Piper usually admired how Tag declared his suggestions like statements instead of questions, but tonight his polished delivery made her cringe. She'd dated enough frogs in her twenty-six years to know Tag Sinclair was a catch. On paper, that is. Her exacting parents adored him, and he treated her well, rivaling the likability of a standard Disney prince. But Piper couldn't remember many of those storybook princes making the princesses laugh, and those couples rarely had much in common besides dazzling smiles and impeccable harmony.

Still, if Tag pressed her again for a more serious commitment, like he'd done on their last few dates, she'd likely give in. Piper: the perennial people pleaser.

Tag stepped toward the front door of her apartment, but Piper placed a freshly manicured hand—painted in OPI's Rosy Future, the pastel shade she'd adopted as her signature color years ago—on his chest, stopping him. In heels, she nearly matched his five-eleven frame, but his perfectly coiffed corn silk hair gave him an extra inch. A blond Ken doll with the same lack of sex appeal.

"That sounds lovely, but I still need to pack for Allie's wedding. I should call it a night."

Tag pouted. "But I'm leaving for the Cape tomorrow and you won't see me for weeks."

Sometimes Piper wondered what Tag even liked about her. Was it the designer clothes? Her ability to hide her imperfections beneath expensive makeup? Or maybe her family's name took her from a seven to a ten in his eyes. Did he even see the messy, miserable girl underneath it all, trying to look like she had it all together?

She mirrored his disappointment with a pout of her own, but the tightness in her chest loosened. "You'll be having so much fun on your family vacation, you'll hardly miss me," Piper reassured him. "Thanks so much for dinner. I had a great night."

Tag's shoulders slumped beneath his gray Cole Haan suit, but he smiled at her. "Me too."

He planted a perfunctory kiss on her lips. Piper closed her eyes and tried for the hundredth time to feel a spark or tingle of excitement instead of Tag's slightly dry and too-firm lips pressed against hers.

Nothing like the thrill of kissing Wyatt.

Wyatt.

She hated when his name popped into her head almost as

much as she loathed him. Piper pushed back from Tag, rattled, and grounded herself by taking in his dark chocolate eyes—so different from Wyatt's piercing gray gaze. With a sharp shake of her head, she banished all thoughts of Wyatt and gave Tag one last kiss on the cheek before walking away.

Letting herself into her apartment, she tossed her black YSL bag on the kitchen counter. The purse, a gift after her official enrollment at Emory's medical school, was more her mother's style than Piper's, but she received compliments every time she carried it. Her mom's influence also adorned her apartment—Barbara Adams took interior design very seriously. Piper preferred a cozy couch with cushions that swallowed her in a hug when she sat down, but the Barbara-approved tufted velvet rolled-arm sofa in cream matched the cold leather love seat, and she'd learned to pick her battles against her mother long ago.

Piper flung her closet open wide and pulled out her trusty black Samsonite suitcase. This last school term had all but sucked the life out of her, but a poolside drink at her best friend's destination wedding was exactly what the doctor ordered—or at least what this struggling medical student would prescribe.

She was debating between a fitted sage green cocktail dress and a bright yellow maxi for the rehearsal dinner when Allie's face displayed on her phone screen—an image from an ill-advised shopping mall glamour shot taken during middle school. In it, Allie's bright red tresses were teased so high they almost weren't in the frame. It was one of Piper's favorite photos of her friend because it captured her impish grin.

"Allie!" Piper answered with delight. At first, only muffled voices sounded through the speaker, then Allie shushed someone and came on the line.

"Piper! I miss you." Her words slurred together, coming out as "emishu," like she was three margaritas deep.

"I miss you, too." Piper tossed both dresses into her suitcase and added a turquoise sundress for good measure. "Promise me we won't go three months without seeing each other again! My heart can't take it. How're the Bahamas so far?" She could already taste the salt air on her lips.

Allie sighed dramatically. "My in-laws are the sweetest people, but if I have to explain the vegan options one more time, I'll lose my mind. And don't even get me started on Oliver's sister, who has decided now is the right time to swear off alcohol and tell anyone who will listen the reasons drinking will kill you." She took a drink, ice rattling in her glass. "Oliver is so calm about everything that he's driving me crazy, too."

"I'm sorry, Allie. I didn't realize everything was getting this stressful." Piper cradled the phone to her ear and dug her swimsuits out of a drawer, laying them out on the bed and assessing her options.

"It's okay. It will all be better once you get here tomorrow."

"I can't wait." Piper scooped up the assortment of one-pieces and bikinis and added them to her bag. "Hey, did Ethan make it in yet?"

"Yeah, we were just missing you over a cocktail. It's going to be so nice having us all back together—a Lonely Only reunion!"

It wouldn't be a real reunion. They'd need Wyatt for that. He'd been the last to join their close-knit group of only children in the neighborhood—the Lonely Only moniker created in first grade by Allie and Piper—and the first to leave. After dumping Piper in high school, he'd cut them all out like a cancer—likely because he couldn't stand the sight of her. There was no way Wyatt would show his face at the wedding after so many years vanished from their collective lives. Right?

Allie jumped back in before Piper could press for more details on the guest list.

"Oh em gee. I met Ethan's new boyfriend, Jack!" she practically squealed. "He's hot, but don't tell Oliver that. I swear he's a doppelgänger of Chris Hemsworth, and you know how I feel about him."

Piper laughed. "I do." The only reason Allie ever watched a Marvel movie with Oliver was to get a look at her celebrity "boyfriend."

"It's too bad Tag can't come. I was looking forward to meeting him."

Piper's chest constricted. "We're far from an official couple and definitely not at the 'come to my best friend's destination wedding' stage." *And likely never will be.*

"Are you worried I won't like him and will scare him away?" Allie teased. She'd chased off a few losers who had dated Piper in college, taking her role as best friend and guardian of Piper's well-being seriously.

"Actually, you'd love him. Everyone seems to, including my mother, who's delighted we're dating. He's very charming."

"So, what's the problem?"

Trust her best friend to see right through her bullshit.

"I don't know." Piper lay back on her bed. "He's handsome and he's a family friend, but it hasn't really clicked yet. I mean, we spend time together, but we mainly talk about school or where we should eat dinner, or the news. I keep thinking that there should be something more, you know? Like more in common, more laughter. More connection. But maybe that's only in a paperback romance."

Allie was unnaturally quiet for a moment. "I can say with confidence that Oliver makes me laugh every day, and I swear he knows me better than I know myself."

Piper blinked back unexpected tears. She wanted what Allie had. Or wanted it again. To feel that connection where your eyes meet across the room, and you know what the other person is thinking without saying a word. Or to laugh at an inside joke so hard tears slide down your face. To know they love every part of you, even the chaotic parts, and you can truly be yourself around them.

She considered, not for the first time, that maybe her first heartbreak had rendered her broken forever, her heart iced over so thoroughly that not even a blowtorch could crack it open.

"Maybe Tag's your person, maybe he's not," Allie continued. "But promise me you're deciding based on what makes you happy, not anyone else, okay? Follow your heart. That's all that matters."

"Yeah, yeah, yeah," Piper said, brushing Allie off before saying goodbye.

She'd heard the advice from her headstrong friend many times, but Piper knew better. Blindly ignoring her parents' warnings about Wyatt and following her heart had led her straight to heartbreak central. Somewhere along the way, she'd stopped trusting herself. Stopped trusting her heart.

Maybe she'd settled for Tag because she knew her heart was safe with him—her heart couldn't break if she never gave it away again.

Chapter Two

Now

Piper despised being late. Thanks to a busted suitcase and her alarm not going off, she'd made it to the Atlanta airport barely an hour before her flight—two hours behind her carefully curated flight schedule. There'd been no time to shower, so a UNC ball cap covered her runaway waves, matching the workout sweats she'd fallen asleep in. At least she'd remembered her bridesmaid dress.

Allie, who'd sent a barbershop quartet to ask Piper to be her maid of honor, had selected a bridesmaid dress with at least four layers of tulle and a small train, matching her over-the-top personality. Piper's style was more Audrey Hepburn than Lady Gaga, but at least it was one less outfit to plan.

Overpacking was her worst travel habit, and cramming the lavender monstrosity along with a week's worth of clothes for the long weekend had been more than her ten-year-old suitcase could handle. Fortunately, her next-door neighbor had come to the rescue, lending her a carry-on to transfer everything into at the last minute.

Rushing through security with the borrowed neon pink suitcase left Piper out of breath and damp with sweat. A Starbucks sign beside her assigned gate glowed as if beamed down straight from heaven. Thank goodness. This was nothing an iced vanilla latte couldn't fix. As she paid for her coffee, audible groans rose from the waiting passengers. She craned her neck to read the nearby monitors, which flashed bright red notifications.

Flight delayed.

Bonus! Now she could settle into her regular airport routine of browsing bestseller bookshelves and selecting the perfect combination of travel snacks. She wanted to be in the right headspace when she landed at the all-inclusive resort—sweaty and stressed out wasn't the intended vibe.

At first, Piper enjoyed the newfound extra time, picking out peanut butter pretzels, a few granola bars made mostly of chocolate, and a new steamy beach read—the kind her mother disapproved of. Her initial wave of relief morphed into worry though when the delay lengthened for a second, then a third time. Passengers paced and muttered. Piper rocked on her heels, gaze glued to the monitor, as the intercom announced the flight cancellation due to a mechanical issue.

Crap.

Gathering her goodies, Piper hurried into the line of disgruntled passengers in front of the check-in counter to learn her options for a new flight. Ten minutes of waiting slid into thirty, the line moving as slow as a sloth on Benadryl.

When her phone buzzed, Piper answered the call like it was a lifeline. Few people could make her smile right now, but Ethan Hartung was the rare exception.

"Hey, Piper-doodle-do," Ethan chirped. "How are you? No offense, but you look like shit."

In her small, mirrored image on the phone screen, Piper's eyes were bloodshot, and her face shone ghostly pale compared to Ethan's freshly tanned skin, which he was exposing a lot of right now in his Speedo.

"It's been a stressful few weeks. How's the beach?"

Ethan panned his phone around so she could take in the expanse of ocean and sand behind him. He held up a bright pink drink with an umbrella jauntily placed on top. "It's perfect!"

Piper squinted into the phone. "What are you drinking? Isn't it a bit early for a cocktail?"

"It's a prickly pear margarita. They harvest the fruit and make the syrup locally, which means I'm basically supporting the culture." Ethan turned the phone around, showing her a spiky cactus bulging with big red berries a few yards away. "And it's never too early, especially not on vacation, which you are hopelessly in need of." He took a long pull from the frothy drink.

"Is it that bad?" Piper wiped some lingering mascara from under her eyes.

Ethan wrinkled his nose. "I'd say this isn't your best look, but I'm not just talking about this morning. I'm worried about you, Piper. You've turned down all my recent invitations to be my plus-one to fabulous parties."

"Last-minute weekend getaways aren't exactly compatible with med school."

Ethan settled onto a chaise lounge and pushed his blond hair back with his sunglasses. "You know they wouldn't be last minute if you planned a trip to New York to see me instead of waiting for me to score tickets to something and invite you up. It's been over a year since I've seen your face in person!"

"Well, say a little prayer you'll see it tonight. My flight got canceled." She tilted her head to the left, revealing the line of people behind her. "Don't tell Allie yet. I'm going to figure it out."

"You'd better!" He lowered his voice to a stage whisper. "Allie's become a Bahamas Bridezilla. And I can't witness your mom getting White Russian drunk again without you here."

Piper winced. "Yeesh, sorry about that."

"You can make it up to me when you arrive. Ask about flights leaving from Charlotte or Charleston. And try calling the airline directly while you're waiting in line." He tipped his drink toward the camera. "Good luck!"

Piper hung up and called the airline as suggested. They placed her fifty-eighth in a virtual queue moving as slowly as the real-life line she stood in. How had this day gone from escaping to a tropical island to waiting in two lines simultaneously?

By the time Piper got to the front of the physical ticket line, the counter attendant's mouth was locked in a permanent scowl.

"There are no more flights to the Bahamas leaving from Atlanta today," she snapped. "I can put you on a four P.M. flight tomorrow or put you on standby for our eight A.M. flight."

A 4:00 P.M. flight would get her there without a moment to spare before the rehearsal dinner and her maid of honor speech. Plus, she'd miss a full day on the beach. With standby, she might not make it to the Bahamas at all. Both options had her missing the bachelorette party tonight.

"Tough crowd, huh?" Piper tried to charm the lady behind the counter, but her commentary elicited only a bored eyebrow raise.

"Listen, Rita," Piper tried again, reading the name off the badge on the disgruntled woman's shirt. "My best friend in the entire world, she's more like a sister to me, is getting married this weekend, and I'm the maid of honor. It's really important I get to the Bahamas."

Rita stretched her lips into a tight, toothless smile. She typed something on her computer, then frowned and turned back to Piper with a sigh.

"What? What's wrong?" Piper asked.

"The four P.M. just booked up. You want me to put you on standby?"

Standby guaranteed nothing. "Please, Rita. I have to be there. Is there anything out of Charlotte? Or Charleston? I'll drive."

"Ma'am, do you see that line of people behind you?"

Piper nodded.

"All of them want to get to the same place as you. I've already filled the seats on the Charlotte flight leaving this evening. I'd suggest you let me book you on the standby flight I have before those spots fill up too."

Piper rubbed her forehead. "Couldn't you guys find a flight that isn't full and send the plane down to the Bahamas instead?"

Rita raised that eyebrow again. "That's an excellent idea, ma'am. Why don't you fill out a comment card and suggest that to my manager?"

Piper was confident Rotten Rita was being sarcastic, but she made a mental note to find out if the comment cards were real.

"If you want me to book you on this standby flight, I'll need your passport and boarding pass."

Behind her, passengers in sundresses and beach hats were on their phones complaining loudly or scrolling on iPads to book alternate flights. She dug up her credentials and handed them over to Rita, who clicked away on her keyboard.

"There. All set." Rita handed Piper back her license with a stiff smile. "See you tomorrow."

As Piper walked away, Rita repeated her opening greeting to the next unlucky customer. Piper pulled a bottle of Advil out of her tote and popped a few pills to squelch the migraine threatening to take over. What was she going to tell Allie?

"Rita didn't cut you a break either, huh?" a man asked from behind her.

His deep voice sent shivers down her spine like a rickety roller coaster, catapulting her back to the very best and worst moments of her life. A voice she hadn't heard in eight years—since the night Wyatt Brooks broke her heart.

The airport noise faded away like the end of a song as Piper pivoted and faced the man she swore she'd never speak to again. Sure enough, as if plucked straight from her worst nightmare, Wyatt stood before her.

The years apart had treated Wyatt well. Though age had erased all traces of boyhood from his face, he had the same serious expression she remembered. He'd cut his hair, replacing his unruly curls with sleeker, more polished waves. A dark five o'clock shadow enhanced his square jawline, highlighting his pillowy lips. Lips that never failed to raise goose bumps on her sensitive skin. When she finally dragged her gaze upward, his gray eyes matched the slice of overcast sky visible through the large glass windows beside them.

Seeing the casual perfection of his familiar face was like pressing on a bruise. Her mind swirled. What was he doing here? She shivered, rubbing her arms. How could she be both hot and cold at the same time?

He bit his lip, staring at her with those heavy-lidded eyes, his hands shoved deep into his pockets. For far too long, they didn't move. Didn't speak. Then Wyatt stepped forward, one arm outstretched as if to embrace her.

Backing up so fast she almost tripped over her suitcase, Piper folded her arms tight over her chest. He couldn't erase years of damage with small talk and a hug. Snapshots of memories flashed before her eyes: summers catching fireflies, riding bikes, fishing in the creek . . . falling in love. One minute they'd been planning a future. The next, he'd discarded her as easily as a used textbook and moved on to someone new even faster.

She cleared her throat, finding her voice. "What are you doing here, Wyatt?"

Adjusting her baseball cap, Piper combed a hand through her thick golden hair, shaking a few tangles loose. She'd pictured this moment a hundred times, but in all her imaginings, she looked fabulous, not wearing wrinkled day-old clothes and sporting a ballcap over dirty hair. Not that it mattered.

Wyatt dragged a shaky hand over his jaw. "Same as you, I'm assuming. Trying to get to Allie's wedding."

Piper absorbed the information as if it were an earthquake, the vibrations resounding through her body. How had Allie left out this critical detail? Warmth crawled up her neck. Of course he was going to the wedding. It was stupid to think otherwise. He was Allie's cousin, after all. Her hatred of him didn't make him any less a part of Allie's family. Still, she made a mental note to absolutely strangle her best friend for not giving her a fair warning.

"Okay, so you're going to the wedding, too." She blinked, still processing that Wyatt was standing in front of her. "But what are you doing here, in Atlanta? I thought you lived in Wyoming or something."

"Colorado," he corrected with a frown. "I had a layover here. I'm guessing we were both on the flight to the Bahamas that got canceled. From the looks of it, it's going to be hard getting another flight out of here in the next few days." He smoothed an invisible wrinkle on his shirt. His fitted white tee showed off his ropy arms and broad shoulders, making it clear he'd trained for combat at one point. "Speaking of that, I have an old army buddy in the area. I called him up to see if he wanted to grab coffee when it looked like I'd be stuck here for a bit, and one thing led to another, and he offered me the use of his plane." He shifted his weight, looking as jittery as she felt. "No pressure, but there's plenty of room if you want to ride down to the Bahamas with me." His voice cracked slightly on the last words.

"What do you mean 'offered you his plane'? Who's flying it?" Piper narrowed her eyes.

Wyatt squared his shoulders and, if possible, grew an extra inch. "I've been flying planes for over five years and in much more dangerous situations than a short trip to the Bahamas."

"Wait. *You're* flying?" Piper opened her mouth and snapped it shut, speechless. It was one thing to exchange a few awkward words with Wyatt in a crowded airport; it was quite another to be alone on a plane with him for hours. A plane he supposedly knew how to fly. At the gate, the monitors still read CANCELED, and the line of angry passengers remained. Missing her best friend's wedding simply wasn't an option, but being trapped in a small aircraft with Wyatt felt intolerable.

He took her silence in stride, scribbling something on a piece of paper and pressing it into her palm. "I have to submit my flight plan, fuel the plane, and complete the preflight check, so I'll be at that private terminal for at least an hour before leaving. Come find me if you want a ride."

He hoisted his backpack higher, and the edge of a black tattoo peeked from under the sleeve of his shirt. Piper tried not to stare. What else were his clothes hiding?

Tilting his suitcase onto two wheels, he hesitated a moment before turning to leave. "Piper, I know—" he started, then blew out a breath, worrying the edge of his bottom lip with his teeth. "It's really good to see you," he finished, not quite meeting her gaze. His jaw twitched like he might say something more, but he flashed her a dangerously dimpled smile. The one that had always turned her legs to jelly.

Still did.

Piper could manage only a slight nod as Wyatt disappeared into the crowd, like a fractured figment of her imagination.

Chapter Three

Now

In a blind panic, Piper made her way to a far corner of the terminal and collapsed into a hard plastic seat. Her heart hammered like she'd mainlined a Red Bull, every nerve ending on fire. Outside the floor-to-ceiling windows, planes taxied on the runway—heading everywhere but where she needed to go.

Piper whipped out her phone to demand answers from Allie. On the first ring, she remembered the bride was probably lying poolside preparing for her big bachelorette night tonight, and this might not be the best time to go into full meltdown mode. But anger aside, Allie was the first person she called when stressed out or dealing with a tough decision. This qualified.

Allie picked up on the second ring. "Piper! Please tell me you're calling from the plane. My future sister-in-law keeps taking drinks out of my hand so I don't 'look puffy' in pictures. I can't take much more of this without you here."

Piper's jaw clenched. "No such luck. My flight got canceled, but I'm on standby for a flight out tomorrow morning."

"So, you'll miss my bachelorette?" Allie's voice went up an octave. "Why is everything going so wrong? I can't—"

"Speaking of everything going wrong," Piper cut in before Allie could get lost in a pity party. "You'll never guess who I ran into in front of Auntie Anne's pretzels at the airport." Piper breathed through her outrage. "Actually, I bet you could guess."

"Uh-oh. You sound mad."

"See, you're already making great guesses."

"You saw Wyatt, huh?" Allie at least sounded guilty. "I can explain."

"I'm not sure you can!" The hot stab of tears clawed at Piper's throat. "Allie, this is the man who ripped my heart out of my chest and tore it in two, Hulk-style. Besides blowing up our romance, he blew up our friendship. He abandoned the Lonely Onlys. He dropped your family, too. How is it possible that he's coming to your wedding? And how could you not warn me?"

Allie sighed. "I wanted to. But you were freaking out about midterms and had already canceled your trip home for my bridal shower. I worried you'd bail on my wedding if you found out, and I didn't want to stress you out even more."

"Well, I'm beyond stressed now! How did this even happen? I thought Wyatt wasn't talking to any of us." It was hard to decide which was the bigger blow—running into Wyatt unexpectedly or learning he'd slipped back into Allie's life without Piper's knowledge.

"I'm sorry! I didn't mean to keep this from you. He reached out to me around Christmas last year, apologizing for everything. We've been catching up here and there. I invited him to the wedding because he's the closest thing I have to a brother, but it surprised me as much as you when he RSVP'd yes." Allie coughed over a catch in her voice. "I wanted to tell you, but I didn't know how."

Some of the tension in Piper's clenched jaw slackened. "You know, you can tell me anything. Especially something like this."

"I know. I'm so sorry. Forgive me?" Allie pleaded. "You can't stay mad at the bride. That's the rule."

Piper let Allie squirm for a long pause before giving in. "You know I can never stay mad at you for long."

It was true. One reason their friendship had stood the test of time was Piper's ability to forgive every impulsive action of Allie's that had landed them in trouble over the years.

"Thank God, because I need you by my side on my wedding day." Allie let out a sigh of relief. "But I'm bummed you won't be here in time for my bachelorette party. We've talked about being together for moments like this since we were little."

Despite her lingering annoyance toward her best friend, Piper's stomach churned with guilt.

"I . . . might . . . have a way of getting down there in time." She bit her lip, already regretting the words about to come out of her mouth. "When I ran into Wyatt, he offered me a ride. He thinks he can fly us there tonight on a plane he's borrowing or something."

Allie gasped. "Are you serious? Piper, that would be amazing!"

"In theory, maybe. But I don't love the idea of being in the same airport as Wyatt, let alone trapped in a metal tube hurtling through space with him. I don't know if I can stomach it." In her mind, she was already back in her Wyatt-free apartment, scrolling for flights and coming up with a new plan to get to the Bahamas.

"I shouldn't have brought it up," Piper said, backtracking. "It's crazy to even think about."

"Look, I know Wyatt's not your favorite person—"

Piper barked out a laugh.

"—but he owes you one, right?" Allie continued. "And you don't even have to talk to him. You guys can stay out of each other's way when you get here. I'll make sure you won't have to deal with him."

Piper drew a deep breath as another plane took off into the sky, leaving a jet of white marshmallow trails in its wake.

"I know this isn't ideal, but Piper, I need you here. Please get on the plane. Please, please, please."

Allie possessed a magical ability to talk Piper into absolutely

anything. In the twenty years of their friendship, that had included skinny-dipping in the neighborhood pool, prank-calling
their crushes, and TPing houses on Halloween. Boarding a flight
with her heart-crushing ex was no exception. And Piper wanted
to be there for Allie, no matter what awful challenges she had to
face to make it on time.

"Ugh, okay!" Piper blew out a resigned breath. "I'll get on
the plane. I don't want to miss another minute of your wedding fun either. But you'd better have a glass of champagne
waiting for me!"

"I'll have a full bottle," Allie promised. "Hey, maybe this is a
good thing. You guys used to be so close. This could be the start
of us all being friends again. Or on speaking terms, at least. And
who knows, maybe you'll be thanking me for this later."

"Full. Bottle," Piper emphasized through gritted teeth before
hanging up.

A WAITER DROPPED a tray of glasses at the bar behind her, star-
tling Piper and evoking a round of applause from travelers
nearby. She checked her watch. Yup, she'd procrastinated long
enough. Despite her very valid reservations, there was no backing out now. Besides, Allie was right. She could simply accept a
ride, be cordial, then be on her merry way and put this all behind
her. Maybe if she believed that hard enough, everything really
would be okay.

By the time Piper reached the private plane terminal, she was
late.

Again.

If she hadn't already looked like a hot mess, she certainly did
now as she raced into the bright modern lobby panting from the
exertion. Besides a smartly dressed flight attendant talking on
the phone in a corner, the room was mostly empty, with no sign

of Wyatt. The nervous energy coursing through her veins made her jumpy—a mouse caught in a snake's den.

Before panic could set in, she spotted Wyatt's tall frame coming out of the nearby restroom. His eyes widened when he saw her, his mouth opening in surprise before breaking into a tilted grin.

"You came!" he said. "Are you ready to go?"

Piper nodded without a smile, begging her body to stop the wave of electricity it produced every time she saw Wyatt's face. Everything about this moment was surreal, but even in her worst nightmares she wouldn't have dreamed up this scenario.

She followed him outside to an aircraft on the far side of the tarmac. Tiny and painted bright white with red stripes, the plane looked like it belonged more on a child's mobile than in the sky. It wasn't close to the luxury private jets she'd seen influencers flying in on Instagram, but it was going to the Bahamas, which was far better than anything Rita could offer her.

Wyatt offered to help with her luggage, but she refused, opting to heave her overstuffed borrowed pink suitcase up the steps after him. After putting their bags in a tiny storage closet at the back of the plane and securing the plane door, Wyatt settled himself in the pilot's seat.

He adjusted the instruments on the dashboard in front of him. "Sit anywhere you'd like. It's just us today."

Piper responded by hefting her tote bag higher on her shoulder and choosing a seat as far away from him as possible. With only four rows, the last would have to do. At least she had a lot of legroom. As a kid, she'd been deeply insecure about being taller than the other girls in her class, but she'd appreciated her height more once her limbs morphed from gangly to graceful.

After speaking into his headset to someone on the other end, Wyatt turned around in his seat. "They've cleared us for takeoff.

You may feel a bit more turbulence than you're used to during takeoff and landing in this smaller aircraft, but don't worry. That's normal. There obviously isn't a flight attendant on board, but once we get moving, there's a Yeti cooler under the seats of your row that's loaded with snacks. There's probably a wine cooler in there, too."

Piper peered beneath her seat at the cooler plastered in U.S. Army and Captain America stickers before snapping her seat belt into place. She granted Wyatt a stingy smile. He would not win her over with a wine cooler, but it was kind of hot how confident Wyatt looked in the cockpit. Annoyingly hot. She shuddered, shaking the thought loose. She couldn't believe she was doing this—willingly trapping herself in a tiny space with this man. She could still back out, but the thought of explaining to Allie why she'd missed her bachelorette party stopped her.

"How long until we're in the Bahamas?" *And how long until I'm not stuck with you?*

"A little over two hours."

Two hours until a reunion with Allie and her parents. Two hours until she could pop a bottle of bubbles and celebrate on a sandy white beach. Piper could handle that.

Her parents, who considered Allie part of the family, had turned an invitation to the nuptials into a vacation for themselves, and they'd arrived at the Bahamas resort a week ago. She fired off a quick text letting them know about her change of travel plans minus a mention of Wyatt. They returned her message with a selfie of the two of them giving a thumbs-up sign at a cabana overlooking sparkling blue water. Her mom's oversize Tom Ford sunglasses perched on the bridge of her nose, and her dad was already sunburned even though he was wearing an Emory School of Medicine ball cap. It was so dorky it made her chuckle.

Piper Liked the photo and popped her earbuds in, letting Joni Mitchell's husky voice transport her anywhere but here. Before they'd taxied down the runway, she'd swallowed a Xanax and sunk into the fuzzy sensation of her anxiety melting away. Once they lifted into the air, the drone of the engines cut off any chance of small talk, and she relaxed for the first time all day. She'd navigated the hardest part of dealing with Wyatt and hadn't combusted. Yet.

Piper was still shrouded in her Xanax cocoon when everything changed.

The first patch of turbulence was gentle enough to rock a baby to sleep. A few bigger bumps followed, as if the plane were a smooth stone skipping across a shallow pond. When they hit an air pocket that caused the plane to drop dramatically, Piper shot upright, her stomach jumping to her throat. She dug her fingernails into the leather armrests, leaving half-moon imprints of her rising terror. Had they flown into a storm?

Outside her window, the air swirled, thick and swampy, the clouds a green-gray color that belonged in a witch's brew, not the sky. Raindrops streaked across the glass. She strained for a glimpse of the ocean below, but the thick curtain of clouds obstructed her view.

At the front of the plane, Wyatt spoke into his headset, his attention focused on the dials in front of him.

Piper looped her tote back over her shoulder, unbuckled her seat belt, and walked toward him. Before she could take two steps, the plane dropped, then tipped to the right, knocking her to the floor. Her knees throbbed at the sudden impact, screaming in unison with her heart.

Alarm sirens rang from the cockpit, a cacophony of panic.

Wyatt whipped around, his eyes wide. He shouted over the engine, "Why aren't you buckled up?"

"I wanted to see what was happening up there," Piper yelled back, grabbing at an armrest and pulling herself upright.

"Jesus, Piper! Get back in your seat!"

"Stop yelling at me. I'm trying to!" The force of the plane jerking up and down pinned her to the floor. Tears swam in her eyes. Her heart raced. Was this how she would die? On the floor of a plane with Wyatt Brooks?

The plane dropped like an elevator whose cable had snapped.

"Piper, get back in your seat. Now!"

She could only choke out a sob in response, frozen in place by terror and confusion. Then a pair of muscular arms yanked her up and into the copilot's seat. Wyatt buckled her in securely before fastening himself in next to her, moving so quickly Piper barely registered what was happening.

"What's going on?" Her heart hammered so loud in her ears it nearly drowned out the roar of the plane.

Wyatt didn't respond as he pulled his headset back on and repeated foreign phrases in a low, terse voice. Tension zipped his face up as tight as his death grip on the flight controls.

Piper's knuckles whitened on the tote bag in her lap. "Is there anything I can do to help?"

Clouds whirred by, the tips of whitecaps now visible out the window.

They were flying far too low.

"Hold on," Wyatt said through pinched lips, his hands trembling on the controls. "We're almost out of this wind pattern. Once we get over these islands, we should be—"

A loud crack cut him off.

The belly of the plane slammed into something unforgiving and hard, jolting them so forcefully Piper bit her tongue, her mouth filling with metallic blood.

The sound of a metal lid snapping off a tin can filled the air. A vacuum of wind hit her from behind as the back half of the plane fell away. The seat she'd been curled up in moments ago—gone.

She wasn't ready to die yet.

This couldn't be the end.

Leaves rushed up, meeting what remained of the plane. Her nostrils burned with the acrid odor of fuel. Heat blasted past her, flames licking her face.

Wyatt screamed something, but a horrible noise filled her ears. Then, with a flash of searing heat, everything went black.

Chapter Four

Then

Piper burst into the clubhouse and shut the door behind her, leaning against it while she caught her breath. All week she'd tried to escape her mother's constant attempts to micromanage her summer schedule, and today she'd finally broken free. While her friends enjoyed a break before high school began, Piper's mother—intent on bolstering her resume for college applications—had booked her solid. That included a week at tennis camp and volunteering as a junior aide at her dad's hospital. Piano lessons had followed tennis camp, not because Piper had any interest in learning to play but because it was part of a "strong foundation," according to her mom. Whatever that meant. Not exactly the relaxing summer she'd hoped for.

Today, Piper had slipped out the back door and made a beeline for the tiny house on the outskirts of their property. Less than five hundred square feet and wired for electricity, the clubhouse earned every inch of its number one spot in Piper's universe and was the one place her nature-averse mother wouldn't follow her. Listening for the sounds of footsteps outside and hearing nothing, she sagged against the door and blew out an exaggerated sigh.

"Running from the law?" a voice inquired from the corner of the small room.

Piper's hand flew up to her mouth, stifling a scream. She whipped her head around to see who'd spoken.

The voice belonged to a boy about her age with dirty bare feet, sunburned cheeks, and a mop of brown curly hair. His legs were long, his expression serious. Where had he come from? He fixed his gaze on her, and something flipped in Piper's gut, like a fan starting up, whirring to life. His eyes shone like marbles—endless swirls of light that Piper swore she recognized. Recognized him. A knowing deep in her bones. But that couldn't be right because she'd definitely never seen this boy before.

Piper wiped her sweaty palms along the front of the pressed Lilly Pulitzer shorts she wore with the matching pink top her mom had laid out for her that morning. One day soon, she'd tell her mom she was beyond old enough to dress herself, but for now, it was easier to go along with it.

Since he was still waiting for an answer, Piper cleared her throat. "Not the law, but hiding from my mom, which is kinda the same."

He nodded like he understood exactly what she meant but didn't shift from his spot.

Piper collected herself with a steadying breath and crossed her arms. "So, who are you, and what are you doing in my clubhouse?"

As a passion project years ago, her dad had renovated an existing work shed into the cozy clubhouse, adding a rooftop deck, glow-in-the-dark star stickers, and a working bathroom. It sat nestled in the woods between Allie's and Piper's houses. Over the years, Piper had added a winding path through the woods and a bright coat of lemon-yellow paint to the front door. The unspoken "no grown-ups allowed" rule made the clubhouse special, and she used the sacred space for official Lonely Only meetings with Allie and Ethan.

It was where Piper went to dream, and now, to escape.

"I'm Wyatt. And I live in the house right over there." He pointed toward Allie's house. "Who are you?"

Piper pursed her lips, determining if this boy was a threat. "I'm Piper from the house over there." She pointed in the opposite direction. "And I know you don't live at the McLaughlins' because my best friend lives there."

"Yeah, Allie's my cousin. I'm spending the summer here." He returned her stare, eyes like wet stones locked on hers.

Hmm. Allie had said her cousin was visiting for a few weeks, but she'd failed to mention her cousin was a boy—and one with such striking eyes. The more she studied him, the more she could see the family resemblance. Maybe that explained the weird feeling that she'd known him for years. Though Wyatt didn't share Allie's shocking red hair, he had the same light eyes and smirking lips. But whereas Allie sparkled with new soul energy, this boy carried the weight of the world on his shoulders.

He blinked at her, then turned his attention back to the book in his lap. Fine. There was no harm in sharing the clubhouse with a fellow reader. For now. She pulled out her own book, a worn copy of *The Giver*, and settled into a beanbag in the opposite corner, keeping him within her line of sight.

After ten minutes, curiosity got the better of her. "Whatcha reading?"

He held up the newest book in the Magic Realm series with a bright red cover. The book Piper had stood in line for over two hours to get her hands on, only to be told they'd sold out. The library wait list was already three months long. Her mom had promised to find a copy in time for her birthday next month, but a month was a very long time to wait for a book she'd spent nearly a year anticipating.

"Wait, how'd you get a copy of *The Return of the Queen*? Is it as good as *The Knight's Kingdom*?"

Wyatt beamed at her enthusiasm, his smile changing his entire face, lighting him from the inside out. "So far, it's better, but I'm only about thirty pages in. My aunt Molly gave it to me this morning."

"Who's your favorite character? Mine is Peregrine." She rarely got a chance to discuss her favorite series with another fan—Allie would sooner talk about politics than fantasy books—and Piper couldn't help the questions pouring out of her.

"I mean, she's cool in an obvious way, I guess. I think Dash has way more spirit."

Piper wrinkled her nose. "Maybe, but what about when she risked her life to save Demetrius? That was pretty spirited. And not in an *obvious* way."

"Wait until you read this one." Wyatt tapped the book knowingly. "You might change your mind."

Piper groaned. "Don't remind me. I'll be waiting all summer long to get it—it's sold out everywhere."

"Do you want to read it with me? I don't mind starting over. We could take turns reading out loud."

That was not the response Piper had expected from this stranger wearing a tattered black Guns N' Roses T-shirt. Allie would make so much fun of her for this, but Allie wasn't here. And to Piper, this sounded like heaven. Most other boys her age didn't sit still long enough to have a conversation, let alone read a book. Clearly, Wyatt wasn't like most boys. She nodded eagerly and took a seat on the floor beside him.

He handed her the book. "You can read first. But you have to do accents and everything."

Piper rolled her eyes but accepted the book, running her fingers over the cover, marveling at the intricate design. After trying to get her hands on this book all week, she couldn't believe she finally held the weight of it.

Usually, she'd be nervous to read in front of a stranger, but next to Wyatt, a deep sense of comfort and confidence settled over her. When it was his turn, Wyatt proved to be a master of accents. Though she'd initially pegged him as aloof, his voice was rich with warmth and humor. Reading Magic Realm aloud felt like swapping their biggest secrets with each other. She could have listened to him hash out the adventures of Peregrine and Demetrius all day. It didn't hurt that he was undeniably cute.

She shook her head, shaking off that thought, and forced herself to stop staring at his jawline, waiting for his dimple to wink into view. Wyatt was Allie's cousin, which made him off-limits for romance. Not that romance was happening here. She was getting way, way ahead of herself.

It was nearly dinnertime when Piper glanced at her watch. "Shoot, I need to go. Thanks for letting me read with you." She stood and stretched her stagnant muscles.

"Of course. If you want to keep reading, we could meet again tomorrow." Wyatt dog-eared the page, saving their place.

"Yes, please, that sounds perfect." Piper bit her lip. "I don't want you to have to wait for me."

He gave an easy shrug. "It's okay. It's more fun this way. Besides, I want to be there when you discover Dash is way cooler than your precious Peregrine." He grinned at her, treating her to a dimple sighting.

"Whatever!" she replied, but a smile flitted across her face. "I'll see you tomorrow."

PIPER WONDERED HOW long it would take Allie to find out she'd met her mysterious cousin, but like clockwork, Allie came over right after dinner, letting herself in the back door. Seated at the kitchen counter, Piper was halfway through a bowl of vanilla bean ice cream.

Allie grabbed a spoon and helped herself to a bite before

launching into conversation. "I hear you met my cousin. What did y'all even talk about? He doesn't say much."

Piper guessed people probably said the same thing about her, even though she had plenty to say in the right crowd. "We mostly talked about books."

Allie giggled. "I should have known you two would get along. You're both so serious and weird."

"Am not!"

Allie squeezed her arm reassuringly. "Good-weird! Trust me, I wouldn't want you any other way. And Wyatt's staying the whole summer, so now you've got someone to talk to about your Magic Kingdom books."

Piper looked down her nose at her best friend. "Magic Kingdom is at Disney World. Magic Realm is the book series."

"This is exactly what I'm talking about." To make her point, Allie polished off the last bite of ice cream from Piper's bowl.

Despite Allie's teasing, that summer turned out to be one of the very best. Piper and Wyatt met most afternoons in the clubhouse to escape the Carolina heat. They reread the Magic Realm series, then moved on to a new one. Allie and Ethan had soccer camp during the day, but at night the four would bike to the drugstore to buy Klondike bars, bask in the frigid air-conditioning at the movies, or get the entire neighborhood involved in a game of capture the flag. They officially inducted Wyatt into the Lonely Onlys later that summer, after he took the blame for a broken window that had been Ethan's fault from a rowdy game of kickball.

It wouldn't be until several summers later, after she and Wyatt had become so close that she couldn't imagine her life before he came into her world, that Piper would learn the full extent of how rough his day-to-day world back home was. Why Wyatt acted far older than his years and wasn't as carefree as most kids. And why escaping to Cedar Falls every summer meant more to him than she could ever imagine.

Chapter Five

Now

Time was elastic. The space between dreams and reality shifted every time Piper opened her eyes.

Blink.

Ten years old and having a sleepover with Allie.

Blink.

The world on fire, and all she could see was red.

Blink.

High school prom and dancing with Wyatt.

Blink.

Darkness and the roar of the ocean.

Piper broke free from the limbo of her dreamworld, her mouth tasting like cotton and something metallic. Blood? When she inhaled, her lungs burned as if she'd smoked a pack of cigarettes.

Where was she? Her hands curled into sand by her sides. A man stood by the water's edge, looking out at the horizon. Was she on vacation? Or hungover? Was this a dream? The man walked toward her, and she squinted.

Wyatt?

Everything came rushing back. Getting on the plane with Wyatt, the alarm bells, the plane splitting apart. Her stomach churned, and she rolled over, vomiting in the sand. Doing so awakened the nerves in her body, setting pain in motion.

Every limb ached. Her head throbbed with persistent pain

that radiated outward like cracks on a windshield. A sharp pressure behind her eyes made it difficult to concentrate or even think clearly. Her hand grazed a bandage covering the right side of her forehead, the skin itchy beneath. Where had that come from? A knot the size of a golf ball had formed at the top of her skull, the source of her throbbing pain. Exploring further, she combed her fingers through a warm, sticky substance matting her hair to her head—blood. She pulled her hand away, shaking, her stomach churning. Hurting too much to move away from her vomit, she lay back in the sand and watched the clouds pass overhead.

"Hey, you're awake!" Wyatt knelt beside her and wiped her mouth with a wet rag, relief flooding his voice. "I want you to take two Advil if you think you can keep it down. Let's start with some water and see how that goes." He pressed a gentle hand under her shoulders, guiding her upright, and the world spun again.

Wyatt steadied her and brought a canteen to her lips. "Take it slow."

The fresh water tasted better than ice cream on a summer day, but Wyatt pulled it away before it quenched her thirst. Her vision blurred, sea and sky melting into each other. The water helped, but only a little. Piper lay back, and Wyatt placed the wet rag on her forehead. She wanted to ask him what had happened to her, and the plane, and if they would be okay, but darkness swept over her before the words left her mouth.

It could have been a few hours or a few days, but eventually, Piper woke again with a clear head, no longer imprisoned by intense pain. She sat up inch by inch before raising her arms above her head in a long stretch. Her body creaked like the Tin Man in need of oil, and her head still throbbed, but the sharp pain was gone, making it easier to think. The knot on her head was smaller, and the cut on her forehead—at least she guessed that's what was going on beneath the bandage—itched more than hurt.

Satisfied she was no longer on the brink of death, she looked around. Where the hell were they?

High in the sky, the sun cast palm-frond-shaped shadows onto the sand. The fragrance of salt mixed with something acrid tinged the damp air. From under the tiny hamlet of palm trees where she sat, the rolling ocean stretched on forever. The turquoise water sparkled crystal clear, beautiful in an unnatural, too-bright way, like a real-life Instagram filter.

Only a few yards of sand existed between where she sat and where the ocean lapped the shore. Behind her, a maritime forest presented a tangle of trees, brush, and roots. Down the beach on her right, the shoreline ran along the ocean for miles until it curved out of sight. Meanwhile, a rocky cliff blocked her view of the ocean on the other side, sand quickly giving way to jutting boulders decorated with moss. Everything grew wild, untouched by man, except for the burned-out husk of metal that sat sculpture-like on the sand a short distance away.

Their plane.

Or what was left of it.

She could make out the red stripes of the aircraft, but flames had singed both wings black, and the metal was bent at odd angles. The back half of the plane, the half she'd sat in for most of the flight, was nowhere in sight. Probably somewhere in the Atlantic now. The wreckage reminded her of horrible car accidents depicted on TV—the kind where the Jaws of Life were necessary to pry someone out.

The kind where no one survived.

Despite the warm air, a chill ran through her. She choked back a scream that threatened to wrench itself from her body. She'd been hoping when she became coherent she'd discover they were not, in fact, crashed on a desolate beach. That she wasn't stranded with her ex.

No such luck.

Down by the water to her right, Wyatt dragged pieces of driftwood into a pile. His once white T-shirt was stained with dirt and dried blood—his or hers, she didn't know. Swim trunks hung low on his hips. Strips of fabric were tied around his left arm, and though he favored his right side, he appeared in overall better shape than Piper. Actually, he was in great shape.

Piper swallowed hard, taking in the way Wyatt's muscles rippled under his shirt as he dragged another log down the beach and wiped sweat from his brow. There was no way around it— Wyatt was a bona fide hunk.

She squashed the thought like it was a pesky mosquito as soon as it swarmed in her mind.

Dirt and blood caked her body, and smoke clung to her hair. Everything itched, and she'd never felt so in need of a shower. The endless ocean in front of her beckoned like a siren's call, the crystal water promising relief to her aching body and sunburned skin. She stood, testing her strength. The beach didn't swim in front of her as it had done before. So far, so good.

After checking that Wyatt remained a respectful distance down the beach, she stripped down to her sports bra and underwear and waded delicately into the ocean, sighing with delight as the cool water soothed her skin like an aloe bath. The waves licked away the dried sweat from her body, and the salty water held her buoyant, rocking her like a baby.

Her throat tightened, and before she could stop them, hot tears sliced down her face, splashing onto the water's surface before becoming one with the salty sea. Once her first teardrop fell, it was impossible to hold back the onslaught of fear and shock that poured out of her like a faucet. This couldn't be real. Had she really survived a plane crash? Where were they, and how would they get home? What if they never made it home? Wild thoughts raced through her mind, each one darker, more depressing than the last.

Facing out at the blue water that stretched on as far as she could see, Piper tilted her head back and let out a primal wail, not caring if Wyatt heard her. She screamed at the ocean, the island, and their stranding until her voice grew raw and her body sagged back into the hug of the water.

Her mini meltdown hadn't gotten her closer to rescue, but it had loosened the tight knot of fear in her chest. Minimally. At the very least, she'd worn herself out.

Coming out of the water with the waves at her back was a little trickier than wading in, and she rocked unsteadily on her feet in the wet, shifting sand. Her vision blurred, and her legs betrayed her, but strong arms scooped her into a fireman's hold before she'd even registered she was falling.

Too woozy to protest, she let Wyatt cradle her against his chest as he strode across the beach. His skin smoldered so warm against her wet body that she half expected steam to rise from the places where their bodies touched. She clung to him, hating how much she needed Wyatt's sturdy arms right now. But more than that, she hated how much she'd missed being this close to him, how badly she wanted to pull herself even closer. Wounded, half naked, wet, and defenseless, she'd never been more vulnerable, yet somehow felt unreasonably safe in this moment. In Wyatt's arms. She buried her tearstained face into his strong chest, trying to calm her racing heart.

"It's okay. I've got you," he murmured in her ear.

How long had she unconsciously craved the comfort of his hug, of his warm body holding her? She worried this tiny taste would set her back years of getting over him, but it didn't stop her from breathing in the still familiar scent of his neck.

Too soon, Wyatt set her down beneath a clump of palm trees. Piper instantly missed the warmth of his body and scrambled to steady herself, pulling on the fresh T-shirt he handed her. It must have been one of his because it fit Piper like a dress. She was thankful for the coverage, though it resembled a very "post hookup" look, which did funny things to her mind.

"You look a lot better. How're you feeling?" Wyatt handed her a water bottle.

Piper took a long sip before answering. "Not great." She tried to fight back the new round of tears forming in her eyes. "What the hell happened? Where are we? Unless they grossly mismarketed the resort on their website, I'm guessing this isn't the Four Seasons Resort?" In her hoarse, scratchy voice, the joke came out flat. The tears rolling down her face didn't add any humor either.

Wyatt sat next to her, leaning back against a tree. Dark circles tarnished the hollows under his eyes, making his irises appear lighter than usual.

"Unfortunately, no. If I had to guess, I'd say we're somewhere between the Florida shore and Turks and Caicos." He brushed some sand off his arm. "I don't know why we crashed. That storm came out of nowhere. I swear it wasn't even on the radar, and the wind forced me to fly too low. I think we may have hit some rocks or a tree, and the force of impact completely split the plane." He winced as if remembering the impact. "I leveled us, so we didn't crash into the water or worse, but it was a really close call, as you know."

Piper gulped, wiping a tear from her eye. She far preferred stranded on dry land to shark bait. "I don't remember any of it," she whispered.

"I'm not surprised." Wyatt picked at the cuticle on his thumb. "I must have been thrown from the force of our landing because I ended up on the sand a few yards from the plane. It caught on fire, and you were still strapped into your seat. I somehow got you out of there, but you were out cold, and I could barely find a pulse." He shook his head like he was trying to rid himself of the memory. "There was so much blood coming from your head. It was awful. I've never been so scared in my life. I didn't even notice I'd burned my arm until you started breathing again."

Piper wrapped her arms around herself in a hug. The charred and twisted hunk of metal down by the water made her stomach twist in cold dread. How had they even survived that landing in the first place? She guessed she wouldn't have without Wyatt.

Swallowing hard, she attempted a grateful smile in his direction. "How's your arm now?"

Wyatt glanced at his bandage. "It'll be better in a day or so."

"Well, thanks for not letting me burn up in there," Piper said lamely. How did you properly thank someone for saving your life, especially when that someone was the guy who'd also broken your heart?

He shrugged like it was no big deal. Like he saved people from burning planes all the time. For all she knew, maybe he did.

Piper's stomach growled like a cornered animal, interrupting her train of thought.

Without a word, Wyatt produced a granola bar from a camouflage backpack nearby and handed it to her. Piper tore off the wrapping and bit into the chocolate oatmeal goodness, fighting the urge to cram the entire chewy bar into her mouth. She couldn't remember the last time she'd eaten. A muffin for breakfast at the airport? Had that been yesterday?

She took another bite. "How long have I been out of it?"

"About a day."

So, she'd lost a night—Allie's bachelorette night. Not ideal, but there still might be a way to make it to the wedding. Given their circumstances, it was a wild, irrational thought, but one she needed to keep her sanity. The obstacles to them getting to that point were not insignificant, but she wasn't ready to abandon all hope.

She raised the bar to her lips and tore off another bite.

"Make that last," Wyatt cautioned. "We both packed some

snacks that survived the crash, but we should ration them until we find another food source."

Piper swallowed hard at the gravity of his words and set the rest of the granola bar down. "Or until we're rescued, right? I'm sure by now my parents have the entire Coast Guard looking for us." It was easier to think they were hanging out on a beach with help right around the corner than that they were stuck in some twisted version of *Swiss Family Robinson*.

"Hopefully," he said, his tone less than optimistic. "But in the meantime, we should build a shelter and find food and water. Maybe see if we can start a fire—the usual."

Piper narrowed her eyes. How was Wyatt so calm and confident about this when she wanted to vomit? Again. "The usual? Did you take some sort of survival class that I missed in high school?"

"No, but I spent five years in the army and deployed overseas twice," he reminded her. "You pick up a thing or two."

Piper flushed. Of course! Why hadn't she connected that sooner? Even with two years of medical school under her belt, he probably knew more than she did. But then again, she'd never had to assess her talents and knowledge for basic survival skills in a real-life crisis.

"I still can't believe we crashed," Piper murmured, more to herself than to Wyatt.

This was insane. In what world was she talking survival strategies with Wyatt—"Mr. Love 'Em and Leave 'Em"—of all people? Any second, she'd wake up from this horrible dream and find herself back on the plane, about to land—safely—in the Bahamas in time to celebrate with Allie.

The anxious energy coursing through her body forced her to stand. Another mini panic attack clawed its way up her throat. Piper paced, still unsteady on her feet, and rubbed her forehead, trying to replant herself in the version of reality that involved margaritas and wedding cake—away from this island nightmare.

Her hand came away warm and sticky—she'd reopened the gash on her head. At the sight of blood, her body broke out in a cold sweat, the way it did when she was called on in class and she didn't know the answer.

She sank back down to the sand, taking several long, practiced breaths in through her nose and out through her mouth. Even talking about body-fluid-related medical ailments made her queasy, but she was used to hiding from her classmates how ill-equipped she was for a career as a surgeon. Except back home, she had a prescription for Xanax to get her through the harder days. She also had her parents' daily phone calls cheering her every step of the way. Here, she didn't have the energy to put on a brave face.

"Do we have any more bandages?" Her voice shook as much as her hand, and more tears prickled her eyes.

Wyatt looked at her like she'd sprouted an extra nose but hopped up and returned with a strip of cloth and some bandage tape. "I thought you were studying to be a doctor. Wasn't that the plan? How's a little blood freaking you out this much?"

"I'm only halfway through medical school," Piper said, focusing on breathing. Blood dripped from her head into the sand, making wavy lines appear in her vision like a flickering TV. "Do you want to chat about my career path, or do you want to help me?"

"Hold still. I'm helping."

Piper froze as Wyatt brushed her hair away from her face and wiped some of her blood off with the edge of his shirt. Doing so exposed the smooth skin of his hard stomach, and a deep pull tightened in her gut at his light touch. She concentrated on remaining as still as possible, closing her eyes to avoid being caught ogling his body, but she couldn't block out the tingle dancing up her spine from his touch.

"There, all set." Wyatt stepped back and examined his handiwork. "Try not to touch it again. It could've used stitches, and you'll likely have a scar, but it looks worse than it is. Head injuries always bleed more."

Piper squirmed and wiped her bloodied hands off on the sand. "Can we please stop talking about blood and cuts?"

One corner of Wyatt's mouth twisted upward. "I guess it's a good thing that you needed bandaging instead of me."

Piper wasn't ready to joke about this just yet, but her body relaxed with the sight of blood behind her. She'd forgotten how much of a natural caretaker Wyatt could be. Probably because he'd grown up taking care of his mom. Watching him jump into action to patch her back up reminded her of the many animals he'd rescued over the years, like the baby fox he'd found whimpering in the dark the summer after ninth grade. He'd bottle-fed it until the kit regained enough strength to be released back into the wild. Or the pregnant stray cat who'd trusted Wyatt enough to give birth in the clubhouse under his care. The runt of the litter, Peregrine, was living a life of luxury with Aunt Molly, and her littermates had all been adopted by loving homes. And that didn't include the many times he'd swept in and rescued his friends.

Rescued her.

Until he'd been the one she'd needed rescuing from.

Thinking about her dead and buried relationship with Wyatt was the kick in the pants she needed to snap into action. He may be fine playing cool, calm Island Ken, but she couldn't just sit around chatting with him like they were old friends at a beach party. The window for repairing their relationship had closed long ago, no matter how much she missed him. She couldn't afford to fall for his charm and nurse another broken heart for years. She needed to get to that wedding and get on with her life.

But first, she needed a plan.

Chapter Six

Then

They'd attended the party at Allie and Ethan's insistence. The Lonely Onlys would be seniors in a few weeks, and scoring an invite to a summer party at a recent high school grad's house was a big deal. Through soccer, Allie and Ethan knew half the kids there and flitted off in different directions as soon as they arrived at the parent-free house, leaving Piper and Wyatt to fend for themselves. The sticky crowd of teenagers, blaring music, and cheap liquor was not Piper's idea of a good time, but she wanted to be a good sport and show everyone she could loosen up.

That's how she ended up seated in a circle spinning a dusty bottle of merlot. The wine bottle stopped its rotation in front of a senior boy with a pinched face and mean eyes. All Piper knew about him was his name, Hunter, and that he was popular because he drove an expensive car and was a pitcher for the varsity baseball team. She'd overheard him bragging earlier that night about the number of girls he'd already slept with that summer, and not in a way that made her want to get in line.

"New rules," Hunter said, his gaze roving up and down Piper's body. "Matches get to spend seven minutes in heaven—a.k.a. the closet over there."

Piper pulled up the straps of the figure-hugging minidress she'd borrowed from Allie, hiding as much of her cleavage as possible. Guys like Hunter who were used to getting what they wanted didn't scare her, but that didn't mean she wanted to be alone in a closet with him. But Allie's voice rang in her head, telling her to go with the flow and have fun.

"Lead the way," Piper said, standing to face Hunter, wishing she'd taken the cup of spiked punch offered earlier in the night.

Wyatt, who was uncharacteristically participating in the game, reached out to twist the bottle in his direction. "I think that one landed on me. Maybe next time, Hunter."

Hunter opened his mouth to argue, but when Wyatt stood up and revealed his six-foot-three, broad-shouldered frame, he closed it. Taking advantage of the pause, Wyatt grabbed Piper's hand and dragged her to the closet before she knew what was happening.

"What are you doing?" she hissed as soon as the door shut behind them. Now everyone was going to think she'd chickened out.

"Saving you from having to kiss Jerkface McGee," Wyatt replied. "You're welcome."

"What if I wanted to kiss him? Did you think of that?"

Wyatt squinted at her in the dim light. "I can go grab him if you want me to. I'm sure he'd be happy to shove his tongue down your throat for seven minutes."

He put his hand on the doorknob to open it, but Piper stopped him with a resigned sigh.

"No, you're right," she said. "I didn't want to be stuck with him. But I don't want people gossiping about us in here."

"Why? Because it would ruin your squeaky-clean reputation if people thought you made out with Wyatt Brooks?"

There was an edge to his voice that made it hard for Piper to tell if he was joking.

"I'm not crazy about your third-person reference," she said. "But no, of course not. I don't like the idea of our friendship being reduced to a stupid high school rumor. It's too special for that."

She was grateful for the darkness so Wyatt couldn't see her

blush. Too special for that? Had she really said that out loud? Being in a quasi-romantic situation with Wyatt, however forced it might be, was scrambling her head.

Wyatt's shoulders relaxed. "It's hard to escape a high school rumor. You're better off ignoring them. But in this case, we can decide what we tell people. So, what do you want our story to be?"

"What do you mean?"

"I mean, as soon as our time's up, which I'm guessing is about four more minutes, everyone's going to want to know what we've been doing in here. Did we kiss? Did we make out? Did we talk about politics?"

Piper laughed, but it came out thin and nervous. Standing this close to Wyatt was making her hands sweat. Which was absurd because they spent most summer days holed up in a clubhouse not much bigger than this closet. But in the clubhouse, her heartbeat never took up the entire room.

What was going on? Wyatt was her friend. There'd been no blurring of those lines, but talking about kissing made her think about kissing him. And thinking about kissing him made everything inside her warm and tingly and out of focus.

"I think we can say you kissed me and make it no big deal," she decided, tucking her blond hair behind her ear.

She wasn't sure if that was the right answer or what he'd been expecting, but his eyes lowered, and he leaned in close. She closed her eyes and raised her face up for his kiss, her heart beating so fast it had become one steady murmur, but he bypassed her mouth, grazing his soft lips on her cheek.

"There, now it won't be a lie," he whispered.

The place where his lips touched her face stung like an electric shock. It left her wanting more, but she didn't dare move when she needed all her energy for breathing.

Before she could respond with anything coherent, someone

yanked open the closet door, and they blinked out into the harsh fluorescent lights of the living room.

Had it really been only seven minutes?

"Time's up!" Kiera Gomez crowed from the crowd of teens gathered around the closet. "Something definitely happened in there. I can see it all over Piper's face!"

Even though she was the same age as Kiera, next to her, Piper felt like the kid sister invited to the party out of pity. Blushing a deep shade of red, she brushed past the crowd.

"How far did you get, man?" the guy standing next to Kiera asked Wyatt.

"A gentleman never tells," Wyatt replied, following Piper out of the closet.

"I hope you're not too much of a gentleman." Kiera batted her long eyelashes at Wyatt. Her teeth gleamed white as opals against her brown skin. "Wanna take a turn with me in there?"

Kiera's blatant flirting and syrupy sweet baby voice hurt Piper's teeth. She hated it almost as much as she hated the lopsided smile on Wyatt's face—the one that made his dimple wink. The one he was now aiming in Kiera's direction.

Wyatt smirked. "You need to spin a bottle first."

Kiera held the Bud Light bottle she was drinking from above her head and twirled in a circle, tilting the bottle in Wyatt's direction as she faced him again.

Wyatt gave Piper a helpless shrug as Kiera pushed him back into the closet, but he didn't look upset by this turn of events. And why should he? With jet-black hair down to her waist, Kiera was curvy, confident, and gorgeous. Everything Piper was not.

Hot pins pricked the backs of her eyes. Wyatt kissing anyone else made her want to claw her eyeballs out—which was inconvenient, considering Kiera likely had her tongue down his throat at that very moment. Piper didn't know how to handle whatever this latent crush might be, but she knew she couldn't be here when Wyatt and Kiera emerged from the closet.

Piper found Allie in the crowd downstairs and tugged on her arm. "Wanna take a shot?"

"Who are you, and what have you done with my best friend?" Allie laughed and poured them each a generous shot of Fireball.

Downing them elicited a cheer from the group crowded around the kitchen counter, and someone poured her another. Pretty soon, Piper had lost count of how many shots she'd consumed.

Ethan pulled her onto the dance floor, and she swigged from the drink he handed her, no longer caring what liquid filled the cup so long as it stopped her from thinking about Wyatt's lips on her cheek. And Wyatt's lips on Kiera's.

Later, when Hunter found her outside the bathroom and suggested he drive her home, she didn't think twice about taking his hand and following him out of the party. At least someone here thought she looked kissable tonight.

While Hunter dug his car keys out, Piper slumped against the hood of his Jeep Cherokee, debating if she should let Allie know she was leaving, but her legs were too heavy to go back inside.

Wyatt found her at the same time Hunter found his keys.

"Piper, there you are! Come on, we're going home." Wyatt grabbed her hand and hoisted her upright.

Hunter grabbed her other hand. "I offered to take her home myself."

Piper swayed like a rag doll between the boys. "I don't need you to rescue me again, Wyatt," she said, slurring her words. "You can go make out with what's-her-face some more. I'm fine here."

Wyatt leaned down and spoke directly into Piper's ear, his voice low. "Piper, you're drunk, and there's no way I'm leaving you with this idiot. Now, you can walk to my truck by yourself, or I can make a scene and carry you. It's up to you."

Piper blew a wisp of hair out of her face. "Someone's cranky."

She yanked her hand out of Hunter's and half walked, half leaned on Wyatt as he escorted her toward his truck. Hunter followed for a few steps but gave up after a sharp glare from Wyatt.

Wyatt opened the passenger door and helped her into her seat. "What happened? I leave you for an hour, and you get wasted? You're usually smarter than this."

"Maybe I'm not as smart as you think." It wasn't the best comeback, but it was the only one she could think of.

"Buckle your seat belt."

"Yes, sir!" Piper gave him a mock salute. Then she threw up out the window.

After some water and a large order of McDonald's French fries, Piper's head stopped spinning. Wyatt kept the windows rolled down as he cruised the back roads of their neighborhood, letting her come down from her drunken high.

"How come you're not drunk, too?" Piper asked.

"Because I don't drink."

"Never?"

Piper had heard stories about Wyatt's escapades with his football teammates and assumed he partied regularly back in his hometown, but now that he'd said it, she couldn't recall ever seeing a drink in his hand.

Wyatt focused on the road. "It got me into trouble last year. Nothing serious, but if things had gone a different way, I could have spent the night in jail. Maybe worse." He tightened his grip on the steering wheel. "I can't afford to mess up like you can, Piper."

She frowned, confused. "What does that mean?"

He flicked his gaze in her direction. "You live in a different world than me. In yours, everyone goes to college. Everyone recycles. Or gardens. Your dad golfs at the country club and tips well. Your mom shows up to your parent-teacher conferences sober."

That drove his point home swift as a bullet. Wyatt hadn't willingly shared the news of his mother's third DUI last month, but Piper had learned the details from eavesdropping on hushed conversations between her parents. She'd gleaned that his mom had lost her license and been sentenced to a year in prison, and because she was Wyatt's only living parent, she'd effectively left him to fend for himself. The thought broke Piper's heart.

"I'm sorry." She worried her bottom lip between her teeth, not sure what else to say.

"Don't be. It's not your fault. Just like it's not your fault my mom would rather go out drinking than hang out with me." Wyatt's words were laced with bitterness.

She reached for his hand, emboldened by the alcohol left in her system. "It's not your fault either."

"I know. The whole situation sucks, but at least I get to finish out high school with you guys, thanks to Aunt Molly." His shoulders visibly relaxed. "I don't know what I'd do without her."

"You know she'll let you stay as long as you want to. You're family. She loves you. We all do."

Her eyes widened at her inadvertent declaration. She'd only meant to reassure him that he wasn't alone in this, not profess her love. She peeked at Wyatt, hoping he would blame it on the alcohol and not make a big deal about it.

He squeezed her hand, the sides of his mouth curving upward, but said nothing. They stopped at a notoriously long red light, and he turned to her. "So why *did* you drink so much tonight?"

"I don't know." Piper considered making something up, but he'd shared some vulnerable truths with her, so she felt safe sharing her inner thoughts. "Honestly, it was weird seeing you and Kiera playing seven minutes in heaven right after we'd been in the same closet." She slid him a shy glance. "It's stupid, I know."

A loopy grin split Wyatt's face. "That is stupid."

"You don't have to look so happy about it." Piper huffed.

"If we're being honest, I didn't like seeing you almost go home with Hunter."

"But I didn't, thanks to you."

He smiled again. "True. You wanna know a secret?"

She nodded.

He leaned over and whispered in her ear. "I didn't kiss Kiera, so I guess we're even."

Then the light turned green, and he turned his attention back on the road before Piper could process the slow-as-molasses warmth spreading through her body.

"Do you think you're ready to head home?" Wyatt asked after they'd completed a third loop through the neighborhood and turned onto her street.

Piper groaned. "Yeah, but my parents are going to kill me. If they ground me forever, promise you'll bust me out."

"I've proved my rescuing capabilities tonight, haven't I?"

"My very own hero." She clasped her hands together like a damsel in distress and fluttered her eyes, knowing it would make him smile.

Chapter Seven

Now

Allie must be going crazy with worry. At this very moment, they should be indulging in mani-pedis at the resort spa before getting dressed for the rehearsal dinner. When had everyone realized their plane was missing? How many phone calls must her father have made by now to anyone with influence? How formidable had her mom been demanding a rescue team comb the Caribbean for her only daughter? She had to figure out a way to get off this island.

Springing into action, Piper stood too hastily, dizziness washing over her. Like a shadow, Wyatt hopped up and reached an arm out to steady her.

"Whoa, take it easy."

"I'm fine." Piper waved him off, willing her balance to return, no longer sure if her unsteadiness stemmed from her head injury or Wyatt's proximity. "You mentioned some of our stuff survived the crash? Is there anything that can help us?" *Anything for me to wear besides your T-shirt?*

"Come see for yourself." Wyatt led her to a thicker patch of trees bordering the beach. "I think our luggage from the back of the plane is long gone, but I pulled a few things out of the wreckage."

Piper spotted the tan stripes of her beach tote propped against the trunk of a gnarled tree. Next to it, Wyatt had laid out an assortment of items—a couple of tiny water bottles, some blankets, and a first aid kit. She knelt in the sand and inspected her belongings. The tote's handles were burned, but the inside, where she'd stored her toiletry bag, remained intact. Most of her makeup and shower bottles were smashed beyond repair, but her toothbrush and toothpaste looked usable. She ran a tongue over her teeth, tasting the slimy film that covered them. That would be her first order of business.

At the bottom of her tote sat the teal bikini and flowy white cover-up dress she'd thrown in with plans of heading straight to the pool, along with a pair of socks, white tennis shoes, and the book she'd bought at the airport. She dug further, hoping to unearth one of the granola bars she'd tucked away.

"I pooled our snacks and stuck them in my backpack," Wyatt explained. "I'm not sure what animals around here might think we're hosting a picnic."

Her iPhone, tucked into a side pocket, had somehow survived without a crack but had no charge left. It might as well be a paperweight now.

"Is your phone dead, too?" Piper asked.

Wyatt nodded. "I tried both our phones yesterday before they died, but I couldn't get a signal. And the location and communication equipment on the plane is completely fried."

"So, we don't have any way of letting someone know where we are?"

"The first aid kit included a handheld radio, but I think it's busted."

A bubble of hope floated inside her. "A radio! Wyatt, why didn't you lead with that?"

He shrugged. "It's useless. I tried making contact all day yesterday and got nothing."

She squinted at him. "Did the badass army guy doze off during Radio 101?"

"Says Miss Halfway Done with Medical School but Scared of Blood."

Piper bit her tongue to keep from falling back into the easy banter of their past. "Let me see it."

Wyatt opened the metal first aid kit and handed Piper the black radio. It wasn't all that different from the radios they'd used in Girl Scouts when geocaching in the woods. In college, Piper had gone through a phase of being obsessed with all things from the 1930s and '40s, including black-and-white films and old-time radio shows. She'd joined the university's radio station club, where she'd produced a thirty-minute broadcast show every Thursday night for a year and had even reassembled an old radio to learn the inner workings. It was all the best parts of medicine: sitting with a complicated problem and patiently working to understand it until the solution revealed itself—but without the blood. She may not know how to forage for food, but she could handle a radio.

Piper carried the radio back to the shady grove of palm trees and settled into the sand. Tuning to different channels, she tested for a signal and listened to the static coming through the speakers. Like most people, radios took a minute to warm up and reveal their answers.

Wyatt continued arranging piles of driftwood as the sun dropped low in the sky, bathing the narrow strip of beach in a dusty rose glow. Soon it would be dark, and she'd be alone with Wyatt on this island for another night. A shiver ran down her spine at the thought.

After an hour of patiently scanning through channel after channel, something other than static poured through the speakers.

A connection.

"Yes!" Piper cheered. "I knew I could make this work."

Wyatt rushed to her side as Piper clicked the talk button and stated their names and situation in a clear, steady voice.

"This is Piper Adams and Wyatt Brooks. Our plane crashed somewhere in the Caribbean on the way to the Bahamas. We need rescue. I repeat, we need rescue."

She listened, waiting for a response, but only silence answered. Speaking louder, she repeated herself. Still nothing.

Wyatt leaned forward and gripped Piper's shoulder, encouraging her to try again. Tingling warmth spread through Piper's body at his casual touch and she forced herself to focus. Holding the radio between them, she spoke the same words for the third time. They both held their breath and waited.

A voice broke through the silence. "This is Rosie Sanchez. I'm with the Coast Guard Search and Rescue team. Do you copy?"

Relief washed over Piper like a cold shower. "Yes! Copy!" She shared a wild grin with Wyatt. "This is Piper Adams, I'm with Wyatt Brooks, and our plane crashed. We need rescue."

"Is anyone hurt?" Rosie asked.

"We're okay. A little banged up, but otherwise fine."

"Okay, good. I'm glad you could contact us. Here's the situation: There's already a rescue effort underway, but it may take a bit of time to find your exact location. Do you have water? Food?"

Piper knew she should be relieved to hear rescue was coming, but she'd been hoping they'd be located this evening. She hesitated long enough for Wyatt to take the radio from her.

"Copy that," Wyatt spoke confidently into the radio. "Yes, we have a few bottles of water and some snacks."

"Great. I need you to make that last and sit tight. Can you do that?"

Piper snatched the radio from Wyatt. "Sit tight for how long?" She could hear the desperation in her voice and wanted to add that being trapped here with her ex was like staring at an open wound, one that hurt far worse than the cut on her head. Somehow, she doubted the rescue workers would prioritize who they helped according to personal history complications.

A beat of silence followed before Rosie came back on the line. "We'll get to you as fast as we can. In the meantime, try to preserve your batteries by only reaching out if it's necessary. You can check in for an update if more than two days pass. My recommendation would be to find some shelter and hunker down until we can get there. And stick together."

Wyatt took the radio from Piper and thanked Rosie, assuring her they would be okay for a few days. He exuded excitement and renewed energy, a sharp contrast to Piper's internal freefall. Despite the deep relief that help was on the way, dread pooled in her stomach at Rosie's "stick together" comment. Wyatt may be strong and capable and somehow more handsome than she remembered, but she wasn't sure she could survive another day with him and walk away with her heart intact.

With a darkening sky and no rescue on the near horizon, Piper slunk to the opposite side of their sandy base camp and sat against a tree looking skyward. Above the swaying palms, the stars blinked on one by one, marking the end of the longest day of her life so far.

At home, Piper needed a sound machine to quell her ever-racing mind at night, so she hadn't expected sleep to come easily, but the ocean waves and warm breeze had swiftly lulled her into dreamland. After watching Wyatt pull together a few leafy green palm fronds to sleep on, she'd done the same, curling up on the warm sand a healthy distance away from him. She may have slept well, but there was no hiding from the sun in the morning. It blazed through the slats of the palm trees, too dazzling and too hot, forcing her awake earlier than she'd have liked.

When she opened her eyes, she immediately knew three things to be true: they were still stranded on this island, her stomach ached with hunger, and Wyatt's arms were wrapped around her like they'd spent the past ten years falling asleep nestled together.

Her back fit perfectly against his chest, her head resting on the crook of Wyatt's arm, while his other arm lay possessively over her side, his hand pressed against her stomach. She clamped a hand over her mouth to keep from gasping out loud at the rush of electricity flowing up and down her body from his sleeping touch. Eight years ago, they'd woken up curled in this same position, and the similarity of the moment brought back a wave of nostalgia. Wyatt stirred, and his arm around her tightened, hitching between her breasts and pulling her closer.

She relaxed against him, relishing the sweet comfort of his embrace. She'd missed this, missed *him* for so long. And now he was here, his arms around her, his sleepy, warm body pressed against hers, hot breath against her ear. Every part of her wanted to turn and wrap her arms around his neck and cling to him, bury her head in his neck, and never let him go. But she was terrified of how much she'd miss it when he woke up and realized his mistake.

No, she couldn't board this train of thought destined to dead-end in disaster. She needed to keep her wits about her if she was going to make it through another few days on this island—and another few days with Wyatt.

So she pretended to be asleep until Wyatt woke with a stretch, then padded away down the beach. Despite the growing heat of the sun, she missed the warmth of his body, the weight of his arm around her. Missed it more than she should.

After enough time to feel believable, Piper wiped the sleep from her eyes, rolled over, and scanned the beach for Wyatt. Several yards away, Wyatt sat on some driftwood he'd placed around a large flattened rock, flanked by similar sized pieces of wood rescued from the ocean. The arrangement gave Piper the impression of a table with benches—if she squinted hard and used a lot of imagination. She used her rescued toiletries to brush her teeth and tame her hair into a braid, then walked over and plunked down across the rock "table" from Wyatt on a driftwood "bench," determined to wipe their sleepy morning snuggle from her memory.

On the rock lay strips of something green and slimy.

Piper scrunched her nose. "What's this?"

"It's seaweed." He popped a strip into his mouth. "I let it dry out in the sun all day yesterday. Help yourself."

"Are there any other options?" She was more of a fries with ranch dressing than a side salad kind of girl.

He held out a tiny bag of almonds and shook a few into her hand. The nuts were gone too soon, but she knew better than to ask for more.

"I'm glad you're up," Wyatt said like Piper was a teenager who'd overslept. "We should explore, find food, and figure out the best place to set up a camp like Rosie suggested on the radio."

Piper's temple throbbed with the beginning of a headache. "I don't know who you were listening to, but I heard Rosie clearly say we should hunker down and sit tight."

"And I heard her say we might be here for longer than we'd like. We should check things out before it gets much hotter. Come on, where's your sense of adventure?"

"Somewhere over the Atlantic would be my guess," Piper mused with a frown, the glow of waking up in Wyatt's arms fading by the second. "You may think this is all some fun escapade. But I didn't sign up to spend my vacation eating bugs with you. In fact, I didn't plan on you being on my vacation at all."

Her harsh words stopped him, but only barely. "I'm sorry. When I'm stressed out, I make dumb jokes—you know that. And I'm not suggesting we go foraging for insects."

"What *are* you suggesting?"

Wyatt pointed to the cliffside down the beach. "We need to get a new perspective. Maybe if we get a better lay of the land, we can give the Coast Guard a better idea of where to find us." He popped another piece of seaweed into his mouth.

Annoyingly, he had a decent point. The almonds had barely satisfied her hunger, so she tore off a piece of the dried green substance and took a tentative bite. It tasted like dirty grass, which she guessed it technically was, but it helped calm her appetite.

"Not bad, right?" Wyatt asked.

"It's not the worst thing I've ever had, but it's not getting a five-star Yelp review."

He passed her a half-full water bottle, and though she could have guzzled the whole thing down in seconds, she took only a small sip.

"If you go exploring with me, we might find something better," he pointed out.

Piper knew what a lost battle looked like, so she gave in. "Fine. Let me change into something else first."

Wyatt took in the oversize T-shirt she still wore, gave her a crooked smile, and turned his back to offer her some privacy.

Desperate for some sense of normalcy, Piper "bathed" with a few makeup remover wipes and changed into her clean bathing suit and beach cover-up. Pouring a dollop of sunscreen into her hand, she rubbed it onto her face and shoulders. No sense in getting skin cancer while waiting to be rescued. After lacing her tennis shoes, she sucked in a breath of salty air and joined Wyatt by the water.

Here went nothing.

Chapter Eight

Then

About a month after she'd overmedicated on Fireball shots at the spin-the-bottle party, senior year of high school began. In the madness of back to school, Piper had pushed away all thoughts of Wyatt's lips hovering over hers in the closet that night. Well, almost all thoughts. Now that he was officially finishing high school at Cedar Falls, her breath would catch every time she saw him in the halls as the sensation of their almost kiss came roaring back. But most of the time, she remembered the strength of their friendship, the fact that he was Allie's cousin, and how important it was to her not to do anything to jeopardize the Lonely Onlys.

On this particular October Saturday, Ethan's dad gave each of them a crisp one-hundred-dollar bill and, with strict instructions to have as much fun as possible, dropped them off at the state fair. They spent the mild fall day gorging on fried Oreos, turkey legs, and every flavor of cotton candy. Somehow no one puked after the Tilt-A-Whirl or the log flume. Though the sudden descent made her want to die, Piper rode a few roller coasters. But only Wyatt was brave enough to try the Gravitron, where the floor dropped out from under the passengers while they were spinning at high speed.

They waited until dark to ride the Ferris wheel. When they reached the front of the line, Wyatt slid into the four-person car beside Piper, his weight next to her as warm as the glowing fair lights. Allie and Ethan filled out the other side.

The wheel started off slow and peaceful. Jovial music blared through speakers, and the lights from other rides glittered like Christmas lights all around them. This was a snapshot moment, the kind she wanted to remember forever—surrounded by her best friends, under the safe blanket of night with the warm autumn breeze on her face.

Their car swung to a halt at the very top of the wheel with a sickening grind, shattering her perfect moment. Ethan peered out over edge, rocking the car until it swung precariously.

"This is so cool. I think we're stuck!" Allie whipped her phone out to record a video. "Now we get to ride even longer!"

Piper peeked over the edge and regretted it immediately. They were higher than she remembered from previous years, the people below as small as ants. She gripped the metal sides tight. Why weren't there seat belts or a safety harness on this thing?

Wyatt leaned down to whisper in her ear. "Hey, keep breathing. In through your nose and out through your mouth."

She did as he instructed, fighting the panic rising in her. Was there less oxygen up here? Why couldn't she get enough air in her lungs?

Ethan shifted again, jostling the car from side to side. Piper gasped.

"Watch it," Wyatt growled at Ethan.

"What if the wheel's broken, and we're stuck up here forever?" Piper asked, her voice small.

"Come on, P. They'd bring the fire ladders or something to get us down," Ethan said.

"Great, so I can break my neck falling down a fifty-foot ladder?" Piper buried her head in her hands.

Ethan peered over the edge. "I'd say it's more like two hundred feet."

"Cool it, Ethan," Wyatt warned, sliding closer to Piper and snaking his arm around the back of her seat. "Piper, I won't let you fall."

Allie turned back around. "Are you okay, Pip? You're looking green."

Piper shook her head, moving as few muscles as possible to keep the car's balance.

The car lurched forward a foot, then stopped again, drawing whistles and cheers from the other passengers. Piper whimpered and turned her face in to Wyatt's chest, matching his breath to calm herself.

Wyatt tightened his arm around her. "Hey, remember when Ethan used to get nervous about riding his bike up the big hill when we were in middle school?"

Piper lifted her head, squinting at him.

Wyatt grinned. "What was the song we used to sing so he'd forget to worry about not making it to the top?"

"Wyatt," Piper warned. She could see where this was going, and she wasn't in the mood to sing.

"Oh wait, I remember." He winked at her, then launched into the opening verse of "Ain't No Mountain High Enough," the words coming out low and confident. He wiggled his eyebrows at her as he drew out the "babe" at the end of the chorus.

Laughter bubbled out of Piper.

"Come on, help me out with the rest." He nudged her.

Piper shook her head, nerves still freezing her in place.

Across from them, Allie didn't skip a beat and picked up in her clear soprano where Wyatt had left off. After a few lines, Ethan jumped in, belting off-key loud enough to attract cheers from their fellow passengers.

Wyatt mimed handing a microphone to her. "Come on, Piper!"

Her fear gave way to laughter, her lungs filling with enough air to speak. Gamely, she sang the well-known lyrics with her friends as they all launched into a resounding reprise of the chorus.

Nearby Ferris wheel riders joined on the next verse, and before long, a cacophony of voices rang out in the glittering night. Somehow Piper's nightmare scenario had morphed into a sing-along straight out of a movie, and she had Wyatt to thank for that.

Piper snuck a glance at him. His face glowed with the tango of flashing bulbs all around them. She loved this side of him—the goofy, carefree parts he rarely showed others. His secret self. He caught her gaze and rewarded her with a dazzling dimpled smile that sent the oxygen whooshing out of her lungs again.

Before the song ended and Piper could panic again, the ride shifted into motion, bringing them back to the ground unscathed.

After climbing out of the Ferris wheel car, Allie pointed to the giant roller coaster one ride over. "Look, there's no line for the coaster. Let's go again!"

"Yes!" Ethan pumped a fist in the air.

Piper shuddered, her lungs constricting again. She'd had her fill of adrenaline-inducing rides for the night.

"I want to check out some games before the fair closes," Wyatt said. "Piper, wanna come with me?"

She nodded, already backtracking away from the coaster after Wyatt, and called to Allie and Ethan, "We'll meet you guys at the exit in thirty minutes. Have fun!"

Once Piper and Wyatt reached the games area, the crowd had thinned. Most fairgoers were trickling out or setting up to watch the fireworks that marked the night's end. They played Whac-A-Mole and balloon darts with little success, then tried their luck at the ring toss.

"Damn it." Wyatt threw his arms up in defeat as his last ring ricocheted off a peg. "I swear they rig these games!"

"Probably." Piper laughed at the scowl on his face. "Come on, Wyatt. Do you really need a stuffed banana with a mustache that badly?"

His gaze flicked to the ground. "I wanted to win something for you."

Piper's cheeks grew hot, the straight-from-a-movie romantic gesture making her blush. Not that this was a romantic gesture. She couldn't think that way. "I'm all out of tickets. How many do you have left? Maybe fourth time's the charm."

He pulled the remaining tickets out of his pocket and scanned the games. "I've got enough for us to both do the basketball toss."

They were the only two players in the game, and to their surprise, Piper won by one point. Smiling, she selected a small bug-eyed stuffed frog as her prize.

"We used your ticket." With a flourish, she presented the plush amphibian to Wyatt. "You earned this."

He shook his head but accepted the prize with a smile, tucking it reverently into his jacket pocket. "Come on, let's go meet Allie and Ethan."

He placed his hand on her back, guiding her toward the exit. The gesture was subtle, but he might as well have stuck her with a hot poker. Warmth radiated from his touch, making it hard to think about much else. When they joined the crowd gathered to watch the fireworks, Allie and Ethan hadn't arrived yet.

"Hey, thanks for earlier, on the Ferris wheel," Piper told Wyatt. "And for getting me out of another horror show of a ride. And for being so nice to me tonight."

Wyatt chuckled. "What do you mean? I'm always nice to you!"

He *was* always nice to her, but something about this felt different. More meaningful. But how could she explain that? An explosion of color and sound overhead interrupted her before she could try.

Wyatt kept his arm around her until the last firework exploded.

Chapter Nine

Now

Aside from the buzzing mosquitoes and leaves rustling in the trees, they walked in silence. After about five minutes, the beach dead-ended at a rocky cliff that loomed over the sand like a cresting wave of rock. About as high up as a Ferris wheel, the rock face had plenty of footholds. Though it wasn't a sheer drop-off, one wrong step would be treacherous.

No way Piper was climbing up there.

Next to her, Wyatt crawled upward like a bear. He glanced down at Piper. "What's wrong?"

"I'm not a big fan of heights."

"That's right." A ghost of a smile flickered across his face. "You stay here. I'll go check it out."

"How do you know it's safe?" Piper made a mental list of the lacerations, broken bones, and internal damage that could happen if he fell. None of which she was equipped to handle. "What if you slip and fall?"

"I have experience with this. Trust me."

Piper wanted to point out that the last time she'd trusted him he'd crashed a plane, but now didn't seem like the time. Wyatt hadn't waited for her permission anyway. Dead set on being reckless, he ascended the jagged cliff like a skilled rock climber. Reaching the top, he swung one leg over the flat surface and pulled himself to safety with ease, then disappeared from her sight. Piper unclenched her fists.

As the minutes ticked by and he didn't reemerge, Piper paced back and forth while visions of Wyatt hurt, or worse, played in her head. She shouted his name, but the sound evaporated over the roar of the ocean. Neither of them knew what lurked up there. Anything could've happened to him. Being stuck here alone hadn't crossed her mind until now. Besides trying to stay alive, most of her energy had gone into her resentment of Wyatt's sudden reappearance in her life. But now, confronted with the possibility of figuring this out on her own, Wyatt's company was the lesser evil by far.

After longer than she'd have liked, Wyatt's hunter green shirt caught her eye at the top of the rock. Piper held her breath while he slowly picked his way down, slipping only once on loose rocks. She didn't exhale until his feet were back on the ground. Dirt streaked his legs, and his taut arms glowed with sweat.

"We're definitely on an island that's maybe five or six miles long." He wiped beads of perspiration from his forehead with the back of his hand. "I could see the ocean on all sides from up there. And I think I saw a clearing in the woods, a short way from the beach, that we should check out. There could be a pond or water-fall or something. Maybe food."

Great. Somehow the climb had given Wyatt more energy when all she wanted to do was take a nap after that spike of adrenaline from worrying about him.

"I don't know, Wyatt. On those wilderness shows where people get dropped off in the middle of nowhere to see who can last the longest, the people who don't move around a lot always win. I think we've done enough for one day."

"Then it's a good thing we aren't on reality TV. I think we'll both feel better if we find something to eat or water, and that won't happen if we go back and sit on the beach."

As if on cue, Piper's stomach whined. Traitor. She crossed her arms over her chest.

"How about we look for thirty minutes?" Wyatt suggested. "If we find nothing, we'll head back to our base camp and conserve our energy."

A bead of sweat rolled down Piper's back, and she fanned her face with a hand. Hot air, drenched with humidity, had replaced yesterday's light breeze.

The woods behind them beckoned, cool and inviting. It couldn't hurt to take a quick look.

Piper blew out another breath. "Fine. Lead the way."

With no clear path to follow, they threaded their way through the dense tangle of trees, stepping over roots and ducking under limbs. Piper followed in Wyatt's footsteps, carefully avoiding the iguanas warming themselves in patches of sunlight every few yards. The large prehistoric creatures only glanced in their direction as they passed by. Instead, it was the birds overhead that squawked, high-pitched and urgent, alerting flock-mates to the intrusion into their private sanctuary.

Piper had spent many summers traveling the world with her parents, but she'd never wandered the wild land of a foreign place before. The trees jutting up at odd angles and birds with feathers painted in unexpected colors, looking like she'd stumbled into a Dr. Seuss book, were just unfamiliar enough to put her on edge.

They were far from home.

Eventually, the sand gave way to dirt, moisture hung in the air, and they stepped into a sun-filled glade. In the center, light reflected like a mirror off a shallow pond. Jackpot.

Walking over to the pond, Wyatt scooped up a handful of water and sniffed it. "I don't know if this water is good enough to drink, but it's a solid backup if we need it."

Piper leaned against a wide tree trunk to catch her breath. Beyond the pond, trees grew sparse, interspersed with large green plants dotted with impressive spikes resembling cacti. Each plant was adorned with bright red bulbs like a crown of rubies. Why did this strange plant look so familiar to her? She walked over and inspected one. Avoiding the long, spiny needles, she plucked a red bulb the size of a golf ball and raised it to her nose. A combination of strawberry and orange blossom scents tickled her nostrils—fruity but not too sweet.

"Careful!" Wyatt shouted, coming up behind her. "We shouldn't eat anything we don't recognize. They could be poisonous."

"I think I do recognize this." She held the berry up to the sunlight. "Ethan was drinking something, a margarita maybe, made of these when I talked to him before my flight."

Wyatt raised a doubtful eyebrow. "Ethan was drinking a cactus margarita?"

A few yards away, a small bird with an orange beak and iridescent green throat trilled loudly from its perch on an identical spiky plant. Another bird joined him, pecking at a red berry's shell until juice flowed freely.

"Look! If the birds are eating them, it's safe to say we can, too." Piper plucked another berry off the cactus plant, proud of her observation.

Wyatt cocked his head to one side before breaking into a wide grin. "You're right. Lunchtime!"

Piper smiled smugly. Maybe she wasn't so bad at this survival thing after all. They picked as many berries as they could carry, and Wyatt used the Swiss army knife he'd rescued from the plane's safety kit to cut open the hard rinds to reveal the pulpy pink meat inside. They celebrated by sitting in the shade in peaceful silence, letting their sweat cool while gorging on the sweet fruits, which burst like watermelon in their mouths.

A momentary truce.

Before they left, Wyatt pulled his shirt off over his head and used it as a sling to carry more berries back to the beach. Following behind him, Piper tried ignoring the way his back muscles rippled with every step and how perspiration beaded and ran down his spine before disappearing into the waistband of his swim trunks. She swallowed hard, wishing she could follow them all the way down.

This kind of dangerous thinking would only lead to trouble.

To distract herself, she focused on the motions of every bird and lizard, hoping to uncover another hidden food source. Up ahead, a small gray bird pecked at something shiny in the brush to their left.

"Hey, wait up," she called out to Wyatt.

She squeezed her way between two trees for a closer look at whatever lay on the ground. The bird tilted its head, then flew away to watch from a nearby branch. Piper brushed some leaves away and uncovered a navy suit jacket with brass buttons that glinted in the sun.

"Are you missing a suit?" She held it up for Wyatt to see.

Shading her eyes, she craned her neck upward and searched for more of their belongings among the overhead trees. About seven feet above her head, she spotted Wyatt's half-opened suitcase hanging from a limb, its contents spilling onto the ground like a busted piñata. Waving in the gentle breeze, a pair of blue boxer briefs clung to a nearby small branch. Against her will, Piper pictured Wyatt wearing them—and nothing else. A new sheen of perspiration dampened her brow, and she used the hem of her cover-up to wipe it away.

Wyatt grabbed the offending underwear and stuffed them into his back pocket before turning his attention to his suitcase. He eyed the tree. "I bet I can climb it."

Piper glanced sideways at him. "Just because you can climb something doesn't mean you should." Did he have to solve every problem by sheer force or manpower?

She picked up the matching suit pants lying nearby and held

them toward him. "Can you use this as a lasso or something and shimmy it off the branch?"

His eyes lit up like she'd challenged him to a dare and got to work, holding the pants by the end of one leg and whipping them upward, until he caught a corner of the suitcase and grabbed hold of the other leg.

While Wyatt finagled his luggage off the tree limb, Piper scanned the treetops. If Wyatt's suitcase had landed here, maybe hers had, too. Sure enough, after taking a few more steps to her left, a flash of pink winked into sight above. Closer to the ground than Wyatt's had been, her suitcase sat barely out of reach, wedged into a V-shaped crux of a thick branch and the trunk.

A little higher up, golden orbs hung like crystals of a chandelier from the top of the tree. One of the yellow orbs rested at Piper's feet on the forest floor. She picked it up, weighing it in her hand. It was the size of a football but much heavier. A fruit of some sort?

She drew her arm back and chucked the fruit at her luggage. It connected with a satisfying thunk, but the bag shifted only slightly.

"Piper?" Wyatt called out. "Where'd you go?"

"Over here!" She scooped up the fruit and tried again, still missing her bag but knocking a few more golden orbs down this time. They tumbled to the ground, one rolling to a stop in front of Wyatt.

He scooped it up to examine closer. "Hey, I think these are papayas!"

Piper grabbed another papaya and heaved it at her luggage, pushing it forward another inch. Wyatt followed suit, his impressive swing knocking the suitcase down with a single try. It landed with a crack, the frame bending into more of a triangle than its original rectangle. Miraculously, it stayed zipped.

"Thanks," she said, trying to hide her annoyance. She'd had it under control before he jumped in with his big muscles and Energizer Bunny attitude.

"No problem. I can't believe you found our luggage and more fruit!" He gathered four papayas and zipped them into his suitcase. "We need to remember where this tree is in case we need to come back. Aren't you happy we hiked into the woods?"

Piper didn't bother answering him. Happy didn't come close to describing her current bug-bitten, hot, and sweaty condition, but she didn't hate the idea of something real to eat. And a change of clothes would help, too. She had no intention of needing to return to this spot, but she took in the shape and size of the trees around them as a reflex.

After she'd wrestled her bag over a protruding root, Wyatt stepped in to help. His large hand covered hers on the suitcase handle, and a jolt of energy shot through her at his touch.

Piper shook her head at him. "I've got it."

If the wheels still worked, that might have been true. But by the time they reached the sandy shore, her suitcase had doubled in weight, and her arms were on fire. Relenting, she let Wyatt help her.

"Looks like you never learned to pack light, huh?" he joked, maneuvering both suitcases over the sand. "I guess some things never change, but I'm surprised you have a pink bag. Didn't you swear off this color for all time?"

It was a harmless statement, and he'd hit the mark about her hatred of pink. She'd boycotted it in ninth grade as an act of rebellion against her mother, who'd spent years putting Piper in outfits with lace, bows, or anything in the rosy shade. But the casualness of his comment irked her. Wyatt couldn't just pick right back up where they'd left off like they were close friends who talked all the time. These little details were too personal, more intimate than he deserved. Dropping his knowledge of her into conversation made it hard for her to remember why they weren't friends anymore. Except she remembered all too well.

And remembering made her want to scream at the sky—like Taylor Swift double-tapping the coffin of her short-lived romance with Jake Gyllenhaal ten years later.

Wyatt could claim to be a survival expert, but she refused to let him add "Piper expert" to his list. He'd lost that privilege when he broke her heart and moved on with Kiera the same day—going as far as inviting Kiera to meet him at their sanctuary, the clubhouse, throwing his treachery in Piper's face and twisting the sharp knife of betrayal past the point of repair.

"Stop acting like you know me." The words shot out of her mouth like a rocket. "You don't anymore."

Wyatt stopped in his tracks and turned back toward her, his brows knit low and eyes glossy. "I may not know you as well anymore. But you used to know me better than anyone on this planet, and I'd bet the same was true about me for you. That doesn't just disappear."

"Maybe not, but you did." She'd delivered a low blow, but Piper was too hot and too hungry to care about being civil.

Wyatt sucked in a sharp breath. "If I recall correctly, *you* were the one who said you never wanted to see me again. That I shouldn't speak to you under any circumstances. You were very clear about that."

"Yeah, I didn't want to talk to you after you shattered my heart! That's what people say during a breakup when they're hurt." Piper glared at him. "I knew we were over as a couple, but I didn't think you'd let our friendship die, too. I thought you'd reach out. Apologize for rubbing Kiera in my face, at the very least. Would it have killed you to send a birthday text or Instagram message?"

"I'm not on Instagram."

This Piper knew from her many late-night searches on social

media, hoping to glean some clues about his life, but she wouldn't tell him that. And it wasn't even close to the point. "Look. I may not have a choice, but I don't have to like that I'm stuck here with you. And I don't want to pretend we're friends when we aren't."

"Fine." Wyatt held his hands up in surrender. "But for what it's worth, I am sorry."

But Piper didn't know which he was apologizing for—breaking her heart or acting like he hadn't.

Chapter Ten

Now

I'm going to work on a shelter," Wyatt announced when they reached their crash site.

Piper shook her head. Did he ever sit still? "I'm planning on sleeping at our five-star resort after we get rescued, but by all means, knock yourself out." Anything to keep Wyatt busy and away from her.

He dragged their luggage over to the pile of their rescued belongings. Piper followed at a distance. Cutting open a papaya, he took a big bite of the bright orange fruit, then swiped a hand over his mouth, wiping away the juice dripping down his chin. He handed her the other sticky half before trotting off toward the woods to do who knows what.

With Wyatt out of sight, Piper forced the zipper to her suitcase open and nearly cried in relief at the assortment of clean garments inside. From this angle, overpacking looked more like a skill than a bad habit. She shimmied into clean underwear and a matching bra, layering white terry-cloth shorts and a navy tank top over them. Grabbing her airport-purchased paperback romance, she found a shady patch of sand overlooking the water.

With a clear view of the expansive sky and the ocean rolled out in front of her, Piper readied herself to jump at the first sign of a boat or plane. She could almost imagine being here on purpose, enjoying a break from the world. Almost. The dull ache in her head and lingering hunger made it hard to ignore the truth—she'd crashed on a remote island with the last person she thought she'd ever see again. The man who'd made her believe in love, then stomped on her heart, the pain shimmering below the surface even after all this time.

Raising the papaya to her lips, Piper took an eager bite. The juice from the sweet fruit soothed her parched throat, giving her a respite from the thirst that had been clawing at her all morning. It tasted like a tropical vacation. A real one, not a plane-crash-imposed one. The beach breeze dampened the sun's heat to a warm kiss. Tilting her face up toward the sun, Piper breathed in the salty air and soaked in this small moment of peace, her jaw slowly unclenching.

She could vividly picture the cheers from her friends and family when she arrived at the resort venue, rescued from their unintended layover and ready for the wedding. Her father would insist on a full medical exam before allowing her to have any fun, and her mother would fuss over her, then send her straight to the spa. Allie wouldn't care that her maid of honor had a sunburned nose and puckered forehead gash. Knowing Allie, she would paint a fake cut with lipstick on her own forehead to match and take the attention off Piper, who loathed everyone looking at her—something her best friend adored. Believing in the possibility of still attending the wedding helped quell the panic threatening to overtake her again, so Piper closed her eyes and let herself slip into the tantalizing fantasy.

"Is this any good?" Wyatt asked, yanking her from her daydream.

"Huh?" Piper jerked her head up.

"Your book. *The Wrong Duke*," he read the title of the paperback in his hands.

"It's great, actually. A Regency take on *You've Got Mail*."

Wyatt smirked. "Not really my thing, but I'll take your word for it."

Piper snatched the book back from him and wiped sand off the cover. No longer high in the sky, the sun was sinking rapidly behind the tree line. She'd slept away most of the afternoon—and they were still stranded on this awful beach.

Hot tears stabbed the backs of her eyes. Her visions of rescue had all been a cruel dream. Instead, she remained trapped in this waking nightmare. The realization hit her like an icy gale, the emotional blow harder to recover from than the physical one she'd already sustained. She turned her head so Wyatt couldn't see the devastation on her face. He noticed it anyway.

He knelt beside her. "Hey, everything's going to be okay. I promise."

"You don't know that." Her voice came out small and pitiful.

"You're right, but I can promise we're going to be okay tonight. How about that?" Wyatt offered her a hand. "Come on. I built a fire. We can split a granola bar and some more berries."

She didn't want to be on the beach in the dark by herself with her even darker thoughts, so Piper wiped the tears from her face, reluctantly took his hand, and let him pull her up.

Sure enough, a few yards behind her spot on the sand, Wyatt had built a small but impressive fire. It helped that the logs and kindling he'd gathered had baked in the sun all day. It also helped that the army knife he'd rescued produced fiery sparks, which he demonstrated for her excitedly. They had nothing to cook and didn't need the fire for warmth, but the bouncing light and crackle of firewood comforted her. Especially as the sky darkened and their food rations for the day disappeared.

The night came alive with the chirping of insects and birds engaged in fierce debate. Their electric discord put Piper on edge. Sitting by the glowing fire as the sun dipped below the treetops reminded her of camping with Allie and their Girl Scout troop in elementary school. Making s'mores, singing songs, and waking Allie up in the middle of the night after a bad dream. Then moving their sleeping bags next to each other to ward off the boogeyman.

Grief and longing hit her with ferocity as intense as the fire.

She missed Allie. Her heart hurt over missing the wedding, which would have happened hours ago. She missed her parents, Ethan, and her bed. She wanted to go home. Fresh tears leaked down her cheeks, and she didn't bother swiping them away.

"I can't believe we missed the wedding." Piper sniffled. "Allie's like a sister to me, and we've dreamed of this since we were little. We probably ruined their big day."

"I can assure you, their day was not as ruined as ours."

Piper glared at him through the tears now flowing down her face. His attempt at humor only upset her further.

Likely alarmed by her tidal wave of teardrops, Wyatt squeezed her arm, then pulled away as if remembering his place. "Hey, I'm upset about missing the wedding, too." He worried his bottom lip with his teeth. "Allie's my family also. I hate we aren't there celebrating with them. And I hate that we're stranded here another night."

Piper wiped her face with the back of her hand.

"But I don't hate that I'm here with you." He pushed a hand through his hair. "To tell you the truth, I was going to the wedding to see you. To talk to you and apologize to you face-to-face. I've missed you, and I'm sorry I didn't reach out sooner." He caught her gaze, the fire dancing in his eyes. "I'm sorry for all of it."

Piper squinted, studying him. Her breath caught in her throat. Did he mean that? She'd always assumed he'd left her behind without a second thought. She hadn't prepared for the possibility that he might regret his actions. That he might miss her as much as she'd missed him. She didn't know how to respond, which was just as well because the tears still trickling down her cheeks gave away more than she wanted.

The ocean darkened, matching the sky, and the flames dwindled.

Piper's shock and grief diminished with them. Eventually, she found her voice. "I still don't understand why you disappeared from my life, from everyone's life, like you did."

Wyatt poked the fire with a stick, staring intensely into the flames. "I wish I could explain it. At the time, I thought I was doing the right thing." Sparks flew up into the night with every prod. "I was an angry kid with no one in my corner. Sure, I'd escape to Cedar Falls when I could, but it wasn't my reality. Being on my own was all I knew, so I thought it was better that way. That everyone would be better off without me." Wyatt swallowed, his voice thick. "But messing up what we had and losing you was the stupidest thing I ever did. If it takes a plane crash to see you, I'd do it again in a heartbeat."

Piper sucked in a deep, noisy breath, stemming her tears. Her heart rate doubled. She didn't fully trust Wyatt with her heart yet, but she believed him. Or at least believed that he meant what he said, which was a start.

"For the record, I would have preferred a phone call to this." She fanned an arm out at the endless expanse of ocean. "But thank you for saying that."

"I'll make a note for next time." His dimpled smile winked like a new beginning.

While they'd talked, a three-quarter moon had replaced the sun in the star-speckled sky, beaming without its brighter celestial counterpart.

Piper stood, the fire casting shadows all around her. "It's getting late. Why don't you show me this shelter you've been working on?"

Wyatt led her across the moon-shadowed beach toward the forest behind them, where the trees thickened and the sand gave way to reedy grass and patches of moss. He'd found a small clearing just wide enough to stand with arms outstretched and not touch anything, as if the trees had all parted to make room for a queen's entrance. It wasn't spacious, but Wyatt had arranged what looked like two cots cobbled together from miscellaneous clothes from their rescued luggage. About four feet above the ground, he'd covered the space with big palm leaves lashed together with vines and reeds, propped up by thin limbs that feathered out from the craggy trees. It was a far cry from the luxury resort but had a certain cozy appeal.

Almost too cozy—like they were having a slumber party—though, to his credit, Wyatt had made the two sleeping spaces distinctly separate.

Piper looked over at him, impressed. "You did all this?"

"Yup, I broke a sweat while you were having a spa day."

Piper smacked him on the arm.

"Kidding! Want to test it out? That one's yours." Wyatt pointed at the makeshift bed on the left, the one fully covered by the palm awning and more padded than his sleeping area.

Inside it was roomier than she'd expected, with enough space to sit up comfortably. She lay down and tested out her mattress. Though the cushioned bedding was light-years away from her memory foam mattress at home, she'd slept on worse.

Wyatt crawled into the shelter next to her and sprawled out on his own cot with his hands laced behind his head. "Not too shabby, huh? It's not an all-inclusive resort, but the rate is very affordable."

She smiled at his joke. "What am I lying on?"

"A selection of the three weeks' worth of clothes you packed for this trip. Including the largest dress I've ever seen."

Piper rolled over. Sure enough, the soft purple bridesmaid dress doubled as the top layer of her "bed." She guessed she wouldn't be needing it now. At least the layers of tulle were doing an excellent job of providing comfort. Wyatt had also crafted a pillow for her by stuffing a T-shirt with clothes. Her black silk slip dress still with tags poked out from one armhole.

The injustice of the beautiful dress she'd bought last week for Allie's bachelorette demoted to a pillow struck her as the funniest thing she'd ever seen. Everything about this moment slipped sideways, leaving her topsy-turvy in an alternate dimension. The beach view looked the same, but instead of dancing in Allie's bridesmaid dress, she was lying on it. Instead of drinking a prickly pear margarita served in a decorative coconut shell, she'd dodged cactus needles to eat its berries.

And instead of avoiding Wyatt, she was literally sleeping next to him.

Laughter bubbled up from deep within her, and she gave in, hysterics shaking her whole body.

Wyatt arched one eyebrow, an amused smile playing at the corners of his mouth.

"This dress. Allie would kill me if she knew I was using it as a mattress." She collapsed into a fresh fit of giggles.

Wyatt threw his head back and joined her with a deep chuckle. "Only the best for visitors on Hell Island. Hey, maybe we'll start a new trend—wedding attire that doubles as mattresses."

Piper giggled even more profusely, egged on by Wyatt's joy, until they both clutched their stomachs, aching from the belly laughs.

Laughing with Wyatt transported her back to high school and how easily it had always come between them, layering joke on top of inside joke until they were the only ones who understood what was so funny in the first place. Slipping back into their old patterns would be effortless—until he broke her heart again.

"We should get some rest," Piper said when she'd sobered up.

Wyatt propped himself up on his elbow, resting his head on his fist. "You're right, Captain Conservation."

Piper pulled a sock out of her pillow and lobbed it at his face.

He ducked gracefully, still grinning. "Thanks for the laughs. I needed that."

"Me too." She returned his smile and fluffed up her pillow to get comfortable.

Shadow covered Wyatt's face. Nestled into their new base camp, Piper felt his presence more than she could see him. Did sleeping on the ground remind him of serving in the army? Or of their Lonely Only slumber parties in the clubhouse as kids, nestled in sleeping bags on the wooden floor like a puddle of puppies?

"You know, it's not true," Piper said after a few minutes of silence. "What you said earlier about not having anyone in your corner. I hope you know you always had Aunt Molly and the Lonely Onlys. And me." *Especially me.*

Wyatt swallowed. "I know. I have a bad habit of pushing away the people I love most, but I'm working on it."

She would need some time to unpack that statement, but he wasn't trying to start a conversation.

"Night, Piper. Wake me up if you need anything."

"Night," she whispered, watching the inky fingers of night drag darkness across the sky.

Chapter Eleven

Then

In October of junior year, the Lonely Onlys stepped into a new era of freedom when Ethan got his driver's license and keys to his dad's old 4Runner. Looking for any excuse for a road trip, they'd devised a plan to surprise Wyatt for his upcoming birthday. Through a little reconnaissance, Allie determined he didn't already have plans with any of his high school football team friends, and Piper baked a chocolate cake with buttercream icing using one of her mom's well-worn recipes from scratch.

An eclectic playlist (Broadway hits for Allie, country for Ethan, and indie for Piper) and lots of snacks fueled the two-hour trip to Mason, North Carolina, where Wyatt and his mother lived. Their excitement faded as the houses grew smaller and more unkempt. Allie double-checked the address she'd plugged into Google Maps as Ethan pulled in front of a dilapidated house with broken shutters and a chain-link fence. The porch sagged like a sad smile. Weeds grew wild through the gravel driveway, and constant guttural barking emanated from the skinny dog tied to a post with a frayed rope next door. Piper could feel the eyes of neighbors watching them get out of their too-shiny SUV sporting fresh haircuts.

Ethan turned the car off and looked over at Allie with a frown. "Is this it?"

"I'm not sure. I haven't visited since they moved to this neighborhood a few years ago. Wyatt always comes to us."

When Wyatt opened the door and found them huddled on the porch, he took a quick step back, lips pressed together tight. They'd surprised him, all right. Wyatt held open the door and let them pass, leading them through a tiny living room to the messy kitchen, where he'd been boiling water to cook a box of off-brand mac and cheese.

"What are you guys doing here?" He dumped the macaroni into the pot and stirred, his shoulders tensed.

Surreptitiously clearing a few empty Natty Light bottles out of the way, Piper set the cake down on the worn kitchen table and presented it to him with a flourish. "Happy birthday!"

Wyatt's gaze darted from the cake to Piper, then around the room at his friends, still struggling to put all the pieces together.

"It is your birthday, isn't it?" Allie asked, still taking in the dimly lit kitchen.

Wyatt raked a hand through his dark curls. "Yeah. I just can't believe y'all are here."

"We wanted to surprise you. We even got you a gift!" Ethan pulled out a graphic novel edition of the latest Magic Realm book and handed it over. "I probably should have wrapped it, but happy birthday, Wy."

Allie cleared her throat. "That's from all of us."

"So is this." Piper handed him an eight-by-eight framed picture of a sketch she'd drawn of him as a hero from the series, holding a sword with a falcon perched on his shoulder.

Wyatt looked at the book, and the framed sketch in his hands, shaking his head. "Wow, Piper, this is unreal. All of this is so great. Thank you, guys. Truly. I appreciate you coming all this way, but my mom will be home soon, and I don't want to stress her out."

Allie brushed him off. "Don't be silly, Wyatt. We need to at least stay long enough for cake. And I haven't seen Aunt May in ages."

Everyone knew better than to argue with Allie, so Wyatt jerked his head in the approximation of a nod and set his gifts down on the kitchen counter.

Piper pointed to a picture secured to the fridge by a magnet. "Is that your dad?" Faded by years of light and covered in a fine layer of dust, the photograph featured a handsome young man with brown curly hair, slate blue eyes, and a dimpled smile that matched Wyatt's. She'd asked mostly to distract Wyatt from his obvious anxiety but curiosity gnawed at her.

Wyatt looked at the picture and nodded again. "Yeah, that's been on our fridge for as long as I can remember. I think it's the last picture my mom took of him before the accident. Right after I was born." His mouth twisted to one side, and he wiped the dust off his dad's face with his thumb.

Piper knew Wyatt's dad had died in a motorcycle accident, but he rarely talked about it. She wanted to ask if he still missed his dad or remembered the sound of his laugh, but Ethan and Allie glared at her. The room had fallen silent.

"Piper," Ethan hissed. "It's Wyatt's birthday. We're supposed to talk about happy things, not his dead dad."

Allie punched him in the arm. "Ethan, that's not helping!"

Wyatt interjected before a fight could break out. "No, it's okay. Really, I . . ." He trailed off as the front door swung open.

"Wyatt, are you here? Whose car is in the driveway?" Wyatt's mom rounded the corner. When she saw the crowd gathered in her home, she stopped short. She wore a low-cut T-shirt with the name of the restaurant she worked at, Checkers, printed across the front. Her jeans were too tight, even though she was as thin as a toothpick.

She looked like a faded version of Allie's mom. Smudged lipstick overshadowed her pale face, and her auburn hair was tangled in a messy bun. Piper could see the resemblance, but whereas Molly burst with life, life had sucked May dry.

Wyatt crossed his arms. "You're late, Mom. You told me you would be home by five thirty."

She waved him off. "A few of the girls stayed after their shift for a drink. I only had one and came right home. I swear." Her slurred words and glassy eyes said otherwise.

Wyatt's jaw tightened, and his nostrils flared.

"Hi, Aunt May." Allie stepped forward with open arms, diffusing some of the tension.

"Oh, my word, it's my favorite niece. I almost didn't recognize you. You've grown so much since the last time I saw you!" May hugged Allie, then stood back, taking her in. "You're so pretty. Every time I see you, you look more like your mom."

May's smile faltered. She ran a hand over her face. "I must look a mess. Wyatt, why didn't you tell me your friends were visitin'? I woulda put on something nicer."

Piper waved from her corner of the kitchen. "Hi, I'm Piper, and this is Ethan. We're sorry to barge in like this, but Wyatt didn't know. We wanted to surprise him."

May tilted her head to the side and raised an eyebrow. "Surprise him? What's the occasion?"

Allie laughed out loud but quieted when she realized May wasn't joking. Piper understood with a sick wrench in her gut that Wyatt's mother had forgotten his birthday.

"We wanted to bring the birthday party to him," Ethan said, unaware of the sudden awkwardness filling the room.

A hand flew up to cover May's mouth, and a quick "oh" burst from her lips as her eyes grew wet with shiny tears. Piper stared at the ground, unable to bear Wyatt's reaction. How was it possible for a mom to forget her son's birthday? Her parents insisted on making her birthday a weeklong affair with multiple cakes and more presents than she knew what to do with. She couldn't imagine them forgetting entirely.

When she spoke, May's voice shook. "Sweetheart, why didn't you remind me about your birthday? I've been saving up to get you something real nice, but you know how crazy work's been lately. I can't believe it's already October." She looked over at the calendar on the fridge, stuck on August.

Wyatt had poured all his attention into mixing the marigold powdered cheese with the wet noodles. The loud slurp slurp slurp cut through the awkwardness.

"It's okay, Mom," he said. "You know I don't really care about birthdays. Why don't you have a seat? I made some macaroni, and my friends brought cake."

His mom twisted her hands together. "No, no, we need to celebrate." She turned toward the group of teens. "Do y'all want something to drink? Maybe some brandy? I think I have something left over from a party a few weeks ago." She rummaged under the sink before extracting a bottle half filled with dark liquid and decorated with tropical flowers. Opening it, she gave it a sniff. "Coconut rum, my favorite. Smells like the beach. Who wants some?"

An adult had never offered Piper an alcoholic drink before, but May did it so casually that it couldn't have been the first time. She wanted to hide behind Allie and hug Wyatt at the same time. No wonder Allie's mom invited Wyatt to Cedar Falls instead of sending Allie down here. Piper had never been so grateful for her parents' strict rules and standards.

"Mom, stop. You can't serve them alcohol."

May rolled her eyes. "My son, the rule follower. Fine, I'll toast for all of us." She tipped the bottle into a coffee mug and swung the mug out in front of her. "Cheers to my baby boy. Happy birthday, Wyatt!"

"Cheers!" Allie replied enthusiastically, waving an imaginary glass in the air. Piper and Ethan followed suit, unsure how to handle the souring situation.

"You guys should probably go." Wyatt's voice was low and rimmed with anger as his mother downed her rum and refilled her mug.

The sticky-sweet smell of coconut filled the small room.

May shrieked, "No, they can't go yet! We need to cut the cake."

By his sides, Wyatt's hands clenched into fists. "Fine."

This was not how Piper had imagined their fun birthday surprise going—with Wyatt's mother drinking and Wyatt teetering somewhere between putting his fist through a wall and retreating into scary silence. She wanted to pull him toward the door and take him away from this place. Bring him back home to Cedar Falls, where Molly would make him a cake for breakfast, and they'd all embarrass him with a song at Charlie's Diner.

The group hunched around the table, and Ethan lit a handful of polka-dot birthday candles.

May wrung her hands, hovering above them. "I can't believe my baby's turning sixteen."

"I'm seventeen, Mom." Wyatt's voice didn't betray any outward disappointment in his mother, but under the table, his hand shook so severely Piper reached for it, lacing her fingers through his.

"Make a wish," she whispered.

He squeezed her hand and closed his eyes before extinguishing every last candle.

Chapter Twelve

Now

Piper didn't care if Wyatt spotted a McDonald's in the jungle; nothing would coax her from her stakeout on the beach today. Okay, maybe she'd leave for a McFlurry, but nothing less. Otherwise, she'd sit here under her trusty palm tree, eyes trained on the ocean horizon, ears tuned toward the sky until rescue came. And they were coming today. She just knew it.

Wyatt, who'd missed the memo to relax, bustled about the beach, creating a giant SOS signal with stones, dragging driftwood into piles, and putting the finishing touches on their shelter. He never went far, always hovering nearby like a deranged helicopter parent. Every thirty minutes or so, he'd plop down next to her, swig some water, share survival facts, or give her an update.

"Remember the rule of threes," he quizzed her. "We learned it in basic training. Humans can live for three weeks without food, three days without water, and three minutes without air, but hopefully that last one won't be an issue."

"Nothing but sand, rocks, and a snake hanging out in a tree," he told her after trekking up the beach toward the other side of the island.

The Wyatt of her youth had never been so chatty, but she chalked it up to nerves. A feeling she fully understood. Waiting for rescue felt like having a boa constrictor coil around her body, every passing hour tightening its hold and draining her of hope.

By the time the sun passed its peak in the sky, Piper had finished her book, taken a nap, and eaten her allotment of fruit for the day. In the water, Wyatt attempted fishing with a wire he'd procured from somewhere, but the fish weren't biting. It seemed they shared Piper's lack of enthusiasm for eating the island bugs he used for bait. Giving up on his mahi ambitions, Wyatt waded back to the shore and hovered over her, dripping water on her legs in tiny, methodical splashes.

"Hey, do you want to play a game with me?" He sounded as hopeful as a kid asking to join a four-square tournament at recess.

She squinted up at him. "Did you pack a deck of cards or something?"

"It's more of a game I made up. Will you please try it? I know you must be as bored as me."

He wasn't wrong. Before he'd stepped out of the ocean, she'd been chatting with one of the crabs peeking out from its dark hole in the sand, trying to coax it closer. Not a great sign of her mental health at the moment. She needed a distraction.

"Okay, I'm in." Piper stood and stretched her stagnant legs, gesturing for Wyatt to lead the way to whatever game he'd devised.

A few yards down the beach, he'd drawn a series of large circles, all of them sharing the same top point by a sprightly palm tree, each one enclosed within the other from large to small, the smallest only two handprints wide. He handed Piper something soft and heavy. A homemade sandbag.

She recognized the Moroccan trellis pattern of her sand-filled Bombas. "What am I looking at? Are these my socks?"

"Yes. Don't worry, you have at least five more clean pairs stuffed in your pillow."

Her socks made her think about her underwear—and the brand-new underwire bra she'd packed for the trip. "Wait a second. Where did you get your fishing wire?"

Wyatt winced. "You won't like the answer to that question, but I promise it will be worth it if I catch a fish."

Piper rubbed her temples, careful to avoid her bandage. Maybe she could use Wyatt as fish bait after she finished murdering him.

Wyatt, sensing he was losing Piper's good favor, hurried to tell her the rules. "So, you get three tosses on each turn, and the goal is to get twenty-five points first. Landing in the biggest circle gets you one point, and it goes up to seven if you hit the smallest one. But you have to go in order. You can't hit the bull's-eye until you've hit all the other circles. Make sense?"

Piper crossed her arms. "No, this sounds complicated."

"Think of it as a mix between bocce ball and darts. You'll get it if we play." He picked up one of the socks and nudged her with his shoulder. "You can go first."

By the third round, neither of them could remember how many points they'd scored or who was winning, but for once, Piper wasn't thinking about her hunger or the lack of rescue. Wyatt hollered every time he hit a bull's-eye and cheered even harder when Piper did. It was impossible not to smile around him, and she was having fun despite their surroundings. In fact, she hadn't experienced this kind of joy in far too long.

With Tag, Piper checked her posture and paid close attention to her vocabulary, like a kid trying to be on her best behavior around adults, acting sophisticated and well mannered. Playing the part of a serious medical student on the path to great success to match his ambitions. And the ambitions of her parents. While Tag clearly liked her, he didn't find her jokes funny, and she rarely understood the dry references only he laughed at. Their dates usually consisted of a steakhouse dinner with red wine or using Tag's parents' box seats at the symphony. All things that required fancy footwear. She couldn't picture him willingly throwing dirty socks into the hot sand, wearing day-old clothes drenched in sweat—or imagine him smiling from ear to ear while doing so, like Wyatt.

Guilt swooped in like a seagull snatching up leftover bread— she'd barely thought about Tag since they'd crashed. Did he even know she was missing? She'd intentionally not made things official with him, and they often went days without talking. They'd built their situationship on convenience more than conventional romance. Neither had time to meet anyone new, so a suitable nonserious dating partner had been the perfect arrangement, but it was strange she hadn't thought of him until now. Right?

Comparing Tag to Wyatt wasn't fair. She and Wyatt were estranged friends at best, while Tag reliably took her on dates and always returned her phone calls. Not to mention, Tag had never broken her heart beyond repair. So why was she unspeakably grateful to be stuck on this island with Wyatt and not Tag? Playing this made-up game on the beach showed her what she'd been missing: silly fun, uninhibited laughter, and an undercurrent of deep friendship.

It also made her wonder—who was missing Wyatt right now? Undoubtedly, he had someone special back home. Besides the whole heartbreak-history-and-crashing-them-on-the-island-in-the-first-place details, he'd been an exceptional survival partner. Always making sure she had enough to eat before he had a bite of food, handling her reluctance to open up to him with positivity and grace, and doing his best to take care of them both.

All traits of an ideal boyfriend.

There was no way someone in Colorado hadn't noticed that, too. Not to mention his army-shredded body and dimpled smile. And those soul-drowning eyes.

Wyatt nailed a bull's-eye and performed an elaborate touch-down dance, rescuing her from her pesky, spiraling thoughts. "Eat my dust, Adams."

"No way!" she protested. "This is the beginning of a new round. You can't get a bull's-eye until you hit the bigger circles!"

"No. That was me *winning* the end of a round."

Piper pursed her lips. "This reminds me of that summer you got everyone in the neighborhood to play a real-life game of Quidditch. A spectacular failure."

Wyatt huffed. "It's not my fault nobody paid attention to the rules."

"Yeah, *that* was the problem. Not that your rules were overly complex."

"Don't lie. You loved every second."

"Maybe." She grinned at him. "Mostly because you took it so seriously. I'm getting strong déjà vu vibes now."

Wyatt chuckled. "That was the summer you broke your arm, right?"

Piper nodded. She'd broken her arm playing kickball during an end-of-school game in front of the entire ninth-grade class. "Yeah, and I couldn't go to the pool because my mom worried my cast would get wet even though it was waterproof. Allie was a junior lifeguard, and Ethan was away at soccer camp and totally ditched me."

"Ditched *us*," he clarified. "Who came and hung out with you almost every single day? That was the summer you got really into Harry Potter, if I recall."

"I remember I wasn't the only one."

"You're right. I'd give anything to be sitting on my couch eating popcorn, watching *The Prisoner of Azkaban* right now," Wyatt said, scrunching his mouth to one side.

"I'd give anything to have a Portkey back home."

"Or a Nimbus two thousand," Wyatt added, not to be outdone.

"Too bad we're a couple of muggles stranded on an island."

Wyatt threw back his head and laughed, the lines by his eyes carving deep grooves.

Piper laughed along with him. "God, we were such dorks."

"Some things never change."

Was it her imagination, or did she detect a catch in his voice? A surge of fondness for her old friend rushed through her. They'd once been so close, their lives and stories intertwined like vines of ivy knotting together as they grew. Even though her defenses remained fortress-high around Wyatt, spending time with him was like revisiting all the best parts of her childhood.

Around them, the wind picked up, whipping sand into tiny dunes that rippled along the shore like echoes from a stone dropped into a glassy lake. So engrossed in their game, they hadn't noticed the sky darkening overhead until fat raindrops splashed down around them. At first, only a few juicy drops splattered the sand, but soon water poured from the sky like a faucet pushed all the way up.

Wyatt pumped his fist in the air. "Yes! An afternoon thunderstorm!"

Back home, Piper would have run for shelter, but she let the rain soak her skin, cleansing her. There was no hairstyle to ruin or makeup to protect. Here, a rainstorm meant life-sustaining water. She tilted her face upward, tasting the drops on her tongue. Within minutes they were both drenched. Wyatt's white T-shirt, made translucent by the rain, molded to his well-defined pecs like a second skin. His face glowed with unbridled joy as he held his mouth open to the sky, arms wide, water running from his hair in rivers.

Their gazes met, pure elation buzzing between them. Wyatt's eyes matched the swirling gray sky, his wide grin hopeful and bright. Impulsively, he grabbed her hands, twirling the two of them in a chaotic circle, the storm enveloping them in a curtain of rain. Her heart crashed into her ribs. It had to be the stormy crackle of electricity in the air making her pulse race.

Dizzy, she dropped his hands to catch her breath as they stopped spinning. "How can we collect it?" she shouted over the rain.

Wyatt held his hand out to her. "Come on. I have an idea!"

Piper hesitated, looking past his hand to his rain-soaked, earnest face. At those eyes shining with renewed hope, and something else. Love? Her heart thundered faster.

The deluge around them wouldn't let her overthink the moment, so she locked her hand into his and he took off running, pulling her toward their shelter. As they raced hand in hand through the rain, she stole a glance at him, her breath catching at the glow of his smile, the chiseled lines of his face.

It was definitely more than the weather setting her nerve endings on fire.

At the shelter, Wyatt grabbed a handful of clothes from their makeshift mattresses and hung them on a tree limb to absorb rainwater they could wring out. Piper mirrored his actions, working steadily alongside him. Pulling his drenched shirt over his head, Wyatt added it to a tree branch. Piper tried not to stare, but the ropy muscles rippling across his strong back every time he moved transfixed her.

Wyatt was beautiful.

She peeled off her own soaked cover-up, revealing the teal bathing suit underneath. After hanging her cover-up on a limb, she took a step back and bumped into Wyatt, who'd moved behind her when she wasn't looking. Turning around only pushed her closer to him, her bikini-clad body sticking to his wet, bare chest. His gaze flicked down at her swimsuit, and his eyebrows shot up.

A shiver rippled through her body.

Wyatt grasped her shoulders and took a small step away from her. "Are you cold?"

"No, it's just the rain. I'm fine," she whispered.

He brushed a wet piece of hair off her face, his thumb grazing her cheekbone a fraction of a second longer than needed. Piper ducked her head so he wouldn't see her cheeks burn.

Escaping the moment, she dropped to the sand and repositioned a group of palm leaves, collecting even more water, distracting herself from the dizzying effect of Wyatt's presence.

Eventually, the rain lessened to a soft mist, but the wind continued howling like an angry ghost. Judging from the murky clouds, the storm wasn't clearing out anytime soon.

Wyatt swiped a hand over his scruffy jawline. "This wind keeps blowing sand into my beard. The army drilled the clean-shaven look into me. I don't think I've ever gone this long without shaving. Do I look like a mountain man?"

Piper regarded his days-old stubble, shielding her eyes from a surge of sand the wind kicked up in their direction. Dark hair framed his jawline, outlining his full lips, somehow making him even more attractive despite his hollowing cheeks.

"I think you look more beach bum than mountain man. Literally. But the stubble suits you."

"Did Piper Adams just compliment me?" His lips curved up in a smile.

Piper scrunched her face. "Don't let it go to your head."

"Maybe I'll keep this look going after we make it home and see if the women come knocking." Wyatt leaned against a tree trunk.

There was no reason for the jealousy blooming in Piper's chest, but she couldn't ignore its sharp pang. "I'm sure you don't have any trouble attracting women with or without the facial hair." She remembered how many girls at their high school had crushed on him, including her.

"Maybe not," he admitted. "But so far, no one's made me want to settle down."

Piper didn't know how she was supposed to take that statement. On the one hand, the thought of Wyatt with a serious girlfriend hurt her stomach. But his comment lumped her into that category of women who hadn't inspired him to commit.

"Or maybe you haven't stuck around long enough to give anyone a fair chance." She hoped he wouldn't hear the sudden edge to her voice, but his head snapped in her direction.

He leveled his gaze at her. "It's possible. But I think it's more a matter of having a hard time finding anyone who comes close to you."

Piper's eyes widened, and she crossed her arms, protecting herself from the barrage of emotions his confession released. "That's a funny thing to say considering you didn't give me, or us, a fair chance either."

Wyatt shook his head. "That wasn't it. It's more complicated than that. And it doesn't matter now, anyway." He dragged a hand over his cheek, frustrated. "Enough about me; your turn. I bet you've got a guy back home losing sleep over your disappearance."

Piper bit her lip. So they were really having this conversation. "I do. He's a fellow med student."

He nodded like he'd been expecting that answer. "I bet your parents love him." His mouth curved upward, but the sad smile tugged at her heart.

Before she thought better of it, the truth came tumbling out. "They do, but we're really more like friends. Otherwise, I would've dragged him to Allie's wedding, and he'd be trapped here with us."

Wyatt's smile brightened ten full notches. "I guess lucky for him, he didn't sweep you off your feet enough to score an invitation to Hell Island." Then with a cheeky wink, "And lucky for me that there's a chance I could win you back."

Piper blushed at his boldness, her insides liquefying. "I assure you that will not be happening." She meant it, but a part of her, a growing part, liked Wyatt's flirting, liked it a lot, and she couldn't help but smile.

The careful lines she'd drawn around their relationship or lack thereof blurred like a photo shot out of focus.

Chapter Thirteen

Then

Instead of Allie's sleek Mazda pulling into her driveway for school carpool that morning, Wyatt's beat-up Chevy truck grumbled up the drive, sputtering in protest when he put it into park and waved out the window at her.

"Allie had an early morning practice, so I thought I'd see if you wanted a ride."

Of course she did. Piper had her license and the keys to her mom's old Lexus, but she wasn't a confident driver and avoided navigating the Tetris-stacked parking lot of the high school. Wyatt knew that.

Because it was unseasonably mild for mid-February, Piper wore only a light coat over her navy tweed skirt and white blouse. Knee-high leather boots kept her warm enough. She climbed into his truck, and her eyes widened at the biceps stretching Wyatt's T-shirt like rubber bands ready to snap. He hadn't bothered with a jacket on this chance warm day and clearly had been keeping his newly buff body under wraps with sweaters all season.

Despite her efforts not to stare, Wyatt caught her anyway.

"I need some new shirts." He looked down at his tee, a stain of pink coloring his cheeks. "I know this looks like I'm auditioning for a role in *Grease*, but I've been following some of the suggested workouts to get prepped for boot camp. It's only about six months away now."

"No. It looks good, err, fine. It looks normal." Piper rolled her window down to cool her burning cheeks as Wyatt drove toward the school. "I can't believe you're leaving so soon." *I'm going to miss you.*

Every time she pictured Wyatt holding a gun or, worse, having a gun held against him, her bones ached. But thinking about him away from her for so long hurt like a fresh wound. They'd always been close, but ever since he'd pulled her into the closet at that summer party, the magnetic field between them had strengthened, drawing her even closer.

"Did you see *Magic Realm* is filming in Charlotte today?" he asked, changing the subject.

"Yes!" Piper had seen the posts on social media last night about crew trailers setting up. "I can't believe they're making a TV show. And not far from here! It's going to be so good."

"We should go."

"Go where?"

"To Charlotte to watch them film. Today."

"We can't, Wyatt. We have school," Piper protested.

"Piper, you've already gotten into Carolina, and I'd bet my truck you're making straight As in all your classes. One missed day won't change that. In fact, I think it's required for a senior to play hooky at least once."

Piper wrinkled her nose. "Isn't that what senior skip day is for?"

"So, you only want to break the rules on a day when it's encouraged?" Wyatt chuckled. "I should have guessed."

"What about you? You're finally turning your grades around. I don't want you falling behind."

"I got a B on my last stats test, and I'm passing all of my classes thanks to your tutoring. I think I've earned a day off."

Piper shot him a long, stern look.

"Come on, Piper. When are we ever going to get to do this again? Please come with me."

Piper leaned back against the headrest and looked upward as if she'd find the answer on the car's ceiling. He was right. They were running out of time to make memories and do all the fun things senior year had promised them. Plus, how cool would it be to see the *Magic Realm* set?

She answered Wyatt with a toothy grin. "Let's do it."

But he was already a step ahead, turning onto the highway away from school and toward the city.

Using social media, they found the filming location at an open soccer field marked by orange blockades and piles and piles of cords plugging in everything from cameras to lights to fans. Bright-colored crepe paper streamers hung above tents with fairy lights, everything decorated to look like a Renaissance May Day celebration. In the middle of the field stood an actual maypole. They weren't actively filming yet, but crew members arranged set pieces and tested lights, scurrying like ants across the field.

"This is the scene where Peregrine crashes the party to warn Dash he's in danger," Piper whispered as they crept closer. They joined the crowd of onlookers peering over the fence that lined the field, waiting for action.

Trailers crammed the parking lot to the right of them along with a white tent filled with people in jewel-toned costumes alongside production assistants dressed in black speaking urgently into their headsets.

"I know! Come on, let's see if we can get in on the action." Wyatt walked toward the crew village.

Piper hurried after him. "What? No, Wy, I'm not sure we're supposed to be here. We should stay out of the way."

"Trust me. It can't hurt to ask."

With more confidence than a high school truant should have, Wyatt sidled up to the table labeled BACKGROUND CHECK-IN and gave the frazzled production assistant behind it an endearing grin. "Hi, we're here to check in. Wyatt Brooks and Piper Adams."

Piper stood arrow straight and avoided eye contact with the PA running a finger down a printed sheet of names in front of her.

"Sorry, I don't have your names. What casting agency sent you?"

Busted.

"Um, the 'we're huge fans and would love to be extras, and you don't even have to pay us' agency." Wyatt flashed his dimples.

Did his smile have the same effect on others as it did on Piper?

The PA sighed and cracked her neck. "Normally, this is when I'd call security, but I had a few extras call in sick this morning, so it's your lucky day." She handed them each a blank W-4 and an NDA. "Fill these out. You'll get a check at the end of the day. Don't talk to the actors. Absolutely no pictures. And don't do anything that will make me regret this, okay?"

The dimples had worked, but that wasn't a surprise. They filled out the forms before she could change her mind. Piper shared a "can you believe our luck?" look with Wyatt, whose eyes were as wide with excitement as hers.

Once she'd collected their forms, the PA handed them each a green slip of paper that said "party guests." "Wardrobe is in the trailer to my left. Give Janine these." She gave them a half smile. "And have fun."

Before Piper knew it, Janine had fit her in a green velvet dress with a long cape and Wyatt in matching green pants, a belted white tunic, and thick brown boots. Someone else whisked Piper away to hair and makeup and, after an hour of powders and hair spray, transformed her into a bewitching *Magic Realm* maiden. The young woman staring back at her in the mirror looked confident, beautiful—and ready for a party. The dress nipped in at the waist, accentuating her curves, and with the artful makeup, her green eyes sparkled like emeralds.

When Piper walked out, Wyatt's face lit up. The low whistle he gave her made the sixty minutes sitting in the hair and makeup chair worth it. Wyatt looked good, too. Better than good, he looked like a cross between Robin Hood and the Jolly Green Giant in the best way possible. Someone had applied a product to his hair that tamed his curls into a Hollywood-worthy coif, and wardrobe had used his new muscles to their advantage, brandishing his biceps like weapons by rolling his sleeves up past his elbows.

Being an extra amounted mostly to waiting around. But waiting in an official *Magic Realm* costume with Wyatt all day felt like a holiday and way better than AP Statistics. Eventually, the director called them to the set. He explained they were guests of Queen Meadow and her stepson, Dash, at a fanciful May Day party that would be one of the show's opening scenes. After spreading everyone out, he arranged them in small groups, relaying instructions on where to walk and what to pretend to laugh about or say.

"Ah, my lovebirds," the director said with a glimmer in his eye when he reached Wyatt and Piper. "The camera will follow you two into the party before we go wide on the full scene. I need you to walk hand in hand like you are having the time of your life. Can you do that?"

Piper's mouth went dry, making responding impossible.

Next to her, Wyatt slung an arm around her shoulders and gave the director an unfazed smile. "You've got it."

"Excellent! I want you to start right behind the camera here and then walk to the maypole."

He led them back to a man with a camera strapped to his body like a baby. "Okay, find your marks. Camera rolling, and action!"

The slate dropped with a clack, and everyone moved into place like a merry-go-round coming to life. Piper had been so excited about this opportunity hours ago, but now her shoes were heavy as lead, her limbs stiff.

Wyatt slipped his hand into hers and tugged her forward. "Can you believe we're on the set of *Magic Realm* right now?"

She knew he was trying to calm her nerves as the camera followed, and she appreciated it.

"Look how perfectly they cast Peregrine," he continued.

She nodded, eyeing the redheaded, leather-clad actress standing off to the side, about to make her entrance.

Wyatt dipped his head to whisper in her ear. "You would have made a pretty great Peregrine, too."

Piper chuckled at the far-fetched statement. She was nothing like the warrior princess who didn't let anyone stand in her way.

"Cut!" the director shouted, and everyone traipsed back to their original places. "Lovebirds, walk a little closer together, yeah? Maybe kiss her on the cheek. Don't overthink it. It's a beautiful spring day, you're at a fabulous party, and you're in love!"

Piper swallowed hard and focused on a blade of grass. Using the suggestions as an invitation, Wyatt wrapped an arm around Piper's waist and leaned closer the next time they started the scene. He pressed a kiss to her temple as they approached the maypole, sending a cannonball of heat through her body. Thank God the camera was only catching them from behind because she knew her face burned fire engine red against her green dress. Being this close to Wyatt set her at ease and on fire simultaneously.

They walked the scene over and over again, each time growing more comfortable with the movements of the camera. And with each other. Every time Wyatt's lips grazed her cheek, her forehead, her hair, it transported her to that tiny closet, her heartbeat echoing off the walls. Here, in broad daylight, it somehow felt even more intimate. Like they were getting away with something outrageous right under everyone's noses. Everyone could see them, but no one was paying attention. It was easy to forget they were only acting like a couple. And hard for Piper not to want it to be real. Hard for her not to turn her head until his lips met hers.

The director yelled his final cut for the day, and Piper sagged in relief. The tantalizing closeness of Wyatt pretending to like her romantically had been sweet agony, but the moment they separated to change out of their costumes, she missed the weight of his hand in hers. She hadn't been pretending when holding his hand made her whole arm tingle or how his sweet kisses made her heart sing. That had all been very real.

By the time Wyatt pulled his truck into Piper's driveway, the sun was a distant memory in the sky. He turned to her, truck idling in park. "Thanks for risking your perfect GPA to attend a royal May Day party with me."

"That was one hundred percent worth skipping school for." Piper could see her mom staring out the window at them with a frown. "But I'm so screwed if my parents find out. Do me a favor and don't tell anyone we did this, okay?"

"Promise," he said, making an x symbol over his heart.

She stepped out of the truck and shut the door but leaned back in through the window. "You know, if the army doesn't work out, you should consider a career in acting. You were great back there. Made it look so easy."

He shook his head. "Nah. I'm a terrible actor. It was easy because it was with you."

Piper glowed up at him, too tongue-tied to respond before he backed out of the driveway with one last wave. She didn't know where they went from here. She only knew her growing feelings for Wyatt were as fragile as the first ice over a freezing pond, crystals spiderwebbing across a sheet of glass—one wrong step would plunge her into icy water.

THEIR SECRET SKIP day didn't stay hidden for long. The next day, the local paper printed a story about the TV show filming locally, featuring a picture of the two of them holding hands in front of the camera, smiling widely at each other. Distracted by Wyatt's smile, Piper hadn't even noticed anyone taking pictures. Her father acted amused, but her mother was livid—storming into Piper's room demanding an explanation, worrying that Piper was headed down a "bad path."

"Mom, I skipped one day. You can't possibly think I'm heading for a life of crime now," Piper defended herself.

"I don't know. That's how these things start."

"What things?"

Her mom ticked an example off each finger. "Hanging out with the wrong crowd, getting knocked up, doing drugs, dropping out of school."

Piper rolled her eyes. "None of those things are happening, Mom. Relax."

"Don't tell me to relax, young lady." She folded the newspaper up forcefully, her mouth twisted into a deep frown. "It's a slippery slope and you are already on it."

Meaning she categorized Wyatt as the "wrong crowd." Which was going to be a problem, since Piper very much wanted to hold his hand again.

Soon.

Chapter Fourteen

Now

N o! No, please," Wyatt cried. "Take me instead!"

Piper shot up, blinking back sleep, searching for something to protect her from whatever must be invading their shelter. They'd gone to bed early when the wind and rain started again, and it was apparent rescue wasn't coming today. In the dark beside her, Wyatt whimpered, his arms thrashing at an invisible monster. Lightning cracked close by, and in the suspended flash, she could see his eyes were shut, his face screwed up tight.

He must be having a nightmare.

As her heartbeat returned to normal, Piper's eyes adjusted to the darkness. Out on the open beach, the clothes they'd strung up on tree branches bucked in the wind like wild ponies staking their territory. The sea, stygian and murky, matched the black sky, except for the undulating waves against the horizon, making it hard to tell where the sky ended and the ocean began. She hoped their palm-thatched shelter would be enough to protect them when the fresh torrent of rain hit. From the clap of thunder nearby, she guessed it would be soon.

Wyatt moaned again. "Stop, no. Make it stop, please!"

His anguished voice constricted Piper's chest like an iron band and made her heart ache. Whatever he was dreaming about, it sounded awful. She couldn't listen to him cry out like this all night without doing something.

She shook his shoulder. "Wyatt, hey. Wake up."

He bolted up with a start, his eyes wild and searching in the dark.

"You had a bad dream."

He continued swiveling his head, searching for a hidden threat.

"Wyatt, it's okay. You're okay," Piper reassured him.

His feral stare found hers in the dark. Then, to her horror, a guttural sob broke from his chest, and he hung his head between his legs. Chills ran down her spine. This wasn't your average nightmare. It was something far scarier. Could it be PTSD? She knew little about his experience in the army, but she imagined a plane crash could trigger even the slightest case. Or a boom of thunder rocking the ground.

Wyatt's shoulders shook with his sobs. She extended her arm to pat his back but stopped short, her hand suspended in the air, unsure if she should comfort him or leave him alone. His pain ricocheted through her body, tearing her in two. Tears welled in her eyes, and Piper bit her lip, clenching and unclenching her hands, not sure what to do.

"Wyatt, talk to me. Tell me what's wrong."

He didn't answer, that awful choking sound emanating from his body. Instinct took over, and she pushed herself to his side of the shelter. Hesitating only a moment, she enveloped him in a hug, her desire to take away his pain overtaking everything else.

Wyatt buried his face in her neck, still shaking. All Piper could do was hold on and try to absorb some of his suffering. She whispered all the comforting things she could think of, rubbing his back in slow, soothing circles. A bouquet of sparks lit up her insides every time his warm breath fanned her skin.

The storm shifted closer.

Eventually, Wyatt collected himself, wiped his face, and sat back, hugging his knees into his chest.

Piper gave him some space but kept a hand on his knee. "Are you okay?"

Wyatt took in a shaky breath. "I will be. I'm sorry if I scared you."

"What happened? You were talking in your sleep. Do you remember what you were dreaming of?"

His lips pressed into a thin line. "I wish I didn't, but I sometimes get these awful dreams, memories really, of my deployment. It's been a while since I've had one, but it's like I'm back there every time. It feels so real."

As if on cue, thunder cracked nearby like a branch breaking from a tree, and Wyatt jumped, his eyes sliding back to a haunted place.

Piper shivered. She knew about PTSD in the secondhand way that everyone from her generation knew about it, but witnessing it up close was bone chilling.

"I'm sorry you have to deal with that." She meant it. This wasn't something she'd wish on her worst enemy, a descriptor she'd have tagged Wyatt with only days earlier, but it no longer fit as snugly. "Is there anything that helps?"

"Not, really. I have to ride it out." Wyatt sat back against one of the larger tree trunks that made up the back corner of their shelter, cracking his knuckles one by one, his whole body taut. "I promise I won't wake you up again. You can go back to sleep."

Piper curled her mouth to one side. "And you're, what? Going to sit here all night?"

"If I close my eyes, I'll see it again." He hung his head like the image weighed him down. "And I can't go back there."

The muscles in his cheek bulged where his jaw locked tight, his fists clenched by his sides. She couldn't imagine what he'd seen overseas. He hadn't had an easy childhood leading up to the military, so his nightmares probably made hers look like a Disney movie. It wasn't fair. He carried so much alone—and he didn't have to.

"Then I'll stay up with you." She wouldn't get much sleep with this storm, and every nerve in her body was wide awake from being pressed against Wyatt moments earlier. "Does talking about it make things better or worse?"

Wyatt rubbed his eyes. "It's hard for me to talk about, but my therapist says the more I let things out, the less power I give the memories to take over my brain. Trust me, though, you don't want to hear about everything going on in my head."

Piper hardly recognized the shell-shocked version of Wyatt sitting in front of her. Where was the strong, confident, annoyingly sure of himself guy she'd witnessed these last few days? His vulnerability made her arms ache to wrap him in another embrace.

"How about you try me, and then we can decide," she challenged him.

The rain trickling through the treetops grew steadier, a pitter-patter becoming a constant drone. A few drops made their way through the thatched covering of their shelter, but most of the water ran off the sloped surface above them. Both of their water tumblers, positioned under the rain flow in anticipation of fresh water, were almost full again.

To avoid the splatter of rain on his back, Wyatt scooted in closer. Piper mirrored him, hyperaware of his proximity in their shared space.

"Understand that joining the army was one of the best decisions I ever made," Wyatt began, taking a moment to find his words. "It was tough, and there were brutal early morning hours, but it gave me direction and purpose. I'd never had much I could be proud of before, but working with my unit, and rising in the ranks, was something I could call my own. No one could take that away from me."

Lightning flashed again, matching the fierceness in Wyatt's eyes. "Being deployed, that was a whole other beast. Mostly it was pretty boring. A bunch of dudes in the desert with spotty internet and minimal food choices is not the big war adventure you think it will be. It was hard—I had all this anger and fight inside of me and nowhere to put it."

That confused Piper. "You were hoping for a fight?"

"We're trained for combat. You see movies and think you know what to expect. You think you want that and can handle it. But when the war reaches you, you realize it's nothing you can prepare for."

He took a deep breath and dragged a hand over his growing stubble. "We realized we were in a war zone when grenades flew over the walls of our compound. The mission had been a simple recon for evidence of foreign troops in the area because there were rumors their numbers were growing. They caught us off guard. So many men were hit, but we had to move out fast to keep the rest of us alive. Those of us who made it out set up a base slightly south where they couldn't reach us, pushing them back with gunfire of our own."

Wyatt stumbled over a lump in his throat. "All night, we could hear our guys . . . calling out for us to come back. To help them. But shots rang out anytime we moved to go back in. In the morning, when we could see the full extent of the damage, all but one of them was dead."

Piper gasped. "Oh, Wyatt. That's . . ." She couldn't find the words to convey how traumatic that experience must have been. Tears dripped off her face, mixing with the raindrops on the ground.

Wyatt rubbed his jaw and continued. "Once backup arrived, we moved into their camp to reclaim our men. Their troops fought back, but we obliterated them. It should have been satisfying to extract justice for our brothers, but when it was all over, I saw it was a bunch of teenagers, kids really. Kids trained for war, but kids all the same."

A tear trickled down his cheek, and he balled his fists into his eyes. "War isn't something that humans are supposed to endure. And I'm one of the lucky ones. An explosive went off near my head a few weeks after that awful encounter and partially damaged the hearing on my left side, maiming me just enough to get me honorably discharged but leaving me otherwise unscathed. Besides the demons in my head," he added with a mangled smile.

Picturing Wyatt in a near-death and dangerous situation made Piper physically ill. It was intolerable imagining a world in which Wyatt hadn't survived. His careless behavior in high school had wounded her deeply, and sometimes she'd wished him the same level of pain he'd inflicted on her, but she'd never wanted this.

She cupped her hand over his bad ear. "I'm glad you made it out alive." In the cover of darkness, it was easier to speak the truth.

He startled at her touch, then placed his hand over hers and kissed her palm, like a reflex. "Me too," he whispered.

His lips scorched her skin, his steady gaze piercing her soul, unearthing old emotions. Emotions of intoxicating love mixed with unbearable hurt. Emotions she wasn't ready to process. She sat as still as a rabbit caught in a hawk's line of sight, held in his penetrating stare, her hand still burning where he'd kissed it.

Wyatt pointed toward the sky above the blackened water. "Oh wow, check that out."

She thought it was a lame attempt to break the weird vibe that was humming between them, or maybe that was all in her head, but when she looked where he pointed, Piper gasped. In the distance, lightning danced from cloud to cloud, igniting the sky with brilliant purple streaks.

She angled her body to face the storm clouds, sliding closer to Wyatt. Jagged bolts of light sliced through the dark like a knight's lance winning a joust. The sky came alive with sizzling energy, making the hairs on Piper's arms stand at attention with every crack of light.

Mesmerizing.

"It's putting on a show for us." Piper stared up in awe. "It's so beautiful."

"It truly is."

She peeked at Wyatt, swallowing hard when she noticed his attention focused squarely on her instead of the glittering sky. His gaze flicked to her lips like he might kiss her. And, for a fraction of a second, she leaned into him, wanting him to. But a louder clap of thunder knocked her back to her senses, and she scooted away, putting a few more inches between them.

Because kissing Wyatt with those heartbreaker eyes would be completely insane.

Right?

Chapter Fifteen

Then

Piper swore every time Wyatt passed her in the halls of Cedar Falls High, his shoulders had broadened, his muscles grown more prominent and his face more chiseled. Preferring solitude, he used his intimidating presence to discourage small talk with his classmates. A rotation of black T-shirts and a permanent scowl added to the effect. Wyatt was there to graduate. Period. He wasn't interested in making new friends or participating in school activities.

That included Senior Prom.

Piper wasted hours in homeroom imagining Wyatt promposing to her in the cafeteria or clubhouse. Not that she had a crush on Wyatt—they were great friends, that's it—but sometimes, when she lay in bed at night, she could still feel the soft weight of his fingers laced in hers, his warm breath tickling her temple. It wasn't hard to imagine him twirling her on the dance floor or how good his lips might feel on hers if they sparked the same electricity as holding his hand.

But it was a silly fantasy. Especially after Wyatt confirmed he would rather shove toothpicks under his nails than go to a school dance, despite the Lonely Onlys' best attempts to talk him into it. So Piper accepted the invitation of her friendly chemistry lab partner, Ryan Chen, and looked forward to the legendary high school ritual even if Wyatt was sitting it out.

Bucking the traditional rules, Allie had invited class clown Parker, who'd moved up the high school social ladder since getting his braces off a few months earlier. Not fully out of the closet yet, Ethan asked Parker's twin sister, Penny, who was equally as fun as her brother and understood she might catch Ethan kissing Matt Thompson in the bathroom at some point during the evening.

When Ryan canceled on her the morning of prom, citing a baseball injury, Piper had been minorly devastated. Not because she had her heart set on dancing with Ryan but because she didn't want to be the only one in her friend group going without a date.

This hit home when Piper arrived at Allie's house for pictures and found everyone coupled up, posing in front of the limo Ethan's parents had rented for the night.

Dressed in a jaw-dropping red sequined gown that made her look like a teenage Jessica Rabbit, Allie waved Piper over and squealed, "You look awesome, Piper. Come get in the pictures!"

Piper hugged Allie and wriggled between the sets of couples in classic prom poses, hoping she looked like she belonged. She'd opted for a classic ball gown silhouette in a pale frost blue over a form-fitted dress. The silk and tulle had made her feel like a princess when she'd tried it on at the store, but standing next to her classmates—dressed in bold colors with cuts that showed off their legs and curves—she felt like a kid playing dress-up on Halloween.

In the row of parent picture takers, her mother caught her attention and smiled wide, gesturing animatedly at her mouth. Piper forced the corners of her mouth up to appease her mom, hoping the fake smile would calm her nerves.

Mrs. McLaughlin looked up from her camera. "Wait, where's Wyatt?"

Piper opened her mouth to explain Wyatt's absence, but Ethan spoke up before she could get a word out. "There he is! Looking sharp in that suit, I might add."

Wyatt sauntered toward the group looking more than sharp. Piper had never seen him in anything besides a T-shirt and jeans, and she couldn't stop staring at how handsome he looked, cleaned up in what she later learned was a suit borrowed from Ethan's dad.

Ethan high-fived Wyatt, and Allie catcalled him, making him duck his head in embarrassment.

"Wyatt, go stand by Piper." Molly pointed, raising her camera back into position.

Wyatt slipped an arm around Piper as everyone turned back toward the cameras. "Surprise," he whispered into her ear. "I heard you needed a date."

Heat crawled down Piper's neck, flooding her stomach with liquid warmth like a chocolate lava cake cut open. "I don't know who talked you into this, but I'm so glad you're here," she whispered back, pinching herself to make sure she wasn't dreaming.

He dazzled her with a smile, and for the first time all evening, a thrill of genuine excitement pulsed through her.

When the painfully long photo shoot ended, Wyatt took her aside and pulled a small box from his jacket pocket. "I don't know the right protocol for this, but Ethan told me to get you one."

He opened the lid, revealing a soft white flower corsage.

Piper's heart did a cartwheel as he slipped the band onto her wrist. "It's so beautiful. Thank you! I feel bad I have nothing for you." She still couldn't believe that Wyatt was standing in front of her, dressed in a classic black suit, putting a corsage on her wrist. It was a scene from a movie. A movie she lived in.

"Just promise you won't let me look stupid dancing, and we're even."

Piper beamed. "Wait, did you just agree to dance?"

She bit her lip to keep from smiling like a maniac. Around her, the whirl of cameras captured quintessential prom memories, but she was too enraptured in the moment to pay attention.

PROM WAS A blur of music, lights, and sweaty high schoolers. Shockingly, Wyatt proved to be a good sport about the whole thing, even dancing to the electric slide when Allie dragged them out onto the dance floor. Word traveled fast that the hot loner Wyatt Brooks was at prom and not shy on the dance floor, and before long girls who'd come with a group of friends or a platonic date lined up for a dance.

At first, Piper had been amused by the unexpected attention Wyatt garnered, but after an hour of watching him indulge every dance invitation, Piper reached her limit. These girls didn't even acknowledge Wyatt at school—what made them think they had any claim to him because he looked good in a suit?

"Save me!" Wyatt mouthed to Piper as Sarah Spencer twerked in front of him.

Two more senior girls not so patiently waiting their turn to dance with him next closed in on him from behind. That was all the prompting Piper needed to step away from her group of girlfriends to break up the twerking contest happening on top of her date.

She tapped Sarah on the shoulder. "I hate to interrupt, but this is my favorite song, and Wyatt promised a dance with me if it came on."

Sarah pouted as Wyatt extricated himself from their circle like a debonair Houdini. "Sorry, ladies. A promise is a promise."

He grasped Piper's hand like it was a life raft in choppy waters and whisked her across the dance floor to a quieter side of the room. "Thank you, I owe you one," he said once they were safely out of sight of his adoring fans.

"Who would've guessed you'd be prom's most popular guy?" Piper tried keeping the jealousy out of her voice.

"What can I say? Ladies love these sweet moves." Wyatt spun in a circle and attempted to moonwalk but didn't have enough rhythm to pull it off.

Piper giggled. "Keep that up and you'll be able to fend everyone off without my help."

The music transitioned to a slow song. All around them, their classmates partnered up like a game of couples musical chairs.

"Oh, slow song!" Piper pointed out the obvious. Why had the air suddenly been sucked out of the room? "Should we go sit down?" She could kick herself. That was the exact opposite of what she wanted to do.

"Actually, this is more my speed. If you don't mind more dancing." A slight wobble colored his voice.

He held his hand out, and she took it, stepping closer to him. One of his muscular arms encircled her waist. The other kept her hand in his tight grasp as they swayed back and forth to a Lumineers song. Her fingers itched to touch his soft, curly hair, to run her palm over the delicate stubble on his cheek. But she satisfied the itch by breathing in his warm pine tree scent.

Wyatt smelled like Christmas.

"Is this okay?" he asked after a minute. "You promised you wouldn't let me look stupid."

She pulled back, gazing up at him. "You're doing great, but trust me, no one is watching us."

Sure enough, the surrounding couples were kissing or holding on to each other as if it were their final moments on the *Titanic*.

"You're right. So, no one's going to notice if I do this." He twirled her around, then dipped her.

"Where did that move come from?" she asked, breathless, her head spinning.

He pulled her upright and back in against his chest. "I may have YouTubed a few dance pointers."

"You're full of surprises, Wyatt Brooks." His face was so close, his sweet breath warmed her cheek.

"I like the way you say my name," he confessed huskily. "And if I didn't tell you earlier, you look beautiful tonight."

Piper's cheeks flamed hot, and she had to concentrate to not step on his feet. She'd never seen this side of Wyatt—this flirty side. It unsettled her. She was disturbed by how much she liked it and how much she wished he would keep looking at her like she was the only girl in the room.

Finally finding her words, she choked out a response. "Thank you. You don't look so bad yourself."

He leaned down until his forehead rested against hers as they continued swaying to the music. Her heart hammered like a kick drum beneath her dress, louder than the song playing around them. Was it possible he felt the same tickle of butterflies she did? This was Wyatt, after all. Wyatt, who'd taught her how to throw a punch and made fun of her British accent. Wyatt, who watched terrible action movies with her, who helped paint the clubhouse furniture yellow, who kept her secrets. Wyatt, who made her feel safe enough to step outside her comfort zone and challenged her to be her best self.

Wyatt, who she could envision spending a lifetime with.

She raised her face, inviting him to kiss her. His gray eyes shone softer than she'd ever seen them. His full lips hovered above hers, but the song faded out, and the tempo picked back up before he could move any closer. Then Allie was by Piper's side, saying this song was their anthem and they had to dance. Before she knew it, a circle of girls singing enthusiastically to every word of the new song surrounded Piper.

When she looked back to find Wyatt, he had disappeared into the crowd.

Chapter Sixteen

Now

Piper twisted a wet T-shirt, wringing rainwater from last night's storm into an empty bottle with a satisfying trickle. Residual rain dripped from leaves, making everything dewy and new.

Wyatt walked up behind her. "Hey, thanks for talking me off the ledge last night." He traded her a papaya half for a freshly filled water bottle.

His hand brushed against hers, and her skin buzzed at the contact, a not-so-subtle reminder of how she'd woken curled once again against Wyatt's hard body, with him holding her close.

"Of course. How're you feeling today?" She picked up the radio and followed him to their usual perches under the shade of the palm tree grove.

He dragged a hand through his hair. "Tired, embarrassed, mostly hungry."

Piper bit into her papaya, the juice exploding in her mouth like a water balloon. "Hungry, I get, but there's nothing to be embarrassed about."

Wyatt shot her a grateful smile. "Thanks. I know, but it doesn't make it any less difficult to deal with." He carved out a chunk of fruit with the knife and popped it into his mouth.

She nodded in understanding, not wanting to interrupt.

Wyatt scooped out another bite, his brow furrowing. "I'm one of the lucky ones. I know too many guys who struggled far more than I did. Including my dad."

Piper stopped midbite. "Your father was in the army?" How had she not known that?

"Yeah, he joined up right after high school like me. He and my mom were high school sweethearts who lost touch when he enlisted. They reconnected before he deployed to Afghanistan a few years later, and, well, I came just about nine months after that."

"Is that why you enlisted, too?"

"That and because college wouldn't pay for itself. My parents were engaged but didn't get married in time to pass any benefits down to me." Wyatt averted his gaze. "I don't remember him, but my mom told me how he'd go on long motorcycle rides at night whenever he had nightmares. She took his death hard, and I became her painful daily reminder of him." The crease between Wyatt's eyes intensified. "I don't think she ever stopped loving him."

Piper swallowed hard. That sentiment hit close to home. "He would be so proud of you. Your mom, too." The tired cliché wasn't enough to convey how much she believed her words.

One corner of Wyatt's mouth turned up, his dimple playing peekaboo. "I hope so. I think my dad would've liked what I've done to support veterans like him. That's how I got into work at this tech start-up."

"Wait, you work at a tech company?" She couldn't picture Wyatt behind a desk at a corporate job, but then again, she knew very little about his day-to-day life. Suddenly, she wanted to know everything. "How'd you get into that?"

He took a swig of water. "I came back from my second deployment a mess. The sound of cars freaked me out so much I couldn't drive. Just leaving my house scared me." Wyatt shuddered, remembering. "A guy at my gym saw my army duffel bag and started a conversation. He, Roger, had been discharged four years prior and had gone through a similar tough transition back to civilian life. He took me under his wing. Set me up with a great therapist, gave me helpful books to read, and got me into meditation. Even connected me with my dog, Badger. It saved my life." Wyatt's tone was serious but not somber.

"You have a dog?" This tidbit delighted Piper more than anything. "You always wanted one."

"Yeah, Badger's my best bud. I miss him a ton." Wyatt's voice grew tight, but he kept talking. "Meeting Roger was pure dumb luck, and I didn't want other vets missing out on the mentorship or resources Roger gave me because they weren't in the right place at the right time. So, I teamed up with a coding buddy, and we created an app."

"An app that connects new vets with seasoned vets?"

Wyatt nodded, his eyes sparkling as he talked. "Exactly. It helps those recently discharged connect with other vets and find a mentor in their area to help them through the tough times. Connects them with a person who understands what they've been through. It also provides trusted resources and even has a feature that provides instant support to someone struggling. Almost like an emergency button. I'd like to think it's saved a few lives over the past year."

"Wow, Wyatt. That's huge. I'm impressed." Impressed was an understatement for the awe and admiration that lit up her brain. Wyatt had done something truly impactful with his life and was miles ahead of her in the figuring-adulting-out race.

He beamed. "Thank you. I got some grant money and government funding to launch it. Then the company I'm at, Invictus Tech, bought it and hired me to keep working on new releases. It's been a wild ride."

"They bought your app? That's unbelievable!"

Piper had always admired Wyatt's steady determination to control his destiny. So many people had dismissed and underestimated him, including their high school guidance counselor, who had pushed for Wyatt to get his GED instead of graduating with the rest of his classmates.

"Bet you didn't think this mediocre student would amount to much, did you?" Wyatt's brow creased, misinterpreting her comment.

"No, that's not it at all! I'm happy others see what I always did." Piper paused, struggling to find the right words. Other teenagers in his situation might have dropped out of school or given up, but Wyatt had studied relentlessly, working hard to graduate with a handful of Bs and an A in history. She angled her body to face him. "I'm so proud of you, Wy."

The tips of his ears reddened. "Thanks. That means a lot coming from you."

His smoky eyes met hers with piercing intensity. Piper didn't look away.

"Anytime. And I'm not saying that because I've got all the time in the world right now." She'd hoped the lame joke would lessen the effect of the butterflies raging in her stomach.

It didn't.

"Enough about me." Wyatt tossed his finished papaya peel into the water. "How's med school? What's it like living your dream?"

Piper puffed her cheeks up and looked skyward, willing a plane to appear overhead and save her from this conversation.

"That bad?" Wyatt asked.

She fidgeted with a strand of hair, twisting it around her finger and into a knot. "I keep thinking it will all click. That I'll wake up and get excited about operating on patients, or Morty the cadaver in our case, but the longer I'm in school, the more I realize I'll never be as passionate about medicine as my father. Or my classmates. It's not my dream anymore."

It was the first time Piper had put words to her emotions. She'd never talked about this with anyone, but Wyatt had the uncanny ability to extract the feelings swimming inside her and bring them into the light.

Saying it aloud released her, like a butterfly breaking free of its cocoon.

"So, what is your dream?" Wyatt asked.

Piper shook her head. "I'm not sure anymore. Is there a job that lets me sit around and read books all day?" She blew out a breath. "All I know is that it's not becoming a doctor."

Wyatt frowned. "Why don't you stop?"

"It's not that easy!" Piper had asked herself that very thing every day for the last two years, but his question made her defensive. "My parents worked so hard to get me here. It's what we planned since I was little, and it would crush them if I threw it all away without giving it a fair chance."

Wyatt pursed his lips. "Do you want my advice?"

"Not really, but you're probably going to tell me anyway."

A smile flitted across his face. "Then feel free to ignore this, but being in the army and being in combat taught me something fundamental but very true. Life is short, and you only get one, so you might as well live it on your terms."

"That's the clichéd advice you learned in the army?" Piper stifled a laugh.

"Don't knock it. That motto has served me well."

Wyatt sounded so confident that Piper had trouble blowing his advice off like she wanted to. She breathed the sea air deep into her lungs. Maybe Wyatt had a point. Even stranded with little food, a head injury, and her ex, life on the island was simpler than life back home. Here doubt about making the wrong choice or fear of someone discovering she was a phony didn't plague her. Here, she could be herself, perhaps more so than she'd been in years. There were no distractions—no TV, no Tag, no social media, and no exams—to prevent her from looking inward. Nothing but the sand and the ocean.

And Wyatt.

Although she'd never get over missing Allie's wedding, she felt more at peace than she had in years. That had to mean something.

"You deserve to live your life exactly how you want to, P. If that means doing something with books or reading or anything else you love, you should." Wyatt nudged his shoulder against hers. "Accept nothing less."

She nodded, swallowing the unexpected lump in her throat, and laid her head on his shoulder. If her reaction surprised him, he didn't show it and responded by kissing the top of her head, then resting his cheek against her hair as they stared out at the horizon together.

Last night, the wall of past transgressions and hurt had crumbled, replaced by a palpable shift toward peace. She liked sitting beside Wyatt and talking to him. Liked laughing with him and loved falling asleep to his steady breathing, then waking up pressed against his side.

It should terrify her, letting Wyatt creep back into her heart, but he was becoming harder and harder to resist.

Chapter Seventeen

Then

"Afterparty at my place," Ethan announced as they piled back into the limo after prom, buzzing with excitement. "My dad said we could hang out in the basement, and I think some guys on the soccer team are bringing beer."

"Some guys" meant Ethan's latest crush, Matt, who'd been by Ethan's side all night. Sure enough, Penny, Ethan's official date, was already snuggled up to one of Ethan's soccer teammates in the back of the limo. Ethan lived a few blocks from Allie in a sprawling ranch with a basement and a pool. His infamous parties usually ended with everyone in the water.

"We're in!" Allie said from her date's lap. "What about you, Piper?"

Piper shook her head. "My parents will never go for it. Y'all drop me off at Allie's, and I'll walk back home."

Taking the path through the woods from Allie's house to hers was easier than making everyone loop back around to drop her at her front door. Plus, she needed a moment to clear her head before going home.

Allie stuck out her lower lip in an exaggerated pout. "What they don't know won't hurt them."

"It's not worth getting into an argument with them over." To be honest, Piper didn't want to ruin her perfect prom memories with a loud basement full of drunk boys.

"You're too responsible, P," Ethan complained.

"Someone has to be!"

She caught Wyatt watching her with a knowing smirk. Her heart skipped from remembering the warmth of his hand on her lower back as he guided her on the dance floor and the tickle of his hair against her face.

Ethan said something to the driver, and the limo pulled in front of the McLaughlins' house a few minutes later.

"Wyatt, keep an eye on these two tonight," Piper instructed.

Wyatt slid toward the front of the limo. "Actually, I'm getting out here, too."

Allie and Ethan barely reacted to the typical Wyatt refusal to socialize, but Piper's heart took off like a jackhammer as he climbed out, offered his hand, and helped her down.

The night pulsed with untethered energy as the limo pulled away. Dancing with Wyatt in a room full of sticky teenagers was one thing. Enclosed in the dark of night, alone, was quite another. Piper couldn't stop the tremble that crescendoed up her ribs despite the balmy eighty degrees. Like he'd practiced the move before, Wyatt removed his jacket and draped it around her shoulders. How could he remain so calm while she might as well be strapped to a gyroscope, flipping and spinning through the air?

She'd been alone with Wyatt one thousand times before. But never like this. The night belonged to them alone, the street filled with only the whisper of wind in the trees.

Wyatt tilted his head in the direction of her house. "Come on. I'll walk you home."

Was that a quaver in his voice?

She followed him through the woods, past the clubhouse. From here, the faint light of her kitchen window beamed like a neon sign. A few feet farther and her parents, if they were in the kitchen, would be able to see them.

Piper skidded to a stop. "This is fine. I don't want to give my parents a reason to lecture me if they see us walking up together."

"Okay." He shrugged like it was no big deal, but a flash of something, disappointment maybe, flitted across his face.

She hoped he didn't take that personally, but she didn't want her parents stopping something from happening between her and Wyatt before it even began.

"Thanks for being my stand-in date. I mean, not that it was a *date* date." Piper tripped over her words. "But you know, thanks for coming with us all and dancing with me."

"I had a great time. Mostly thanks to my awesome *date*." He smiled shyly. "We should do this again sometime."

Piper furrowed her brow. "Go to prom again?"

"Ha, yeah, no, you're right. I guess this was a one-time thing." Wyatt adjusted his shirt.

She slipped his jacket off her shoulders, but he stopped her.

"No, keep it. I mean, you can't keep it; it's Ethan's dad's. But I can get it from you tomorrow."

She put the jacket back on. Why was this conversation so awkward, like they'd both forgotten the English language?

"Okay, thank you. And thanks for walking me home."

"No problem. Have a good night." Wyatt looked like he wanted to say something else but stopped himself.

"Night." Piper waved back as she walked toward her house, kicking herself for being so lame. She was halfway across her lawn when he called her name.

"Piper, wait!"

When she turned toward him, his face was inches away from her. She breathed in sharply.

"I just . . ." Then his lips were on hers.

She kissed him back fiercely, wrapping her arms around his neck and pressing her body as close as possible to his.

He was warm, his lips were soft, and she was sinking.

His hands were everywhere, on her cheek, hair, and the small of her back, holding her against him. It wasn't her first kiss—that honor had gone to Bobby Bensen, her seventh-grade boyfriend of three weeks—but it was by far her favorite. By the time he pulled back, they were both out of breath.

"I just wanted to kiss you." He finished his sentence with a deep inhale, his forehead pressed against hers.

Her smile stretched so wide she was sure she looked like a clown, but she didn't care. "I'm glad you did. I've been thinking about kissing you since that slow song." *And since you almost kissed me in the closet last summer.*

"A little longer for me," Wyatt admitted with a shy smile.

Emboldened by his answer, Piper tipped her face up to his. "Then we should do that again."

But he didn't need a second invitation—his lips were already closing over hers.

Chapter Eighteen

Now

Sharp static poured out of the radio by Piper's side. She'd flipped it on this morning for an update now that they'd passed the two-day mark Rosie had promised. Wyatt strained forward and listened as Piper tuned the station to catch a garbled voice, but nothing intelligible came through.

Piper stood, dusting sand off her bottom. "I'm going to see if I can get a signal on this thing if I go farther down the beach."

She wanted to reach Rosie again, but she also needed a momentary breather from the strong current of Wyatt's charm, which threatened to pull her under. Even now, she wanted to be closer to him, touching him, kissing him. Learning all she could about what he'd been up to since she'd last seen him.

Wyatt scrambled to his feet after her. "Great. I'll try my luck fishing, so we aren't stuck eating papayas again."

They parted ways, and Piper walked down the beach, adjusting the radio's channel dial, wishing she could change the station in her mind, which insisted on thinking about Wyatt. Hearing his voice, joking with him, getting lost in his eyes—it anchored her to a time when he'd consumed her every thought. Being around Wyatt these past few days made it easy to remember why she'd fallen in love with him in the first place—a slippery slope she might not survive sliding down again. In some ways, her ever-present grudge against him had served as a security blanket, protecting her from any more hurt. But as hard as she tried now, she couldn't muster up the same level of anger toward the man on the beach, who'd bandaged her wounds, built them a shelter, and made her laugh hard enough to forget their life-or-death situation.

After she'd scrolled through the airwaves for several football field lengths of the beach, a welcome voice broke through the static. "Hello, hello! Piper, Wyatt? Can you hear me?"

Piper grasped the radio, putting it right by her ear. "Yes! Hi! We were getting worried you'd forgotten about us."

"Sorry to leave you hanging, but some bad weather cropped up that delayed our search," Rosie explained. "Be on the lookout for our planes over the next few days and flag us down if you see or hear us, okay? With any luck, we'll find you by dinnertime tomorrow, but it could be longer."

Tears of relief sprang to Piper's eyes. She choked out an acknowledgment of Rosie's statement.

"Do you guys have enough water? Are you okay sitting tight for the time being?"

"Yes, we're okay. We have water from a storm last night, but we'll be waiting and ready for you. If you talk to my parents, can you tell them I love them?" Piper's heart squeezed tight at how worried her parents must be.

Rosie promised to pass the message along, and Piper switched the radio off, hugging it to her chest. The prickling desperation to be as far away from Wyatt as possible might have faded, but she wanted to be home. She could already imagine taking the longest shower of her life, hugging her parents tight, then sitting down for a southern buffet, warm biscuits melting in her mouth. Her stomach protested at the mouthwatering image, reminding her she'd eaten only airport snacks and fruit for the past few days.

Home by tomorrow night! The idea buoyed her with rejuvenated hope.

Not ready to walk back to Wyatt yet, Piper continued her trek along the shoreline. The low tide pulled the water back like a curtain, giving the sand the stage. As she walked, bright orange crabs, eyes sticking out like antennas, scuttled across the sand, ducking for cover every time the shadow of a seabird moved over the sand. One crab wasn't quick enough, and a white bird with black-tipped wings swooped down and carried it away, another bird following him out over the water, fighting for a crab leg. If Wyatt didn't catch any fish, maybe they'd have some luck with the crabs.

The beach usually dead-ended at the foot of the cliffside, the water splashing against the rocks, but with the low tide, a narrow passage of sand now outlined it. Curious about what was on the other side, Piper walked the tightrope of sand between the rocks and the sea. When she rounded the bend, the same white beach stretched before her, bordered by more gnarled trees bent by the ocean wind. The only visible difference on this side was more rocks dotting the sand.

Her heart sank. Of course it looked the same. What had she been expecting—a grand hotel? A docked cruise ship? She didn't know, but confirmation that they were indeed on a remote island knocked the wind out of her sails.

Her appetite to explore further evaporated—though her appetite for food strengthened—so she headed back to their base camp. She was so focused on getting to the other side of the beach she almost didn't notice the sun glinting off an object bobbing in the water. Shielding her eyes for a better look, she scanned the whitecaps. Sure enough, something close to the shoreline vanished and reappeared with each swell of water.

The object resembled a suitcase or a plastic container, not something that belonged in the ocean. If she squinted hard enough, it almost looked like the Yeti cooler Wyatt had pointed out on the plane, the one filled with refreshments. But that was probably her hunger talking.

Piper wasn't a great swimmer, having failed to overcome her fear of putting her face in the water at YMCA swim camp years ago. So far, she'd avoided the ocean on this extended layover, but by the time she flagged Wyatt down, whatever was out there could be too far for either of them to reach safely.

This was up to her.

Stripping down to her red one-piece bathing suit, Piper gave herself a quick pep talk about the low statistics of shark attacks before wading into the ocean. The water, she noted with relief, was as tranquil as it had appeared from the beach. The calm after the storm. She swam a few easy strokes, allowing her body to get used to the movement. When she spotted the telltale U.S. Army and Captain America stickers on the front of the plane's Yeti bobbing in front of her, she quickened her pace, in disbelief until she had her arms wrapped around it.

Though the cooler was buoyant, pushing it back toward shore required more effort than swimming out to it had, especially where the waves met the beach. Once the ocean no longer supported the cooler's weight, it smashed into her shins repeatedly as she wrestled it onto dry land. By the time she dragged it and herself onto the sand, she was woozy and out of breath but proud of herself.

Unlatching the lid, she held her breath, saying every prayer she knew that there would be something worthwhile inside, then peeked into the cooler through the cracks between her fingers. Ocean water filled the container, and the whole thing stank like dead fish, but several cans of Coke and Miller Lite floated in the water, looking better than a million dollars. Even a bottle of prosecco remained intact, and she counted at least four water bottles. She pushed aside some cans, and her heart almost stopped at the subsequent discovery—two blocks of Cabot cheddar cheese, still packaged, and a plastic carton of Oreo cookies.

Wanting to be sure she hadn't cracked up and imagined it all, she rubbed her eyes and counted to three before looking in the cooler again. Sure enough, the food and drinks bobbed in the water like a game-day buffet. A slow smile spread across her face. Wyatt would be thrilled. More than thrilled, he would lose his mind.

Piper dumped out the excess ocean water, placed the radio and her clothes on top of the lid, and used both hands to drag the cooler back toward their base camp. Halfway there, she gave up lugging it herself and left it in the sand for Wyatt to carry the rest of the way. His muscles were far better suited to this job. As he came into view, she broke into a run.

"*Wyatt!*" she screamed down the beach, unable to contain her excitement any longer. "Wyatt, come see what I found!"

From his fishing post on the shore, Wyatt's head popped up like a gopher, and he splashed out of the water.

"*Piper?*" He sounded frantic as he sprinted toward her. He'd stripped down to his swim trunks, and in the new dawn of a full cooler, she could fully appreciate his overwhelming gorgeousness—all hard muscles and glistening tan skin.

When they met in the middle, she jumped into his arms, wanting to wipe the worried look off his face and celebrate with him. His arms looped around her, hugging her back. The sensation of his chest against her mostly bare body sent ripples of desire through her. As she inhaled his familiar woodsy scent, she fought the temptation to entwine her legs around him and smother his neck, cheek, and lips with kisses.

"What's wrong? Are you hurt?" Wyatt's fingers slid into her hair, assessing her head for bumps. He set her down, searching her face for an answer, adorable in his concern.

Piper shook him off. "I'm fine!"

His eyes remained cloudy with worry. "Why are you wet? Did you go in the ocean?"

"Yes, and I found something you won't believe. But I need your help bringing it back here." She tugged on his arm to pull him down the beach, but he didn't budge.

"Jesus, Piper, you nearly gave me a heart attack running down the beach like a *Baywatch* babe."

She cocked an eyebrow. "A *Baywatch* babe?"

"Yeah, I mean, look at you."

She glanced down. The sun had burned her skin red as her bathing suit, whose straps hung off her shoulders from the weight she'd lost. Saltwater had created beach waves no salon could replicate in her wild yellow mane, probably because no one would request looking so untamed. The high cut of this one-piece made her legs impossibly long, and the loose straps showed more cleavage than she usually would, but she was far from Pamela Anderson.

Still, Wyatt stared at her like he might tear her bathing suit off, his eyes so dark they burned like charcoal. Heat pooled between Piper's thighs. What had she come to tell him again? Her stomach whined. Oh, right, food!

"How's your hunger?" she asked.

His eyes darkened further. "Very loud. Why?"

Piper swallowed thickly. Were they still talking about food? "I have a surprise for you. Come with me."

Wyatt grunted but followed her along the shore.

When the cooler came into view, she turned back to him to say, "Close your eyes."

"Piper," he protested.

"Come on, just do it. Please!"

He obliged, holding on to her arm as she led him forward. This was more fun than she'd expected. Once they were right in front of the Yeti, Piper opened the lid.

"Okay. You can look!"

Wyatt blinked, then narrowed in on the cooler. His mouth fell open. "Is this real? Or did we both die, and this is some kind of weird limbo?" He knelt, pushing aside the floating cans.

"No, I don't think we're on some spinoff of *Lost*—I think the storm brought it from wherever it landed." Piper pulled back on her tank top and shorts.

"You swam to get this? What happened to conserving energy?" He knew about her mistrust of the ocean and sounded proud—and a little amused.

"I guess you're rubbing off on me." She rolled her eyes in exaggeration.

Wyatt grinned. "Hmm, sounds like I'm not such a bad influence, after all."

He ripped open the cheese and sniffed it before breaking off a hearty chunk and handing her a piece of the cheddar. They both moaned in delight as the warm cheese hit their tongues.

"Is it just me, or is this the best thing you've ever had?" he asked.

"It's not just you. And I have more good news." Piper swallowed her mouthful of cheese. "I reached the rescue station on the radio, and they said the storm delayed them, but they're sending out a crew to find us soon. Wyatt, we could be home by tomorrow night!"

Wyatt paused midbite. "That's great." He smiled tightly, but his gaze cut away from her, focusing instead on the endless ocean.

Chapter Nineteen

Then

Allie came over the day after prom bursting with gossip. She threw herself across Piper's bed. "I can't believe prom's over! I missed you at the afterparty. Did you and Wyatt hang out after we dropped you off?"

Piper's breath caught in her throat at the mention of Wyatt. "What? No! He just walked me home. Why?" The moment last night between her and Wyatt felt as fragile as a chrysalis, not yet ready to be passed around and inspected.

Allie cocked her head to the side and pointed. "His jacket's here."

Crap, she'd forgotten about that. "I was cold, and he let me borrow it for the walk home." She hoped she sounded casual. "Tell me more about the party. Did Parker kiss you?"

As she'd expected, Allie jumped at the chance to talk about her night with Parker and take the attention off Piper—and Wyatt.

On her way out, Allie picked up the jacket and slung it over her shoulder. "I promised Ethan I'd help him clean up. I'll bring this to him."

Dang it. Returning the jacket would have been a perfect excuse to see Wyatt again soon, but she couldn't argue with Allie's logic, so she thanked her and said goodbye.

When Wyatt hadn't called or texted an hour later, Piper started second-guessing everything. Maybe last night had meant nothing to him. Maybe back in Mason, he made out with girls all the time, and this was no big deal. Based on the female attention he got last night, it seemed like a safe assumption.

She could call him. Like she did all the time. All the time, until they'd kissed and changed everything.

Before she could drive herself crazy, she picked up her phone and texted, "*Walk?*" then buried the phone under her pillow.

After an excruciatingly long minute, her phone double-buzzed back.

"Meet you outside in 5."

Her body sagged with relief, then switched into full panic mode. Rushing to the mirror, she analyzed her reflection. Gone was the girl with perfect hair dressed in a ball gown, but her cheeks were still rosy from a morning shower, and her eyes glowed unnaturally bright. She was about to discover whether the spark between them was simply a result of the magic of prom and a flawlessly fitting dress.

"I'm going out for a walk!" she called to her mom on her way out the door but didn't wait for a response.

Piper's heart was in her throat. Why was she so nervous? This was a simple walk with Wyatt. Her friend. The friend who'd kissed her last night and who she maybe had a teeny tiny, possibly major, crush on now.

Another anxious thought popped into her head. How would she greet him? Was she supposed to kiss him hello? Piper wasn't a hugger by nature, but if she didn't hug him after last night would he think she didn't like him?

Her fears melted away as soon as she rounded the bend and saw his smile, worry replaced with a new frenetic energy that rattled in her rib cage like a maraca. Wyatt opened his arms wide, and she slipped into his embrace as if they always greeted each other that way. As natural as breathing.

He took her hand. "Come on, let's walk down to the stream."

Again, it struck Piper how easy it was to be with Wyatt—her fingers intertwined with his. And how right it felt. Like a fog had lifted, and in the clearing, it was obvious they should be together.

The shift in her feelings toward him was dizzying and electrifying—all-consuming. Was it possible he felt the same way?

"I'm glad you texted," Wyatt told her. "I should have called, but I thought you might bring my jacket over this morning, and I didn't want to be annoying. Or presumptuous."

"Allie stopped by and took it to Ethan."

He nodded, and the furrow of his brow relaxed.

"It's weird being back in normal clothes, isn't it?" Piper chatted on. "It was kinda fun dressing up for a change and seeing everyone looking so awesome. This is a far cry from my prom look, huh?"

They'd reached the small stream that bordered the Cedar Falls subdivision, and Piper took a seat on a large rock overlooking the water. Wyatt sat beside her and cocked his head to one side as if taking in her appearance for the first time. Piper smoothed her hair back, worrying her bottom lip.

"Don't get me wrong, you looked amazing last night," he said. "But I like this Piper even more. This is the Piper who helps me with English essays, gives me advice about my mom, and takes my side when Allie's annoying. This is my Piper."

Her stomach flipped at his admission.

"Any chance the magic of Ethan's dad's suit stuck around? I've never had more girls want to hang out with me than last night," he teased, a slight hint of fear in his voice.

"I can't speak for the other girls." Piper cleared her throat. "But I always want to hang out with you. You don't need a fancy suit to get my attention."

He smiled at her, broadly enough to show off his dimples. "Good, because I don't own a fancy suit, but I'd very much like to take you on a date. Is that okay with you?"

"It's more than okay with me," she assured him. "Though it may need to be a 'to be determined date' until I get my parents on board."

"A TBDD." Wyatt exhaled audibly, his dimple on display once again. "Hopefully soon because I want as much Piper in my life as possible this summer."

It all sounded too good to be true—an entire summer by Wyatt's side. Piper bit her lip to keep her psychotically wide smile in check. Her parents probably already had a summer schedule lined up for her that included activities to "get ahead in life" like they usually did. They'd made it very clear they didn't want her dating until college, and Piper rarely went against their wishes, but she wouldn't let anything stop her from going on her first real date with the best guy she knew.

"People usually break up before college, and we're just getting started." He pushed his curls off his forehead. "Clearly, timing is not our thing."

"I don't know, this feels like pretty perfect timing to me." Piper angled her face toward him. When their lips met, it was the ultimate affirmation that the spark between them was stronger than prom night magic. Kissing Wyatt officially became her new favorite thing to do.

"It's hard to disagree with you when you kiss me like that," Wyatt murmured between kisses.

"Then I'm going to have to kiss you more often."

"No arguments here."

The all-consuming experience of kissing Wyatt under the warm spring sky was exciting, with an undercurrent of deep familiarity, like their love story had already been written in the stars.

Chapter Twenty

Now

Wyatt snapped open a Coke with a pop, took a sip, and handed it to Piper. The fizzy bubbles danced on her tongue, coating her throat with the sweet syrup—impossibly delicious. It acted as a touchstone to home, of stealing sips of soda as a child from her dad, late-night study sessions with Allie, and her go-to college drink: Captain and Coke. She passed the soda back to Wyatt, biting the inside of her cheek as his mouth pressed against the top of the can in the exact spot hers had. What would he do if she leaned over and captured his lips with her own?

"Hey, can you show me where you found the Yeti?" Wyatt broke through Piper's reckless thoughts.

She raised an eyebrow, curious. "It was right in front of the cliffside. Why? Do you think there could be more where it came from?"

He shrugged. "I'm not sure. Probably not, but I'll feel better if we check."

They left the Yeti with the radio and trekked back toward the cliffside. The tide crawled to shore, moving farther up the sand with every crashing wave, erasing the traces of Piper's previous footsteps and sending crabs skittering for cover. When they met the rocky wall, the sandy path that once outlined the cliff was covered in a foot of water.

That didn't stop Wyatt from barreling forward.

"Watch out for rocks," Piper cautioned, even though she knew there was no point in lecturing him when he had that determined look in his eyes. She followed at a slower, more careful pace, picking around rocks and shells.

"There!" Wyatt exclaimed from the other side of the protruding cliff. "Do you see that?"

The sun staggered toward the horizon, casting beams of light at sharp angles onto the water. Piper caught up with him and craned her neck to follow Wyatt's finger. Sure enough, something metallic sparkled in the water, lodged on a reef or sandbar far out at sea. It was hard to tell exactly what it was over the choppy waves, which had strengthened as the tide turned.

Wyatt shaded his eyes with his hand. "I think it's our plane or what's left of it. Do you see that red stripe? I bet it got brought in by the storm last night."

"Maybe." Piper didn't want him to get his hopes up.

"I'm going to swim out there and see. There could be more food or something to help us out."

Piper's eyes widened. She put a hand on Wyatt's arm, stopping him from diving headfirst into the water. "I don't know if that's a good idea, Wyatt. I know you're a strong swimmer, but those waves are getting bigger, and it could be farther away than it looks. Plus, I doubt you slept well last night."

He waved her off. "If we wait for the water to calm down, it could get washed back out and we'll miss our chance. Besides, I've eaten better today than any day since being here. And for the first time on this island, I'm caffeinated! There's no way I'm not going to check it out."

"Rescue is coming tomorrow. Why risk it when we're so close to getting off this island?" *Why did he always have to press his luck?*

"The same reason you swam out to get the Yeti. We can't count on rescue. They were delayed before and could be again.

I don't want to pass up an opportunity to see what other supplies we might find. What if it's the difference between life and death?"

She should have guessed he wouldn't listen to her. "Then I'm coming with you." She wasn't about to let him do something foolish alone.

He sized her up with a long, even stare as if trying to measure her current level of stubbornness. She lifted her chin and met his gaze.

He let out a breath. "Fine, but if I say the current's too strong, we call it off, deal?"

"Deal."

For the second time that day, Piper stripped down to her bathing suit, tossing her clothes onto the sand, away from the approaching tide line. Wyatt waded in hip deep before cutting a clean line out to the visible tip of the plane, skimming under waves that threatened to smash him to the ocean floor. Following in his wake, Piper struggled to keep up, cursing every wave that forced her under. She didn't take a full breath until they crossed over the barrier of the biggest waves, to where the water was calmer, but not by much.

Up close, she could tell the twisted metal structure was indeed their plane. Only the tail poked through the water, bent like a broken arm, a bright red stripe signaling its identity. Treading water several yards back, she watched as Wyatt reached the plane and dove underwater. He came up empty and swam to the other side of the plane, fighting the current. Diving back down, he stayed under longer this time before finally resurfacing with a sharp inhale.

He waved an orange box in the air at her. "Flares!"

Piper stroked closer, and he tossed her the plastic container. It floated in the water until she could grab it, waterlogged but otherwise undamaged.

"Be careful," he warned. "The waves are acting funny around this reef. The tide's creating an unpredictable current pattern."

"Let's head back then."

But he ignored her, determination gleaming in his eyes. "I saw a bag of something, peanuts or pretzels maybe, sticking out of an overhead bin, or what's left of it. Wait here; I'm going to try to get it." He took a deep breath and tipped headfirst back underwater.

Piper treaded water, her arms aching against the relentless waves, trying not to think about how far out they had swum. From out here, their beach resembled a scene from a postcard instead of their home for the past four days. What would happen if they kept swimming away from the shore? Would they find help? Another beach? Or run into a shiver of sharks before getting too far?

Piper turned back to the place where Wyatt had vanished. Somewhere beneath the waves, her original plane seat rested. Her stomach churned with bile thinking of how close she'd been to a watery demise, strapped to this ocean death trap forever.

A murky undertow caused by the storm marred the usually crystal-clear ocean, making it hard to spot Wyatt. Not being able to see him made her nervous. What was taking so long?

She counted to ten. There was no reason to worry; Wyatt swam like a pro athlete. He was probably working on getting whatever he had seen loose. Even so, panic forced the air from her lungs as visions of worst-case scenarios filled her head. She couldn't lose him. Not now, not like this.

When bubbles broke the surface a few feet to her right, she acted on instinct, letting go of the orange box and diving under, ignoring her fear of being submerged in water.

After a few sharp strokes downward, she spotted Wyatt's dark hair. Why wasn't he swimming in the right direction? Kicking closer, she hooked her arms under his shoulders and yanked him upward as hard as possible.

Together they crashed through the surface.

Wyatt sputtered, then coughed up a mouthful of ocean water before gulping in a shaky breath of air.

"What happened down there? You scared me!" Piper couldn't help the shrillness of her voice. She had more to say, but the dullness in Wyatt's eyes and the pinch of his face stopped her.

Something was wrong.

"A swell knocked me into the plane. I hit my head, and I got all turned around." Wyatt gasped for air. "I think I cut my leg on something, too."

Piper pushed aside visions of sharks sniffing out blood if he'd cut himself. "Come on, let's get you back to shore and take a look."

"Grab the flare kit first," he grunted.

Piper wanted to argue with him, but she knew it would waste time, and she didn't know the extent of his injuries. She swam to the orange container she'd left floating behind and then came back to help Wyatt, putting his arm around her shoulders for support.

He clenched his jaw and kept his gaze anchored on the shoreline, now farther away than Piper remembered, as they painstakingly paddled their way back. When they got close enough to stand, Piper snaked an arm around his waist, encouraging him to lean on her. The pit in her stomach worsened when he didn't fight off her help.

Wyatt stumbled out of the water before sinking onto the beach. A trail of blood dripped down his leg and into the sand from a cut on his shin. Recoiling at the sight, Piper ran and grabbed her T-shirt. Breathing in through her nose and out through her mouth, she snapped into doctor mode and applied pressure to his wound with her shirt. Wyatt remained unusually quiet as she fussed over him, holding his head in his hands.

The bleeding stopped quickly, and when she mustered up the courage to look, she saw that the cut wasn't as deep as she'd feared. More of a bad scratch that should heal on its own in a few days. Thank goodness. His head wasn't bleeding, but who knows how hard he'd hit it or how much saltwater he'd ingested in the shock of being struck. Chances were good he had a concussion, but he was alive and still here with her.

That's what mattered most.

Piper let out a trembling breath. Those few seconds he hadn't resurfaced had crystallized the depth of her feelings for him. Feelings locked away so tight she had believed they'd never break free—but she hadn't planned for a plane crash or a near-death experience. Or how good it felt being close to Wyatt again—or how hot he looked with a few days' worth of stubble.

She'd ignored the shifting energy between them earlier, but now it came into sharp focus. Her desire to keep the barbed wire up around her heart washed away completely. She wanted to take care of him, protect him like he'd been doing for her since they'd crashed—since she'd known him.

Wyatt lifted his head. "Am I going to make it, Doc?"

"You're going to make it. I'm more worried about your head than your cut, which looks okay." Piper tied a strip of her T-shirt around his leg, protecting the cut from the elements. "But I wish we had something better to clean it out."

He groaned. "Is this where I get my 'I told you' so lecture? Because I deserve it. I should have listened to you."

She laughed out loud. "I gave up trying to get you to listen to me long ago."

"Wow. I must really be hurt if you're letting me off the hook so easily." Wyatt meant it as a joke, but he shifted positions and winced in pain at the new movement. He gritted his teeth. "Ugh, I feel like I've been through the spin cycle of a washing machine. I'm going to have the worst headache tomorrow."

Seeing Wyatt—her strong, brave Wyatt—in pain brought unwitting tears to her eyes. "I hate that you got hurt."

He lifted his head at the catch in her voice. "Hey, this is nothing compared to what I've been through. And nothing compared to what could have happened if you hadn't been there to drag my butt back to shore. I'll be fine."

Piper attempted to smile at him, but her mouth wavered with emotion. She kept picturing him beneath the waves, imagining what would have happened if he'd been too injured to swim back to shore. Or if he hadn't resurfaced at all. Her heart wrenched, and a tear spilled down her face. She turned away from Wyatt, embarrassed about crying when she should be comforting him.

Tenderly, he wiped the tear off her cheek with his thumb, replacing the tear stain with prickling desire. When she turned back to him, his face was mere inches from hers. His eyes mirrored her emotions—fear and longing.

She didn't know who moved first, but his lips closed over hers, urgent and warm. The fire that shot through her veins burned her from the inside out, paralyzing her. Tantalizing her. Maybe it was the adrenaline pumping through her blood, the years of history between them, or the incredible sensation of Wyatt's lips moving over hers. Whatever it was, the riptide of desire swept her away, and she didn't fight it.

Though it was under the most extraordinary circumstances, kissing Wyatt still felt like the most natural thing in the world.

Chapter Twenty-One

Now

"W hy haven't we been doing this the whole time?" Wyatt asked when they came up for air.

"Maybe because I've been holding an eight-year grudge against you. Or because we've been worrying about what to eat, or we could both use a shower." Piper rattled off the list near hysterics, though nothing was funny about the moment.

He cupped her face in his hands. "None of that matters anymore."

Piper melted back against his mouth. A small voice inside her head screamed to be careful, but she pushed it aside. All she wanted to do was sink into Wyatt's kiss, bury herself in his deliciously soft lips, and forget everything else. She wrapped her arms around his neck, straining to get closer. Deepening the kiss, his tongue sweetly parted her lips for more. Piper swore her bones were melting, evaporating under the all-consuming heat of Wyatt's embrace.

His fingers traced the shell of her ear, the curve of her neck, breaking their kiss only long enough to pull back and study her face. Almost like he was convincing himself this wasn't a dream. Finding proof that she was real, this was actually happening, in her eyes. She placed a hand on either side of his face, losing herself in his intense gaze, the sand and surf fading away. Energy skittered between them. Piper tugged his face back down to hers, but when Wyatt made a noise that sounded more like pain than pleasure, she snapped back to her senses.

A small circle of blood seeped through the makeshift bandage on his leg. As much as Piper wanted to continue reenacting their high school glory days, Wyatt was in no shape for a full-blown make-out session.

He followed her gaze to his leg. "It's okay."

His sweet face tempted Piper to dismiss her better judgment and get lost in his touch, but his eyes were still dull, his face pinched. Someone had to be the responsible one right now.

Catching her breath, she pushed herself up and held out a hand to him. "No, it's not. We need to get back to base camp so you can rest."

Wyatt grumbled under his breath but let her help him to his feet.

Walking back to their canopy campsite took twice as long as the trek to the cliff, with Wyatt swaying like he'd had a few too many cocktails. When his vision blurred, they had to pause as the sand swam before him. Even with his increasing dizziness, Wyatt insisted on pulling the Yeti back himself, his chivalry charming in a caveman kind of way.

The inky carriage of night raced across the horizon, drawing trails of indigo and darkening the sky. When they reached their shelter, Wyatt collapsed inside, relief evident on his face. Piper brought over the bag of Oreos, a water bottle, and two of their last few Advil, watching Wyatt until he'd swallowed them both down.

She sat next to him and patted his knee. "I'd say you've earned a cookie."

Ripping open the plastic wrapping on the bag of cookies, she handed one to Wyatt. He ate his cookie in one bite and presented her with a wide chocolaty smile to make her laugh. It worked.

She mimicked him, baring her chocolate-covered teeth with a giggle.

Wyatt joined in with her laughter, then winced. "Ahh, it hurts to laugh."

He rubbed his temples with his fingertips, then lay down with a groan. Piper gently slid his head into her lap.

"Here, let me." She replaced his hands with her slender fingers, rubbing soothing circles into his temples.

His shoulders relaxed. The water and humidity had turned Wyatt's hair into unruly waves, reminding her of high school, when his flop of hair constantly fell in his eyes. She relished running her fingers through his soft curls, careful not to press too hard on the top of his scalp, where he'd hit his head.

"Comfortable?" she asked.

"Never been better."

Piper chuckled. Given their current situation, that statement had to be sarcasm, but to prove he meant it, Wyatt found her hand and tugged her face down to his.

Piper fastened her lips to his, the sensation of the upside-down kiss sending her into orbit. She'd missed the feeling of kissing Wyatt anytime she wanted, of the easy affection that once existed between them. Deepening the kiss, Wyatt clasped her hand tight in his, keeping her locked to his lips.

With a groan, Piper pulled away before she wanted to. Wyatt needed to rest, not act out a scene from *Spider-Man*.

Reluctantly, she shifted his head out from her lap, not wanting to leave but unsure what else she could do to help. "I should let you rest. Do you need any more food or anything else?"

"Just you." Wyatt put a hand on her arm, stopping her from moving too far away. "Please stay. Maybe you can read to me?"

He caught her gaze with a familiar look that held more meaning than she could absorb. Tears glittered in his eyelashes like diamonds caught in cobwebs. She couldn't say no to that. She didn't want to.

Piper located the paperback romance novel she'd discarded by her bed, its pages distorted from the rain and salt air. "I thought you said this book wasn't your thing."

"It isn't, but maybe I'll love it, hearing it from you."

Piper rolled her eyes at him but settled herself cross-legged, her back against a tree trunk, her knees grazing Wyatt's shoulder and hip. He rested an elbow on her knee. Now that they'd crossed the line of something more, they both wanted to stay in constant contact.

"You can read wherever you left off," he told her.

"I've actually finished it, but I don't mind starting over." She began at the first line, introducing Wyatt to the world of ball gowns, dances, Lady Arrieta, and her mystery pen pal. Reading to Wyatt unleashed an avalanche of nostalgia behind her rib cage. This had always been their tradition. Something that made them, them.

After an hour, it became too dark to read the words. Piper closed the book, peeking at Wyatt in the fading light.

His eyes fluttered open. "Hey, it was getting interesting."

She smirked at him. "I told you it was good. If you're lucky, I'll read more to you when we have daylight tomorrow. How're you feeling?"

"I think the Advil's helping." He sat up and stretched. "Promise me the Duke comes back for Lady Arrieta. He loves her so much. I want to see them get a happily ever after."

Piper stiffened. "That's the part that makes no sense to me. Why would he walk away from her if he truly loved her?"

"Maybe that's exactly why he left." Wyatt's gaze captured hers in the growing dark, his eyes beacons of reflecting light.

Piper set the book down, folded her legs into her chest, and wrapped her arms around them, a physical shield against Wyatt. Against the awful memories invading her brain like an army. Kissing Wyatt had cracked something open inside her, resurfacing old feelings of love and digging up long-buried pain.

"Is that why you broke up with me?" Her words shot out like a cannon in the dark. Their high school breakup had shocked her, and knocked the wind from her lungs. By the time she'd recovered, Wyatt had vanished without a word. If they had any chance at moving forward, she needed to know why he'd left like that, why he'd walked away from her so completely.

"It's complicated." He tugged on his ear.

That wasn't good enough. She couldn't accept half-truths any longer. "Then uncomplicate it for me. Please, Wyatt. I need to understand. It's time we talk about it."

He blew out a deep breath. "I guess I was trying to protect you."

"Protect me! From what?"

"From me."

Piper shook her head. "Why do you always cast yourself as the villain in our story?"

He shrugged unhappily but didn't elaborate.

Piper leaned forward. She was so close to the truth. "What changed? Tell me what happened. Please."

Wyatt stared at the ground for some time before he spoke, his voice low and tortured. "I overheard your parents talking about me. Saying that I was a 'dead-end road' they 'didn't want you going down.' They were going to insist you stop communicating with me once I left for boot camp. They would've withheld your tuition if you didn't break up with me."

Her brow furrowed. "But why would they say that? They'd known you for years! They liked you. It doesn't make sense." But as she said the words, she recalled her parents' concerns about her spending too much time with Wyatt, how they didn't want her to tie herself down. How he wasn't heading in the same direction. The "right" direction.

"I guess it was one thing for us to be friends, but being involved with me romantically was not part of their plan for you. I confronted them. You overheard some of our argument that morning. I was hurt, but I also understood where they were coming from." He looked up and met her gaze. "Piper, I barely graduated high school, and I wasn't going to college. I had nothing to offer you, and I knew it. You were going to be a doctor and go off and do all these amazing things. Us together would never have worked."

Little pieces of the puzzle snapped into place, but it wasn't enough for her to see the full image yet.

Now that the floodgates were open, Wyatt continued filling in the gaps. "Selfishly, I wanted to keep you all to myself, but I didn't want to hold you back. I wanted you to have the best life possible. And to do that, I had to help you move on."

That was it. The last puzzle piece.

"So, you broke up with me." Her voice cracked, the bite of tears pricking her throat. The memories were old, but the pain stung fresh as her sunburn.

Wyatt nodded, his head in his hands.

Anger pierced through her pain, her nostrils flaring. "So, let me get this straight. You heard my parents saying those awful things, and you immediately gave up on us? Threw it all away. Why didn't you at least talk to me? Tell me what they said?"

Wyatt's face crumpled like he might cry now, too. "I didn't want you fighting with your parents or throwing all your plans away because of me. I wasn't worth that."

Piper's heart beat a furious pulse in her ears. "But you didn't even give me a choice! You decided what was best for me like my parents did."

"I did what I thought was right." Wyatt reached for her hand, but Piper jerked it out of his grasp.

He hung his head. "I'm so sorry."

"What hurt me the most was you dumping me as a girlfriend and a friend the same day. How come you never called? Never spoke to me again?" She stopped holding back tears, letting drops fall wetly down her face. "You acted like our relationship meant nothing to you."

Wyatt's face twisted in anguish. "It meant everything to me. I knew if I called you, I'd beg you to take me back. I'd tell you how much I loved you, and it would have all been for nothing."

Her hands trembled. "I waited for that call for years."

"I wanted to. So many times." Wyatt spoke over his damp eyes. "But then too much time passed to have any excuse good enough to get you to talk to me."

"Until we crash-landed on this island."

He nodded. "Again, not how I planned on reconnecting with you." He wiped his tears away with the back of his hand. "God, I'm sorry, Piper. For being an idiot. For hurting you back then. For getting us stuck here now. For everything."

The fight leaked from Piper like air out of a day-old balloon. "You broke my heart." The simple statement spoke volumes.

"I broke my heart, too." Raw pain colored his words.

Pain that matched her own. A new fat tear rolled down her cheek.

Wyatt reached out and pulled her to his chest. She resisted at first, but he wouldn't let her go, repeating "I'm sorry, I'm sorry" over and over in her ear until she gave in to his embrace. He held her a little too tight, as if she'd slip through his grasp like sand if he let go, but she welcomed the crush. She locked her arms around his waist, burying her face in his warm neck, sobbing until she had no more tears left.

Wyatt's tears mixed with hers, but it was a cleansing cry—

gut-wrenching memories reframed with this new information. Wyatt trying to do the right thing. Wyatt acting out of insecurity and love.

When their tears dried, Wyatt shifted them to the ground, still holding her close. They clung to each other in the vast, dark night, having found their way back to one another at last.

Chapter Twenty-Two

Then

Graduation passed in a blur of emotions and snapshots of black caps framed against a Carolina blue sky. Wyatt and Piper kept their budding romance under wraps until summer to protect it from the scrutiny of the school's halls, which included Allie and Ethan. But with high school over, Piper was ready to share her joy with their closest friends and eager to go on a real date with Wyatt.

She wasn't the only one. After his prom showing, half the girls at school had developed crushes on Wyatt, who'd spent the year losing the final baby weight in his face and gaining bulging biceps. Of course, he'd been entirely unaware of his effect on the girls of Cedar Falls High. Avoiding a spotlight on their relationship had been a mutual decision between Piper and Wyatt, but every time she overheard girls talking about Wyatt, she worried he might be keeping his options open. Worried she wasn't enough for him.

She reached her breaking point while joining a group of Allie's soccer friends at the local coffee shop, Espresso Self, during their first lazy weekend afternoon of summer break.

"Do you know who's gotten so hot that I think he should be my new boyfriend?" Kiera, the almost closet kisser, asked.

Allie clapped her hands in glee. "Ooh, who? Tell me, tell me!"

"Wyatt Brooks."

Piper almost spat out her caramel latte.

"He's your cousin, right, Allie? What's his deal? Can you set me up with him?" Kiera leaned forward with interest, cupping her chin in her hands, her impossibly long eyelashes fluttering.

"I swear, all of a sudden, my loner cousin's more popular than me! When did that happen?" Allie asked with a groan. "But I'm not getting involved in his love life. And if I were you, I wouldn't hold your breath for Wyatt—he keeps his circle tight."

"Piper, you're friends with him, too." Kiera was persistent. "Do you think he'd go on a date if I asked him?"

NO, because he's dating ME was what she wanted to say. "I don't know if Wyatt's your type," Piper hemmed instead.

"Trust me. Tall, dark, and gorgeous is definitely my type." Kiera swirled the ice in her coffee. "Plus, he's got those piercing blue eyes and bad boy vibes. Yeah, he's my type."

"Gray. His eyes are gray," Piper corrected coolly. "And there's a lot more to him than his looks."

"Whatever. I'm just saying that Wyatt is very datable, and I intend to test that theory this summer." Kiera licked her lips in exaggeration, and the group of girls giggled.

Piper bit her tongue but glared daggers at Kiera for the rest of the afternoon.

Piper didn't think Allie had clocked her sour mood, but Allie pounced the second they slid into her car.

"So, are you going to tell me what's going on with you, or do I have to ask?"

"What do you mean?" Piper played dumb.

"Piper, I'm your best friend. Don't think I haven't noticed you and Wyatt sneaking around these past few weeks and looking at each other with the literal heart eyes emoji. I thought you might claw Kiera's eyes out back there. Spill it."

Piper covered her face with her hands as the truth tumbled out. "You're right. Wyatt and I, well, we're still figuring out what's going on between us, but we kissed after prom, and he asked me out on a date, and I kind of like him." She peeked over at Allie between her fingers. "Are you mad?"

Allie smacked her in the boob. "I'm only mad you didn't tell me sooner! Wyatt kissed you? Piper, that's huge!"

"I know. I'm sorry. I've been dying to tell you, but it's so new, and I didn't want to jinx it." A blush crawled up Piper's cheeks. "Is it too weird for you?"

"No, it's kind of perfect. My bad boy cousin and my goody-goody best friend. I love it."

Piper took her first full breath since spilling her guts. "Good! I was so worried you'd be upset."

"No, I'm the opposite—I want to plan your wedding!"

Piper snapped her head up, alarmed. This level of enthusiasm was worse than anger.

"Please don't make a big deal about this. We haven't talked about what this thing between us is. And he's going off to boot camp soon, and I'm headed to college and—"

"And blah blah blah! You're being too practical, per usual. I'll try to stay out of it but promise me you'll let your heart guide you for once instead of that big noggin of yours."

Piper's mouth dropped open, offended. "Hey!"

"What's your couple's name going to be?" Allie continued with wicked delight.

"This is not being low-key! Get this out of your system before you get home."

"Pyatt? Wiper? Yeesh, I'll keep thinking."

WYATT CALLED AN hour later. "You told Allie," he said as soon as Piper picked up, sounding more amused than upset.

"I couldn't keep it from her anymore. Please tell me she didn't harass you. I told her to be cool."

"She mentioned something about calling us Wiper, and Kiera wants to go on a date with me, which made you jealous."

"Ugh, so not cool at all." Thank goodness Wyatt couldn't see her scarlet face. "I'm sorry I told her. She called me out, and I didn't want to lie to her."

"No, I'm glad you did. I thought maybe you didn't want anyone to know about me. About us." Wyatt echoed Piper's earlier fears.

"I was thinking the same thing," Piper admitted. "I don't want this, us, to be a secret."

"Then it's settled. We're out of hiding. Now tell me more about this jealousy," Wyatt said, a smile in his voice.

"It was nothing. I didn't like how Kiera was drooling over you."

"I'm kinda surprised any of those girls even know who I am."

Piper lay down on the bed. "I'm not. You're a catch, and they all know it. But don't get a big head about it."

"I'm the furthest thing from a catch," Wyatt said darkly.

"I strongly disagree."

Wyatt remained silent.

"And so does Kiera," Piper added, trying to break him out of his negative spiral.

"You're the only girl I care about."

Piper smiled, her heart thudding. "So, can I tell Kiera she needs to find someone else to date this summer?"

"Definitely. I'm taken. You're my girl."

Piper would never tire of hearing those words.

Chapter Twenty-Three

Now

Piper had been prepared to harass Wyatt if he prematurely sprang back into action the following day, but he'd slept in late, content dozing in the shade as long as she stayed close by, napping or reading with him. Not that she minded. Peace had settled over Piper like a weighted blanket, Wyatt's confession last night unlatching a gate that released her final strands of resentment.

The morning would have been perfect except for the nagging thought that she should check the radio. They hadn't heard from anyone since yesterday, and no planes had sounded overhead. She had believed Rosie when she said they'd find them soon, but some confirmation would make her feel better.

"I'm going to test for a radio signal down the beach," she announced, bringing Wyatt a water bottle and a block of cheese. "Can I trust you'll still be lying here when I get back?"

Wyatt wrinkled his nose. "I'm not sure how much longer I can stay horizontal, P. Besides a very minor headache, I feel fine."

Piper looked him up and down. Healthy color stained his cheeks, and his eyes appeared bright and focused, a vast improvement over yesterday. "Promise me you won't overdo it."

He sat up. "Define overdoing it."

"Don't do anything I wouldn't do."

"Act like Captain Energy Conservation, got it." He gave her a cheeky salute.

She rolled her eyes at him with a smile. "Just behave, please."

"I'll do my best." He pressed a kiss on the back of her hand, his stubble tickling her delicate skin. "Hey, be careful."

"I always am," Piper reminded him, her voice wavering from his kiss.

Last night had been the best sleep she'd had in ages, drifting off to the gentle rise and fall of Wyatt's breath. What that meant, and what their kiss might mean for their future, she didn't know. And she couldn't afford a meltdown by overthinking it now.

Puffy white clouds dotted the horizon, offering patches of shade as a respite from the blazing sun. The beach greeted her with the sounds of a new day as she walked along the shoreline, leaving fresh footprints in the sand. Overhead, tropical birds warbled bright foreign songs, and the swish of trees swaying in the breeze answered their calls. Waves lapped the shore, their rhythmic slapping like a balm to her ears while salt sprays filled the air with a humid pungency.

Unfortunately, the sound she was hoping to hear, Rosie's voice, never poured through the speakers, her radio mission yielding nothing after hours of turning the dial.

Though she'd hoped Wyatt would take her advice, it didn't surprise her to see him attempting to fish when their strip of the beach came into view as she walked back. Getting Wyatt to take it easy was like expecting a cat not to follow a laser pointer. He hadn't noticed her yet, and Piper admired him from a distance, the sun reflecting off his broad shoulders like a halo. Maybe it was the lack of human contact, but every time she saw him, Wyatt looked even hotter than the time before.

He wobbled, a larger wave almost knocking him over in the water. Why did he insist on pushing himself to the limit all the time? The urge to throttle him for acting recklessly accompanied an even greater desire to kiss him again until his pain melted away. She set the radio back in their shelter, kicked off her shoes, and shimmied out of her sundress to the black-and-white-striped bikini underneath. Like the ocean tides drawn by the moon's gravitational pull, Piper walked into the water toward Wyatt.

The cool water soothed her hot, achy skin, and she waded in quickly, finding the waves friendly. Wyatt heard her splashing and turned around with a sheepish smile. At least he had the good sense to look guilty that she'd caught him away from his assigned spot on the beach.

"Did you get a signal? Any new updates?" he called out.

Piper shook her head, moving closer. "Nothing, but I'll try again later. How's your head?"

"It's good! I've been out here for thirty minutes and almost caught a fish," he boasted. "Give me another thirty, and I'm sure I will."

Of course. The idiot would make his recovery much harder than it had to be, and she needed him to be okay. "Sounds like you've done enough for one day then, huh?"

The annoyance must have been visible on her face because Wyatt raised an eyebrow in her direction. "Is there something else you'd like to say?"

"Wy, I need you to take care of yourself, and it looks like you're not." Her words caught in her throat, and she swallowed over the burning sensation of tears. Seeing Wyatt go under the waves and not resurface had wrecked her. She couldn't go back to that place of despair again.

Wyatt tucked the fishing hook into the back of his swim trunks and was by her side in an instant, pulling her against his bare chest. "Hey, hey, hey. I'm sorry I'm stressing you out. I'm shit at resting, but I'm doing the best I can."

Piper collapsed into his arms, the waves pushing her closer to him with every oscillation. "It's okay," she murmured into his chest. "It's just been a long few days."

"That's the understatement of the year." Wyatt rubbed her

back in soothing circles. "But I'm perfectly fine, I swear. Every-thing's going to be okay. We've made it this far, and we'll be home soon. I promise."

She tilted her head up, vividly aware of how close his lips were to hers. One medium-size wave would send them colliding. "You scared me yesterday." She wasn't berating him but wanted to ex-plain why she was so emotional.

He twisted the end of her braid through his fingers. "By get-ting hurt or by kissing you?"

She met his gaze, relieved he was addressing the potentially life-altering unspoken moment between them. "Both."

"Will it scare you if I kiss you again?" He bent his head, float-ing his lips above hers.

"Let's find out," she whispered.

When he closed the gap between their lips, it was more inten-tional than last time, less frantic but every bit as passionate. Fire flamed deep in her belly, stoked higher by his teeth grazing her sensitive lips. She melted into the kiss. Then, fisting her hands in his wet locks, she dragged him closer. Wyatt sank into the wa-ter and hiked her up, his hands slipping under her butt, and she wound her legs around him.

Supported by the water and Wyatt's strong arms, Piper felt weightless, carefree, all concerns driven from her mind by his devilish mouth.

She'd spent so many years furious at him, constructing iron-clad walls around her heart, but this whole time he'd been build-ing a bridge. Brick by brick, finding his way back to her. Letting her guard down frightened her, but shutting down Wyatt and his heady kisses would require fighting against the current—literally and figuratively. She gave herself over to the heat of Wyatt's mouth, the delicious caress of his tongue. Before long, they were both panting for air.

Eventually, Wyatt set her down, moving an arm's length away, still waist-deep in water.

"Listen, Piper," he started.

Piper stiffened, bracing for a statement about how they were playing with fire, how they'd been down this road before and it hadn't worked out. How they were better off as friends. With a piercing certainty, she found she didn't want to be just friends with Wyatt. She wanted all of him.

Wyatt put his hands on her hips, steadying her. "I know I was the last person you wanted to see, and you have every reason for feeling that way. But I'd be lying if I said I haven't enjoyed every minute with you these past few days." He chuckled. "Well, maybe not every minute, but way more than I have a right to." His graphite eyes found hers, his expression serious. "If you let me back into your life, I won't walk away again."

Piper sucked in a breath, grateful that Wyatt held her upright because her legs quivered like jellyfish. She ricocheted through fear, wild delight, hesitation, then back to joy.

Finally, she squeaked out, "Okay."

Wyatt studied her face, brows furrowed. "Do you mean 'Okay, great speech' or 'Okay, you're cool with me sticking around'?"

"Okay, I'd very much like you to stick around." She beamed up at him.

His responding grin split his face from ear to ear. "Okay."

He tucked a stray tendril of hair behind her ear and traced his thumb over her lips. Her heart whirred at the taste of saltwater from his touch, heat growing in her core. His hungry gaze locked with hers, his gray eyes swirling with stormy desire. She would have gladly complied if he'd wanted to take her right here in the water, but he let the electricity crackle between them without distilling it with a kiss.

The ocean flowed around them, but time stood still.

BESIDE THEM, A silver-bellied fish leaped out of the calm water, its sleek body glistening in the sunlight before it landed with a splash.

Wyatt threw his hands up in the air, releasing Piper. "Argh, the universe is taunting me with these damn fish, I swear. I can't believe you reeled in a freaking cooler full of food, and I can't even catch one fish when they're practically throwing themselves at us."

Another fish followed, flinging its body out of the ocean like an aspiring Olympian. They reminded Piper of hours spent fishing with her granddad at Lake Hyco. He used a reel and rod but gave her a net to scoop up the fish that surfaced when the water was calm. Even with her limited fishing skills, she usually walked away with at least one decent catch.

"Let me see what you're using to catch them."

Wyatt handed her his homemade fishing reel—bent wire he'd torn from Piper's bra tied to a shoestring.

She turned it over in his hand. "Maybe the fish know you hijacked this hook from my best bra, and they're boycotting you."

He laughed. "Maybe so."

"What if the universe isn't taunting you but trying to tell you something?"

"Uh-oh, are the fish talking to you now?"

She punched his arm. "I'm serious. What if you had a net?"

"Sure, that'd be great, but unless I overlooked the fishing net you packed, I don't see how it matters," Wyatt grumbled.

Piper held up a finger, signaling for him to wait a moment. She waded to shore, strode to their shelter, and inspected the once-lavender bridesmaid dress—now bleached a dismal shade of khaki—complete with four layers of tulle that resembled her granddad's delicate fishing net. Without hesitation, Piper ripped the tulle from its seams, enjoying the satisfying sensation of tearing apart the monstrous dress.

Apologizing to Allie under her breath, Piper ran back to the shoreline where Wyatt waited. She proudly handed him the large swath of tulle. "Do you think you could make a net with this?"

He frowned, confusion wrinkling his forehead. "Wait, you did pack a fishing net?"

Piper shook her head, a small smile tugging at the corners of her lips. "No, this is tulle from underneath my bridesmaid dress."

After he'd studied the material for a moment, Wyatt's face lit up. "Piper, I think this could work!"

He busied himself fashioning a net, twisting the wire from his homemade fishing hook into a circle, hooking strands of the tulle as he wound his way around. When he finished, he waded back into the water, taking care not to startle the fish. Wyatt stood motionless with his net poised, ready to catch whatever he could. For several tense minutes, nothing stirred above the ocean's surface. Finally, a fish threw itself out of the water right in front of him, but he wasn't quick enough and swore under his breath when the net came up empty.

Piper couldn't bear watching. She squeezed her eyes shut, only peeking out from under her fingers. After a few more misses, he caught one, staring at the flopping fish in disbelief. From her spot on the beach, Piper let out a cheer. He'd done it!

"Did you see that?" He ran over and deposited the fish next to her on the sand. "I'm going back for more!" He practically skipped back into the water, slightly favoring his unhurt leg.

Piper smiled after him, thrilled to see him so alive after yesterday's near-drowning debacle. Within the hour, they'd lined four slippery fish in a row on the beach and were staring at them in awe.

Wyatt wrapped his arms around her shoulders and kissed her head. "Piper, you're a genius."

She leaned against his chest. "You're the one that caught them."

"We're celebrating tonight with a feast. Take that, universe!" Wyatt shouted up at the sky.

He turned her in his arms, scooped her off the ground, and spun her around in a hug, his warmth enveloping her like sunshine. His happiness flooded her senses with unbridled joy. Setting her back down, he leaned in and kissed her, his pillowy lips parting hers as their wet bodies pressed together.

When they parted, Piper wasn't sure what had made her dizzier, the spinning or the kiss.

Chapter Twenty-Four

Then

The summer she started kissing Wyatt, Piper didn't want to stop. When she wasn't hanging out with her friends, Piper was with him—making out in the clubhouse, holding hands on long walks, or talking on the phone late into the night. Their new level of intimacy grew roots deep as an oak tree's in Piper's heart the way only a first love can.

Even though they'd hung out countless times since their first kiss, Piper bubbled with excitement for their first official date that Friday. And, in an act of generosity, her parents had recently extended her curfew by an hour. It felt like the perfect start to what was shaping up to be the best summer yet.

"You look nice, Piper. Are you going somewhere special tonight?" her mom asked when Piper made her way down to the kitchen the night of their date.

Piper smoothed the pleats of the bright coral maxi dress Allie had loaned her, hoping her hands weren't too sweaty. She'd spent a few extra minutes curling her hair into soft, buttery waves, dusting her face with powder to cover the spray of freckles across her pale nose, and applying a second coat of mascara to make her green eyes pop.

"Thanks, Mom! I'm not sure where we're going, but Wyatt's picking me up in about twenty minutes." Piper made it sound like a casual nonevent, but she couldn't hide the elation in her voice.

Her mom heard it, too. "Are Allie or Ethan going with you?"

For a second, Piper considered avoiding the truth, not wanting the night ruined by a lecture or disapproving look. But she'd never been good at lying to her parents, and she didn't want Wyatt to be a secret anymore. "No, it's just Wyatt and me. We're kind of going on a date."

Her mom exchanged a frown with her father, who was thumbing through mail on the counter. Piper rushed to explain. "I know you've always said you didn't want me dating in high school, but technically high school is over. And you've known Wyatt forever."

"We set those guidelines for a reason, Piper," her dad said, taking his glasses off and rubbing the bridge of his nose.

"Are you saying I can't go?" Piper set her jaw and crossed her arms, challenging them. She rarely went against her parents' wishes, but nothing would keep her from seeing Wyatt tonight.

After a tense moment, her mom relented. "You can go, but please use sound judgment."

Wyatt's truck rumbled into the driveway, cutting off the need to continue this debate.

Piper grabbed her purse and headed toward the door. "I've got to go." At the very least, she could spare Wyatt the third degree.

Her mom cleared her throat. "Be home by ten."

Piper clenched her hands into fists and turned back around. She forced a calm smile onto her face. "My new curfew is eleven."

"That's when you're hanging out with your friends. We don't want you out all night with a boy. It's not appropriate." When her mom used this haughty, clipped tone, matters were not up for debate, but Piper was tired of being told what was appropriate or best for her.

"Wyatt's not some boy. He's my friend. And he's my date." *And possibly the love of my life.*

"It's not about Wyatt. It's just that you're so close to college. We want to make sure you stay on track."

Piper wasn't in the mood to analyze that cryptic statement further. "It'll be fine, Mom. I'll be home by curfew—my new curfew," she clarified and ran out the door before they could argue with her further.

Wyatt was standing on the doorstep, fist raised to knock, when Piper flew out, almost colliding with him. He'd traded his usual black T-shirt for a crisp white button-up rolled up at the sleeves, accentuating his strong forearms, and paired it with navy shorts. His face split into a dazzling smile when he saw her. How could she have seen his face a million times and still be caught off guard by his devastating perfection?

"Come on, let's go." Piper grabbed his hand and dragged him to his truck.

Wyatt dug his heels in. "I should say hello to your parents. I don't want them thinking I'm the kind of guy who honks from the driveway and expects my date to run out."

"Since when do you care what people think?" Piper asked.

"Since it involves you."

That gave her pause. It melted her heart that he wanted to be chivalrous, but contending with her parents after storming out like that would put a damper on the rest of the evening.

"Please, Wyatt. If we go back in, they might not let me leave. They gave me such a hard time about going out tonight, and I don't want anything to ruin our evening."

Wyatt glanced back at the house door, biting his lip, then down at Piper's pleading face. He sighed. "Fine. But next time, I'm coming inside."

He opened the truck door, helped her up, then leaned against the doorframe, drinking her in. "You look amazing, by the way." His voice was low, a shared secret. "I love this dress."

Piper grinned, unsuccessfully hiding how much she loved the compliment. Her nerves from earlier evaporated into the warm summer air. There was nowhere else she'd rather be than next to

Wyatt, with him looking at her like she was a movie star instead of the same awkward girl he'd known since middle school.

"Thanks. You look pretty great yourself." He shut her door, climbed in on the driver's side, and kissed her before turning the engine on. Every time she saw him, she thought it would be weird that they'd crossed the sacred line of friendship, but when they kissed, it felt weirder that they hadn't been doing this all along.

"Where are we going?" she asked as he backed the truck out of the driveway.

"You'll see."

The sun drifted sleepily toward the horizon, clearing the way for a night of possibilities. To stay cool, they rolled the windows down in Wyatt's truck with no AC. The radio was about the only thing that worked. Piper tuned it to a classic rock station, cranked up the volume, and they sang along to Mellencamp's ditty about Jack and Diane.

"Woo-hoo!" Wyatt hollered out the open window and turned onto the main road, picking up speed. He glanced over at her, his eyes sparkling. "This is the best. Driving with you, listening to the radio, feeling the breeze, being free."

Piper delighted in this rare moment of Wyatt expressing childlike glee. The joy radiating off of him was contagious. She reached for his free hand. "I couldn't agree more."

He laced his fingers through hers and held on tight, sending a conga line of tingles down her spine. The road rolled out before them like a red carpet, the night ushering them forward and promising to keep their secrets. The moment sparkled with magic. She could tell he felt it too by the way he held her hand like she might float away if he let go.

Piper would have been happy driving around with Wyatt all night, but he pulled into the parking lot of Charlie's Diner. The diner hadn't changed much in the forty years since it opened, with its sloping roof, yellow Formica counters, a jukebox that played only Elvis, and a menu that offered fries with every meal. It was a Lonely Onlys favorite spot, where the servers knew them by name, and they had an unofficial corner booth.

"Wait right here." Wyatt left the truck running as he ducked into the diner and returned a few minutes later carrying two milkshakes. "Strawberry with whipped cream for you. Oreo with extra cherries for me."

Piper accepted the to-go cup dripping sweat from the heat along with a straw. "I like this date already."

A small crease between Wyatt's brows formed. "I hope you like what's next."

He guided the truck up a gravel path to a grassy knoll, reversed until they faced the dirt road, and parked. Piper watched with curiosity as he pulled out a bag of popcorn from the backseat along with a stack of blankets and stepped out to lower the tailgate. He spread the blankets on the bed of the truck, then motioned for her to join him, offering a hand to help her climb up. Stars glittered above, and below, the projection on a movie screen glowed.

Piper's eyes went wide. "Is that the old drive-in theater? I didn't know you could see it from up here!"

Wyatt reached through a back window of the truck and tuned the radio station to the channel broadcasting the movie before pulling her back against his chest.

"I discovered it a few weeks ago. I know it's not a fancy steak house like you deserve, but they're playing your favorite movie tonight. This way, it's like our own private showing." He handed her the popcorn. "Plus, the popcorn's a lot cheaper."

Piper kissed his cheek and took a handful of popcorn. "Thank you. This is the perfect first date."

She snuggled into him while they watched Harry meet Sally, Sally befriend Harry, then Harry lose her, only to realize they were meant to be together all along. Piper knew every line by heart, which helped, because she spent most of the movie distracted by Wyatt. Whenever he dropped a kiss onto her shoulder, shifted positions to get closer to her, or played with her hair, she worried she might combust on the spot.

A few tears spilled down her face as the sounds of "Auld Lang Syne" filled the air. The ending always made her cry.

Wyatt brushed a tear away. "Are these happy tears?"

"Mostly. This song gets me every time."

Wyatt kissed her last tear away, then kissed her again on the lips. He tasted like popcorn and possibility.

She faced him and framed his face in her hands. "Promise me we'll always be friends. I don't want to go years without talking, like Harry and Sally did in the movie."

His laughter vibrated deep within his chest, but he grew somber when he saw she meant it. "I can't promise we'll be friends—I hope we're always much more than that. But I can promise I won't let a month, let alone a year, go by without talking to you." He brushed a strand of hair from her face, then sealed his words with a deep, time-stopping kiss.

The warm summer air had nothing on the scorching heat radiating from Wyatt's lips. Piper melted into the sensation of kissing him, of feeling the chemistry charging between them like a freight train picking up speed. She could stay here all night, all week, curfew be damned, as long as Wyatt kept his mouth moving on hers.

Unfortunately, Wyatt had his eye on the time. He groaned and rolled over onto his back, putting physical distance between them. "It's getting late. I better get you home."

How was he staying so in control when all she wanted to do was claw his clothes off and press herself against his sturdy frame? She tilted onto her side so she could see his face. "I hate saying goodbye to you. I could stay here forever."

Wyatt took her hand and brushed his lips roughly along her

knuckles. "One day, I'll be out of the army and running my own business, and you'll be a successful surgeon." His voice was raspy, raw with emotion. "We won't have curfews or rules, and I'll be able to take you to the best restaurant in town. I'll take you to Paris or Rome—anywhere you want to go."

She loved the idea of building a life with Wyatt, the picture he painted of their future inked in her soul like a tattoo. "You know I don't need any of that stuff, right?" She stroked his cheek. "Being here with you is all I want."

Wyatt's mouth wrenched to one side, like he wanted to believe her but didn't. "As long as you're happy, I'm happy."

"I'm happy." Piper cupped the nape of his neck and drew him back on top of her, conveying her happiness through her lips on his, feeling like the star of her favorite rom-com with every lingering kiss.

When she slipped through her front door five minutes before 11:00 P.M., her parents were waiting up, but they could say nothing to ruin Piper's cloud-nine mood.

Chapter Twenty-Five

Now

In high school, Piper's feelings for Wyatt had grown gradually, then all at once. Like sinking into quicksand, she hadn't known she was in trouble until way too late.

Quicksand déjà vu flitted through her as they prepared dinner. Every touch they exchanged sent shivers down her spine, each sideways glance filled her with nostalgia and longing. Tonight could easily be the last of their unplanned layover. She'd wanted off this island—their island—from the moment they'd crashed, but now she wished she could stuff sand back up the hourglass of time.

While Wyatt cleaned the fish and started the fire, Piper cleared sand off their rock table and arranged palm leaves to serve as place settings, hoping to make tonight feel less stranded-against-their-will vibes and more romantic camping adventure. She set the remaining red berries on each palm leaf, stepped back, and admired her tablescape—castaway chic.

The place settings inspired Piper to transform herself from the swamp creature she must resemble into a girl on a tropical vacation—a tall order. Most everything in her bag had been used in some practical way or another, except for the slinky black slip dress stuffed into her DIY pillow. She pulled it out and rubbed the soft silk against her cheek. It felt like years since she'd purchased the dress at Zara specifically for Allie's bachelorette party, but in reality it had been less than two weeks ago.

Wyatt was still bent over the fire, so she ducked behind a tree and changed, sliding the dress down her body like liquid silk. She had no bras intact, thanks to Wyatt's handiwork, and the fabric clung to her curves or what was left of them after her island crash diet. The final look would have been considered obscene in a public setting, but there was no one here to see her except Wyatt.

He was the only one she wanted looking.

She found the hairbrush she'd abandoned long ago and coaxed her drying braids into beach waves. Using a piece of a compact mirror that had survived the crash, Piper assessed herself. Back home, she wore makeup like armor, but here, fresh freckles bloomed across her nose and rosy cheeks like wildflowers. The red, puckered scar still marred her forehead, but her soft green eyes glowed with a light she hadn't seen in a while. She sent up a prayer of thanks to Allie for forcing her to attend a series of torturous laser hair removal sessions during college. She didn't expect she'd ever feel completely clean while they were here, but at least she didn't have to worry about shaving.

Glancing over at Wyatt's back, she almost lost her nerve and changed back into her regular T-shirt and shorts. He was going to think she'd lost her mind walking out in a freaking minidress looking like a mermaid washed ashore, but she'd gone this far. Might as well see it through. Running a hand across her stomach, Piper walked toward him with as much confidence as she could muster.

When he looked up, Wyatt's eyes practically bugged out of his head. He stood, almost knocking over the fish he'd laid out on a burned sheet of metal from the plane wreckage that acted as a baking sheet.

"Piper! Whoa." His Adam's apple bobbed.

She flushed and rushed to explain. "It's ridiculous, I know. But you said it was a celebratory feast, and I had this dress . . ."

Wyatt kept staring at her like he'd never seen a girl in a dress. Though, to be fair, he hadn't in days. "No, you look amazing."

His hungry eyes made her mouth go dry. Taking her hand, he twirled her and whistled before kissing her sweetly. Piper's entire body sang. He'd always had that effect on her—making her feel both sexy and safe.

Wyatt tugged at his dirty T-shirt. "I'm underdressed."

"No, you look great." It was annoying, actually, how good Wyatt always looked.

"Let me at least go put a fresher shirt on."

Piper had to bite her tongue to keep from saying she preferred him shirtless but changed her mind when he returned in a light blue gingham button-down shirt rolled up at the sleeves and navy shorts. The clothes were rumpled from pulling double duty as bedding, but they reminded her of what he used to wear to pick her up for dates in high school. Effortlessly hot.

"Well, look at that. You clean up pretty nice, too." She enjoyed how the tips of his ears reddened at the compliment.

"Thanks. Let's eat!" He waved her toward the rock table and distributed fish onto the leaves.

Though Wyatt complained more than once about how much easier it would've been with a YouTube tutorial on deboning a fish, he'd got the job done with dexterity. They had to pick around bones, and the fish wasn't cooked in all places, but it was their best meal yet—made even sweeter with a side of Oreos.

Even though they were eating dinner with bare hands over a rock on the beach, dressing up reminded Piper of life back home. Would they even be speaking in the version of their lives where the plane hadn't crashed? He'd said he wanted to stay in her life, but would he still mean it when rescue came? The idea of losing the perfect bud of friendship and the spark of romance blossoming again between them devastated her.

"Is everything okay?" Wyatt asked like he could read her mind. "I mean, besides the obvious very not okay situation we've found ourselves in."

"Yeah." Piper glanced up with a wilted smile. "I was thinking about rescue coming. It's a good thing, of course, but weird thinking we could wake up in our own beds soon." *Halfway across the country from each other.*

"I know what you mean. It's going to be strange; using a phone, driving a car, not having sand in everything."

"Not being around me 24/7."

Wyatt's gaze cut to her face. "That's the part I'll miss."

Piper's throat ached, tightening like a tie around her neck. When she found her voice, she changed the subject. "Is there anything you'll do differently when we get back?"

Wyatt pursed his lips, thinking. "Besides being a better nephew and friend, I'd like to get more involved in helping foster kids, especially teenagers. It's been on my to-do list for a while, but it's time to actually make it happen."

"Really?" She didn't know what she'd expected Wyatt to say, but that wasn't it.

He leaned forward, shifting toward her, resting his elbows on his knees. "You know, if it weren't for Aunt Molly taking me in whenever my mom got herself in over her head, I would've ended up in the system. And I can't imagine that would have worked out well for me. Nobody wants a moody teenager, but Molly stepped up to be my legal guardian through a kinship placement when I needed her most. I owe her a lot, and the best way I know how to say thank you is to pay it forward."

Obviously, Piper knew Wyatt had moved in with Molly during their senior year, but she hadn't understood the significance.

"I think you could help those kids a lot. You'll be an awesome role model." She could easily picture Wyatt teaching a kid how to drive—or holding a baby with a smile that matched hers.

"You think?" Wyatt bit his lip.

She placed a hand on his knee and caught his gaze. "I know."

He smiled gratefully and took a sip of water from his canteen. "Speaking of family, I did one of those DNA tests a few months ago."

"Really?"

He nodded. "I've always wanted to learn more about my roots on my father's side. After my dad died, my mom cut off all contact with his extended family and moved us to Mason. I don't know the specifics, but I think they fought over custody of me, and she ran. I know she probably did what she thought was right at the time, but as a result, I know nothing about my dad's family." He angled his body, shifting until they sat side by side, facing the ocean.

"Are you glad you did it?" she asked.

"Yeah. It's comforting somehow to see where I come from. To have tangible proof that I'm connected to others, even though I'm basically an orphan. Gives some credibility to my existence."

Piper curled her arm through Wyatt's and leaned her head on his shoulder. "You've always been very real to me."

"Thank you." He dropped a kiss on top of her hair. "I just wasn't prepared for relatives to reach out."

"*What?* Like who?" She pulled back and examined his face.

"My dad's brother—my uncle. And two cousins."

"Wyatt, that's amazing. Are you going to meet them?" Why didn't he sound more excited about this earth-shattering news?

Wyatt shook his head. "I don't know if it's a good idea. What if I meet them and they decide they want nothing to do with me?" Fear laced his voice. "What if they're mad I didn't reach out earlier? I've done okay on my own so far. Maybe it's better that way."

"What if they already love you and can't wait to get to know you better?" Piper kissed his shoulder.

"It's a moot point until we get off this island." He cleared his throat and shrugged her off. "Enough about me. What about you? What will you change, if anything?"

Piper knew better than to press him, but she made a mental note to bring it up again. She wouldn't let Wyatt throw away his chance at meeting family members. Their conversation tonight mirrored the deep, meandering, soul-searching talks they'd often had as teens. Challenging each other to dig deeper with each question. Their time on the island so far had acted as a giant pause button to her life. A life of letting the current dictate her direction instead of steering her own ship. All the extra time to think had helped her get clear about what she wanted out of life or, more accurately, what she didn't.

Piper untangled a knot in her hair. "I don't know. I guess figure out what the hell I want to do with my life if it's not medicine."

Wyatt raised a brow. "So, you'll quit med school?"

She puffed up her cheeks and blew them out slowly. "I think so—if I can figure out what to tell my parents. No big deal." She wrinkled her nose at the thought, though giddiness coursed through her body from saying the words out loud.

He bumped her shoulder with his. "You'll figure it out. As long as you do what makes you happy, not anyone else, it will all work out."

Easier said than done. But she knew he was right. Pulling the plug on her entire life plan no longer seemed as unreasonable or impossible as it had a week ago. She silently added officially ending things with Tag to her second-chance-at-life-to-do list. They'd never confirmed exclusivity, but she wanted to clearly communicate that she didn't see a future with him. Especially with the newfound clarity that her heart still belonged to Wyatt—even if the second chapter of their love story began and ended on this island.

"I'll make a deal with you. If you tell your parents how you feel about becoming a doctor, I'll reach out to my relatives."

Piper snapped her head up. "Yeah? What happened to being better off alone?"

"I'm realizing there could be another way. A better way." His eyes smoldered like the fire, burning into hers.

"Deal." She stuck her hand out to shake.

He enveloped her slender hand in his larger one, not letting go. Rough calluses tickled her palm, and her skin prickled, thinking about what his hands would feel like on her body.

In the shrinking daylight, Wyatt's gorgeous face glowed in the soft flicker of the flames. The serious stubble he sported defined his chiseled jawline and perfect mouth further. Piper swiped her thumb over a fading bruise dusting his cheekbone, just wanting to be near him. With a small smile, Wyatt brought her hand to his lips for a kiss.

"There's something else I'm going to do when we get home," he told her, his voice full of gravel, her hand still nestled in his. "I'm taking you out for a proper meal. One that doesn't involve sea-to-rock cuisine."

The possibility of spending time with Wyatt in the real world made all the blood rush to her head like she'd drunk a bottle of wine. As did the barrage of memories of previous idyllic date nights with him.

"How about milkshakes?"

He beamed wide enough to show his dimples, clearly catching her reference to their first date. "Cheap date, you've got it."

"Oh, I'm not done," she countered, biting back a smile at the word "date." "We start with a milkshake at Charlie's Diner, but you better believe I'll be getting fries, mozzarella sticks, and a plate of mac and cheese as big as my head."

"I'm on board for all of that. Does Charlie's still serve those double cheeseburgers?"

"Of course!"

"Then it's settled. As soon as we get off this island—you, me, and Charlie's finest milkshake."

"Milkshakes, plural. I won't be sharing." Piper stuck her lips out in a flirty pout and squeezed his hand tighter.

Wyatt laughed, the sound echoing up from deep within his chest. "Only the best for my girl."

Piper's own laughter caught in her throat, warmth fanning out from the flame ignited in her core. As a teenager, she'd adored hearing him call her "my girl."

If possible, she loved it even more now.

Chapter Twenty-Six

Now

Seizing the opportunity for a breather, Piper gathered the remains of their dinner with a quick "be right back." For years, she'd placed Wyatt firmly into a box reserved for people she would never let back into her life, which made her warm feelings toward him—growing warmer by the second—confusing.

After burying the fish bones and soggy leaves in the sand, she stood before the ocean, feeding off the power of the waves crashing onto the shore. The breeze cooled her flushed skin. With a stomach full of food, she could appreciate the wild beauty of the beach, admiring the sky as the remaining traces of daylight drained away and a full moon rose overhead.

At this moment, on this beach was exactly where she was meant to be. The certainty of that feeling hit like a lightning bolt, awakening her to a fresh start, a new beginning, a second chance. It filled her with gratitude for every path that had led her here—here with Wyatt. He'd always been her North Star, but she'd blocked his light. And now, by some crazy twist of fate, he was back in her life, his light calling her home.

She strolled back to him, savoring the way the silk dress slithered over her skin in the nighttime air. Halfway back, she caught Wyatt watching her like she was his favorite dessert, gaze fixed on her moonlit silhouette. His face, lit by the flicker of flames, drew her in like a magnet. His unnerving gaze never left hers.

Wordlessly, she sat back down across from him, unsure of what to do or say next.

The tension between them pulsed like a glowing ember.

Wyatt broke the silence first. "I'm going to get something. Wait here."

She protested, but he flashed her a hunky smile that was impossible to argue with.

He returned carrying the bottle of sparkling wine from the Yeti. "I think now is the perfect night to crack this open."

Piper nodded eagerly. She could use some liquid courage. "What are we toasting to?"

"Staying alive this long. Figuring out how to catch and cook fish. Finding this bottle of prosecco." He paused, his gaze lingering on her lips. "Kissing you. Take your pick."

Piper returned his soft smile. "I'll toast to all of that."

Wyatt pulled off the cork with a satisfying pop that made Piper want to "woo" out loud. He took a sip from the bottle before handing it to her.

The prosecco, warm and bubbly, tickled her throat on the way down. She took another swig, then held the bottle up in a toast. "Cheers to awful bridesmaid dresses serving more than one purpose."

"Yes! Remind me to thank Allie for her fashion choices when we see her." Wyatt accepted the bottle, taking a longer sip this time. "Cheers to you finding a Yeti full of food."

"Amen." Piper took her turn with the bottle. "And cheers to us for not killing each other. Yet."

Wyatt laughed. "It was touch and go there for a minute."

"There's still time," Piper teased, but all her animosity toward Wyatt had evaporated with the recent rain.

They passed the bottle back and forth, reveling in the moment's joy and the break from thinking about their next steps for survival.

They'd finished half the bottle when Wyatt held it out in front of him to make a new toast. "I've got another one."

"Let's hear it."

"A toast to you, Piper. I know I put on a strong front, but I'd be lost without you." His voice cracked, and his eyes dampened. "You're the reason I get up every morning and keep going. And I don't just mean on this island. I don't know where I'd be if you hadn't come into my life when we were kids and if you weren't here with me now. I'm thankful for you every day. And I've missed you every day we've been apart."

Unable to speak over the lump in her throat, Piper laced her fingers through his and held on tight. His gaze flicked to her mouth, his pupils blackening his eyes except for the reflection of fire dancing in them.

Her stomach flipped.

Once she remembered how to breathe again, Piper took the bottle and set it securely next to her in the sand. Then she leaned forward, winding her arms around his neck until her face was inches from his. His breath fell warm and sweet on her skin, his gaze locking onto her like a target.

When his lips finally brushed against hers, feather-light and teasing, Piper let out an audible sigh. She buried her hands in his hair and urged him closer, sealing her mouth on his, shivering as his tongue traced a delicate line along her lips. How could his kiss still evoke the same out-of-control spiral of emotions she'd felt as a teenager? Could still make her believe in soul mates and fairy tales and happy endings.

Kissing Wyatt felt like coming home.

Before long, kissing wasn't enough. Wyatt pulled her into his lap, and they became a coiled knot of limbs. His hands were everywhere: tangled in her hair, caressing her back, running up the sides of her body. Focused solely on getting as close to him as physically possible, Piper wrapped her legs around his waist. The combination of prosecco and his kisses made her feel like she was floating above her body. From her position in his lap, she felt him grow hard beneath her.

He wrenched his lips from hers. "God, Piper, if we keep kissing like this . . ."

She interrupted his train of thought with another searing kiss. If they kept kissing, it would lead to more, which was exactly what she wanted—way more than she wanted a milkshake right now. Dragging him down onto the sand and showing him exactly how much she loved being his girl was all she could think about.

Piper untangled herself from his arms and stood, extending an inviting hand to Wyatt.

He put his hand in hers, and goose bumps traveled all the way up her arm and down her body in nervous anticipation. The idea of being with Wyatt again, really being with him, was both terrifying and electrifying, but everything inside her was ready to walk into that fire. Hell, she'd waited eight years for this moment, and now it couldn't happen fast enough.

She led him over to the entrance of their shelter and lifted her face to kiss him again, making it obvious what she wanted. Wyatt needed no further invitation. Within seconds, he'd backed her up against a tree, cradling her hips in his large hands, trailing kisses along the lines of her collarbone and up the sensitive curve of her neck. Piper fisted his hair in her hands, sighing in pleasure as his warm mouth made its way inch by delicious inch to her lips. His mouth collided with hers, and she tugged on the ends of his curls, pulling his face closer, deepening the kiss, their tongues sparring.

Piper couldn't decide if she wanted time to slow down or speed up. She wanted Wyatt to rake his hands over her body, to put out the fire he'd started, the fire that threatened to consume her whole. But she didn't want this moment—Wyatt Brooks kissing her, wanting her, on a moonlit beach—to end. She slid a hand between them and pushed gently on his chest, creating a few inches of breathing room. He rested his forehead against hers, both of them panting heavily.

"We can stop if you—" he started, but Piper shushed him by placing a finger to his lips.

He nipped at her fingertips before she reached for the top button of his shirt and undid it, a teasing smile playing across her face. Standing still, he watched, stormy eyes intense and smoldering, as she undid each button, working her way down one by one until she could push back the fabric, revealing his broad chest and taut stomach. Unable to help herself, she ran her hands along his smooth skin, marveling at the muscles quivering under her touch. How many times had she wanted to touch him, to feel his solid steadiness beneath her hands? And now she had free rein. If possible, her heart thrummed louder.

A jagged scar she hadn't noticed before shone in the moonlight above his rib cage. Deliberately, she pressed her lips to it, then tugged his shirt off completely and traced kisses along the outline of the black tattoo that started at his bicep and extended to his shoulder. His breathing grew uneven, his eyes unfocused when Piper continued kissing down his flat stomach.

Her lips curved into a smile. She loved having this effect on Wyatt and hoped his knees were as weak as hers. She wrestled with his shorts, pulling them down over his hips, dipping her fingers beneath the front of his waistband to the tickle of hair underneath. Before she could explore much further, one of Wyatt's strong hands closed over hers in a viselike grip, the other cupping under her chin, dragging her upward, forcing her to look at him before he ravaged her mouth with his lips, his tongue, his heat.

When her lips were swollen from his kiss, he grazed his teeth along her jaw and nipped at the sensitive spot below her ear. Then he turned his attention to the swell of her breasts, burning her skin with his hot mouth. Bending his head lower, he ravished first one, then the other, through the nearly sheer silk of her dress. Piper gasped, arching her back, heat pooling between her legs. He caught her gaze with a devilish grin. Payback for her earlier assault. When he finally lifted her dress over her head and pulled off the rest of his clothes, she was desperate to feel his hard body against hers.

Shrouded only in the fire's glow and light from the moon, he pulled her down to their bedding and continued worshipping her breasts, her stomach, her thighs, then came back to her lips.

"How is it possible that you're this goddamn beautiful?" he murmured, his lips doing dangerous things to her earlobe. "I've fantasized about this hundreds of times, but this, *you,* are so much better than my imagination."

She shook her head. "You're the one with the hot army body."

He framed her face with his hands. "Never in my wildest dreams did I think I'd get lucky enough to be with you, like this, again. I swear, Piper, I won't screw it up this time."

"Just don't leave," she whispered before pulling his mouth back to hers. She didn't want to think about the past right now. Couldn't think about anything besides how intensely she needed his hands on her skin, his lips on her body. Wrapping one of her long bare legs around him, she hitched herself against his hard length.

A glint of silver flashing in the dark caught her attention. Wyatt had produced a condom seemingly out of nowhere.

"I figured we should be careful given our circumstances," he said, looking sheepish as he rolled onto his back and maneuvered on the condom.

Piper laughed. "You just happened to have that handy?"

"I had it in my backpack. I brought it on the off, off, off chance that something might happen between us at the wedding." He captured her lips with his again. "And I'll admit I've been thinking about this moment for days, so I tucked it into my pillow just in case."

"So, was this all an elaborate plot to sleep with me?" she teased, kissing him back.

"Yeah, I chartered a plane and crashed it, hoping I'd wear you down enough to let me have my way with you."

"Well, it worked, if that helps. Was it worth it?"

"We're about to find out," he growled, moving back over her. "Is this okay?" He cradled her beneath him, his eyes searching hers in the moonlight.

She nodded, panting, and pressed her naked body against his, punctuating her words. When he pushed into her, Piper almost cried in relief. He trembled, clasping her hand in his. She held on like a prayer.

The keening of insects saturated the air, matching the increased synchrony of their breathlessness. They moved like they were trying to lose themselves in each other, to drown out everything else. Like this alone kept them alive. Wyatt's callused hands moved lawlessly over every inch of her body, stoking the fire that had been simmering for days until it boiled over, feverish and desperate.

Until there was nothing but Wyatt. No sand, no plane crash, no island. Nothing but them together.

Afterward, he tucked her under his arm, not letting her go. "Are you good?"

"Never been better." She dropped a kiss on his chest, right above his heart.

"I love your freckles." He kissed her nose.

Piper squirmed. "I usually cover them up, but there's no hiding them here, especially with all the sun I'm getting."

"I'm glad. These freckles drove me crazy in high school. I spent hours finding constellations on your face."

Piper suppressed her maniac smile. "That's very cute and a little stalkerish."

He shrugged. "I never denied being obsessed with you. Still am."

It wasn't quite an admission of love, but it was as close to one as Piper needed now. She leaned in and kissed him once more.

Kissing Wyatt felt inevitable, sleeping together fated.

Aftershocks of happiness shot through Piper like fireworks all night long. Every time she stirred in her sleep, Wyatt's arm tightened around her, or she woke and found herself wrapped around him. Twin flames dancing in the dark. She'd worried that being intimate with Wyatt would remind her of the last night they'd spent together—right before he broke her heart—but it was a salve to her hurt. Wyatt's kisses melted away the last wisps of pain, cracking her resolve like an icy pond in spring.

It had taken eight years and one plane crash to bring them to this moment, but it had been worth the wait. That night, the stars shone solely for them.

It was a tiny slice of heaven, smack-dab in the middle of hell.

Chapter Twenty-Seven

Then

The midsummer evening stretched on forever, alive with warmth and possibility. To add to the sweet buzz of the night, Piper's parents were attending a fundraiser for the hospital and weren't expected back until well after midnight—a dream come true for any teenager.

Less than ten minutes after her parents left, Wyatt arrived on her doorstep for a curfew-free date night. He wore his standard outfit, a fitted black T-shirt and jeans, but had added the new leather boat shoes Aunt Molly had gifted to him for graduation. When he aimed his megawatt smile at her, Piper's breath caught in her throat.

Sometimes she couldn't believe he was hers.

"Hey," he said, his voice husky. "I was just missing you."

In response, she beamed and pulled his face down to hers so their lips brushed, then connected fully. Oh, how she loved kissing Wyatt Brooks. She'd kissed a handful of boys throughout the years at school dances, slumber party dares, and casual dates, but nothing compared to kissing Wyatt.

"I'll take that as a 'you missed me, too,'" he teased when they broke apart.

"I did. And I'm going to miss you even more when you leave." She stuck her lower lip out in an exaggerated pout. In about two weeks, Wyatt would report to Fort Benning to begin boot camp, and she wasn't close to ready to say goodbye. Every moment they had together felt precious.

Wyatt's face fell. "I know. Being apart from you is going to suck, but you aren't getting rid of me so easily. I'll call you every chance I get and visit you at school when I can."

Her heart swelled. "You promise?"

"Promise." He crossed his heart. "But let's not think about that tonight."

"Easier said than done," she grumbled. "What do you have planned to distract us?"

Wyatt held out his hand and led her out the door and down the little dirt path to the clubhouse. Their clubhouse.

"This." He gestured around the small wooden room.

Piper's eyes widened in delight. Candles of all shapes and sizes filled the room with soft light as dusk fell. He'd arranged an indoor picnic with a blanket, pillows, and a wicker basket filled with Tupperware containers.

"Aunt Molly helped me cook some of your favorite food. I burned the corn bread, but the BBQ looks and smells amazing. This way, we won't be rushed." He glanced at Piper for approval.

"I love it," she assured him, clapping her hands.

Wyatt opened a bottle of sparkling cider and poured them each a glass. The corn bread was, in fact, burned, but that didn't stop it from being the best meal Piper had ever had. Though that may have had something to do with the proud smile on Wyatt's face every time she complimented his cooking. And how the flickering candles made his gorgeous eyes glow. There was nowhere else she'd rather be than here in the clubhouse with Wyatt.

After dinner, they arranged the blanket and pillows outside on the tiny top deck to indulge in Molly's famous chocolate chip cookies. Lying back, they watched the sky fade to black, counting the stars peeking through the dark curtain of night, calling out constellations they knew as their eyes adjusted to the dark. Wyatt wiped a stray cookie crumb off the corner of her mouth, then replaced his thumb with his lips. She tasted the salty sweetness of chocolate on his tongue as it swirled against hers.

They danced from topic to topic like a well-rehearsed waltz, sharing their hopes, dreams, and fears about the future and pausing only to exchange kisses. At some point in the evening, as more stars clicked on like stadium lights overhead, the air shifted imperceptibly.

Piper shivered and snuggled closer to Wyatt. The carefree laughter faded from his face, replaced with a smoldering gaze. Each lingering kiss lasted longer than the one before, like each of them was daring the other to break away first, neither backing down.

Pulling his marvelous mouth away from hers, Wyatt propped himself up on an elbow and looked down at her. His focused gaze made Piper squirm.

"I want you to know something," he said in a low voice that cracked with nerves. His hand wavered. He took a deep, unsteady breath, his eyes wet pools so deep Piper thought she might drown in them.

"I think I love you." He shook his head. "No, I know I do." Confidence flooded his voice as he repeated the sentiment, his eyes shining.

Piper's face split into a smile beyond her control, his words melting her into liquid gold. Wyatt never said anything he didn't mean. He was letting her all the way into his heart, and it was the only place she wanted to be. She'd known she was in love with Wyatt since their first kiss. Though she'd been falling in love long before that.

"I love you, too." She interlaced her fingers with his and held on tight.

He squeezed her hand and continued staring at her in awe.

Like she was gravity, and he was an astronaut in space who couldn't live without her—like he could see her soul.

Wyatt Brooks loved her.

They were in love.

His lips connected with hers, more tender than his previous kisses. It wasn't enough for Piper. She twisted her hands into his hair, pulling his weight on top of her.

"We should go inside," he whispered in between kisses.

She nodded eagerly, and Wyatt scooped her up, blanket and all. He continued kissing her as he carried her inside, stopping only long enough to set her down and lay the blanket out, careful not to extinguish any of the flickering candles. Then he wrapped her back up in his arms, his lips moving over hers like if he stopped, he might die. She'd thought when this moment came, she'd be afraid, but wild anticipation fueled her actions. When he knelt on the blanket on the floor and held out his hand for her to join him, she didn't hesitate, swept away in the dizzying passion of first love.

As AMAZING AS making love with Wyatt was, falling asleep in his arms was even sweeter. She hadn't meant to stay in the clubhouse all night, but every time she tried to force her body to rise and get dressed, Wyatt's steady breathing and warm embrace lulled her back to sleep.

When she crept home in the early glow of dawn, her mother's weary face greeted her, a phone cradled to her ear. "She just walked in. I'll call you back later." Her mom turned to Piper. "Piper! Where have you been?"

"I got up early and went for a walk," Piper lied, guilt flooding her system.

"That's funny, because Molly informed me that Wyatt's not in his bed where he's supposed to be either. Want to try telling me the truth?"

Piper's cheeks grew hot. "I'm sorry, Mom. I didn't mean to worry you. Wyatt and I were hanging out in the clubhouse last night, and we fell asleep. Nothing happened!"

Piper touched her warm cheek self-consciously. She felt different this morning; did she look different, too? Could her mom see through her lie and tell her precious daughter was no longer a virgin?

"I don't like this, Piper. I hardly recognize you since you started spending more time with Wyatt. You've been staying out all hours of the night, and I got an email this morning saying you haven't registered for the freshman seminar yet. It's not like you to miss a deadline."

Piper kept her voice calm even though her mom bringing up Wyatt infuriated her. "This is the first time I've come home late! And I forgot the deadline, but I'll sign up today. I'm sure it will be fine."

She spun to go upstairs, but her mom grabbed her forearm, stopping her. "I think you need to take a break from Wyatt. He's a distraction to you."

Piper glared at her. "Mom, he's my boyfriend. He leaves for boot camp in two weeks, and I want to see him as much as possible before then."

How could she explain Wyatt was more than a high school crush? He was her best friend, her soul mate, her one true love. She knew he would be in her life forever, whether or not her mom wanted to believe it.

Her mother's mouth pressed into a thin line. "And what happens when he's gone? When he's in the army? If he's deployed? Have you thought about that? Will you skip school to visit him on base or forget to study for an exam because you're on the phone with him too late? This is your life, Piper—you've got to start taking more responsibility."

Piper swallowed a scream. Had her mom never been in love

before? For once in her life, she was having fun and following her heart. What was the big deal? "I think you're worrying too much."

"And you're not worrying enough. We'll discuss this more later, but you're spending the rest of the weekend grounded."

Piper shook her mom's hand off and stomped up to her bedroom, slamming the door behind her.

Chapter Twenty-Eight

Now

Wyatt's lips tickled the back of her neck, waking her as dawn broke golden and violet across the horizon. He dropped a line of lazy kisses from behind her ear to the top of her spine, branding her skin with a trail of fire. Neither of them had bothered to put clothes back on after last night, and her body instantly awakened at his touch. His hand flattened against her stomach, then drifted south, moving as slow as his kisses. She turned around to face him, sighing with pleasure at the delicious feel of his bare skin against hers, at his hard warmth against her softness.

Wyatt's arms locked around her, drawing her close. "I love waking up to you like this."

Piper responded by crushing herself to him, melting into his languid morning kisses. "Me, too. I could stay here with you all day."

"One perk of this forced vacation is nothing's stopping us." He ran a hand down her back to cup her bottom, coaxing her closer.

Piper smiled against his lips. "You got any more protection in that magic pillow of yours?"

Wyatt grinned, a wicked gleam in his eyes. "As a matter of fact, I do." He pulled back to rummage in his clothes pillow.

At first, Piper thought the sound was her heart beating lustily in her ears. But Wyatt froze in place as a faint thrumming filled the beach, growing louder by the second until it became the distinct and steady drone of a plane engine.

Wyatt gripped her arm. "You hear it too, right?"

Piper nodded, not wanting her voice to drown out the hopeful sound.

They stared at each other for a beat before springing into action. This was the moment Rosie had warned them to be ready for. Piper tugged on a nearby T-shirt and wiggled into a pair of shorts, all cobwebs of sleep and lust wiped from her mind. Wyatt hopped on one foot, then the other, putting on his swim trunks and tennis shoes. Grabbing the flare kit, he raced toward the beach. Piper scooped up the radio and a red beach wrap and rushed after him, tripping over her feet in haste.

By the water, they shielded their eyes against the sun, searching desperately for the plane that would signal their rescue. Wyatt zeroed in on the sky, flare gun loaded, ready to pull the trigger. The engine's whir grew louder, flooding Piper with giddy excitement. After nearly a week on this island, rescue was literally on the horizon. She couldn't see the plane yet, but she waved her red wrap in the air, hoping the color would stand out against the white sand and green trees.

"I've got to get up higher and flag them down." Wyatt nodded at the cliffside to their left. "Our SOS washed away during high tide last night, and the cliffside and trees are hiding us."

Panic rose in her like nausea. "But you're still hurt. Maybe I should go."

But they both knew that wasn't the right call.

Wyatt shook his head impatiently. "I'm fine. Wait here and try to get someone on the radio." Before Piper could protest, he took off sprinting toward the cliffside that jutted out less than two hundred yards away.

Piper fumbled with the radio knob, her hands slippery with sweat, twisting the knob millimeter by millimeter, listening for the sound of a channel clicking into place. The adrenaline and drinking from last night, not to mention the mind-blowing sex, had left her limbs as useless as wet noodles. No voices emanated from the device in her hand.

She could still hear the whirring of the plane as Wyatt inched his way up the rock side. A few seconds later, the loud crack of the flare gun rang out, an orange shimmer whistling across the sky. Was it bright enough? Would they see the trail of smoke? She'd been thrilled about an overcast morning, but now she cursed the gray clouds dotting the sky.

Piper's breath came in shallow pants, her focus darting between the sky and the cliffside until Wyatt jumped the final few feet back to the ground. A few minutes later, he arrived at their beach camp sweaty and out of breath, with a pronounced limp. A starburst of red seeped through the torn bandage on his leg, blood running from a fresh gash on his shin.

She rushed to meet him with a water bottle. "You should sit." She gestured to a spot in the sand.

Wyatt accepted the water bottle but shrugged off her suggestion, pacing by the shoreline instead, seeming unaware of his injury. He scraped a hand over his jaw, his face set in a scowl.

"Did you see the plane?" Piper bit her lip, unsure if she should give him a hug or space.

Wyatt's expression pinched like he'd tasted something with too much vinegar. "I saw it, but I don't know if it saw me. I thought they'd come back and make a few loops around the perimeter of the island, but they kept going. Did you reach anyone on the radio?"

Piper gnawed on her lower lip and shook her head. "I'll keep trying, though."

"We only have two more flares, which is not ideal." He pulled the flare gun out of his back pocket and showed it to Piper. "Do you know how to use this?"

"I'm assuming you point and shoot?"

His brows knit together, frustration obvious on his face. "Make sure the wind is at your back, hold it at a sixty-degree angle, and look away when you shoot to protect your eyes."

Piper wanted Wyatt to put his arm around her and tell her everything would be okay, not give her another survival lesson. "Wind, sixty degrees, look away. Got it." She couldn't help the flippant tone in her voice, something to counterbalance Wyatt's sudden militant edge.

His lips tightened into a thin white line. "If we get separated, or I'm incapacitated, and you hear a plane or see a boat, don't hesitate to fire." His words were an unpleasant reminder of their increasingly dire reality. "Do you understand?" Wyatt asked again. Frenetic dark energy radiated off him, a stark contrast to the flirtation of last night.

"Yes! What's with the lecture?" A lump formed in her throat, made worse by the other question whispering in the back of her head . . . What if no one had seen them? What if they were stuck here for good?

His face relaxed a fraction. "I want to make sure you know what to do if anything happens to me."

Piper swallowed hard at the thought of Wyatt not being around for any reason. "As long as you aren't planning any more daring adventures, nothing will." She worked to keep her voice light and airy. "I think you should let me look at your leg. We should rebandage it."

He looked down as if noticing his injury for the first time. "Oh, yeah. I slipped on a loose rock on my way down." He waded into the water to wash the blood off, hissing as the saltwater hit the open wound. When he reemerged on the dry sand, she saw the fresh cut, ragged and deep, ran lengthwise down the side of his shin—and was still bleeding.

"Sit," she said more forcefully this time.

Wyatt eased himself onto the ground beside her, masking his pain with a blunted groan. He cried out when she pressed her red wrap down firmly on his wound, breathing through her nose to keep from passing out at the sight of blood. Now was not the time to let her nerves get the best of her.

It took longer than she would have liked for the bleeding to stop. When it did, she wrapped the fabric around his leg, tying it tight. Wyatt remained stone-faced, staring out at the horizon the entire time.

She hovered a hand over his knee, wanting to comfort him but acutely aware of the "don't mess with me" vibe emanating from his entire body. She wasn't ready to face rejection if he pulled away from her touch. Instead, she sat back and clasped her hands together stiffly, hugging her legs under her chin.

Silence filled the beach like a palpable phantom. Instead of turning to her for solace, Wyatt was collapsing in on himself, fall-ing further and further away from her with every second. The jux-taposition of postcoital bliss and plane-rescue miss made Piper feel jittery and anxious like a tightrope walker without a net.

After an unbearably long time, Piper jumped to her feet. "You know what might make us both feel better? Some food. I'm going to get us some food." She could hear the manic edge of her voice, which matched the nervous energy leapfrogging through her.

By her calculations, there should still be at least one more pa-paya, some soda, and a full block of cheese left in the cooler. She wasn't sure how to put a smile back on Wyatt's face, but she had yet to meet a problem that cheese couldn't solve.

Piper looked in all directions, trying to spot the Yeti. After taking a lap around their campsite and the firepit, she walked back to Wyatt, confused. It's not like there were many places a large, bright blue cooler could hide on this patch of sand.

"Hey, do you know where the Yeti is?"

Wyatt continued staring slack-jawed out at the white-capped ocean. "I don't know. Where did you leave it?"

Piper sucked in a breath. "I'm not sure where *we* left it—that's why I'm asking. Weren't you storing the fish in it last night? Is that the last time you saw it?"

"Yes, I used it over there." He pointed vaguely toward a spot now underwater. "But you said you would pull it back to the shelter last night."

Piper didn't like the accusatory tone in his voice. "Yes, but you said you'd handle the fish, so I thought you meant the cooler, too."

That got Wyatt's attention. He snapped his head toward her. "So, you left the cooler by the water?" A dark cloud settled over his face. "It's gone, isn't it? The cheese, drinks, everything swept out to sea with the tide." He heaved a shell into the water.

Piper's heartbeat picked up speed, thudding mercilessly in her chest. This was all wrong. She and Wyatt should be holding hands on a plane bound for home or making love in their cozy beach nest, not fighting over a fishy cooler.

She shrugged helplessly. "I'm sorry."

"I can't believe this. First, rescue misses us, and now we're down to what, a piece of fruit?" His eyes had gone dark, his face devoid of emotion.

Piper couldn't find the Wyatt she loved behind the mask. His cold behavior reminded her of his nonchalant attitude when he broke up with her all those years ago. And thinking about that filled her with cold dread.

"The plane could still come back. And we can catch more fish," Piper countered. She understood his bad mood over the plane, and losing their food was less than ideal, but why was he projecting so much hostility at her?

He shook his head, his brow furrowing. "You don't understand. The fishing net was in the cooler. And if that pilot reports this area as having no signs of life, then another plane won't head this way anytime soon. We could be stuck here indefinitely." Wyatt picked up another shell and hurled it into the water. "Damn it! This is all my fault. I should've been paying more attention. Instead of—" His gaze cut to her face, and he trailed off.

A tear slipped down Piper's face, fear twisting her stomach in a cruel knot. She'd broken her walls down for Wyatt but now was reminded of why she'd needed them so high in the first place. Their love bubble had burst so abruptly it left her reeling, her deepest fear playing out right before her eyes, but she'd be damned if he hurt her first this time.

"Instead of what? Kissing me? Sleeping with me?" Her nostrils flared, and she crossed her arms tight against her chest. "You're right. That was a big mistake."

Wyatt frowned. "That's not what I'm saying at all. I meant I shouldn't have let myself get distracted from getting us home."

"But it's what you're thinking. Admit it. We were drinking and got carried away in the moment. That's all it was." Angrily, Piper wiped another tear off her face, sucking in a deep breath to quell any more. This pain reminded her of how quickly their high school love had soured—like milk left out too long. "And I agree, we need to focus on surviving and getting off this island. That's our priority." She had to squeeze her hands together to keep them from shaking—a side effect of breaking her own heart. "We should forget about last night."

She waited for Wyatt to argue. To tell her not to be silly, that they were both hungry and tired and maybe a little hungover, but nothing would stop him from kissing her again, from loving her. That, of course, it hadn't just been the wine or the moonlight—it had been everything he'd wanted for years, and he could never forget it had happened. That last night was amazing, even if they were still stuck on this stupid beach.

But Wyatt's eyes widened like she'd punched him before his

face tightened as hard as stone. "Okay. If that's what you want." He gave her a curt nod. "We can forget it ever happened."

He turned back to the ocean and away from Piper.

PIPER STALKED OFF to their shelter. Another tear leaked down her face, betraying her tough exterior. No way was she sitting on this beach with Wyatt waiting for a plane to save them when he couldn't even stand to look at her. Had last night really been so forgettable to him?

She knew what they had was special. Last night had healed so many pieces of her once-shattered heart, and Wyatt had felt it, too. He had to have, but the dismissive look in his eyes now burned her insides like someone had poured gasoline down her throat and lit a match. The burning was oddly comforting and easier to tolerate than the recent feelings of love and butterflies, so Piper welcomed the charred chaos.

Back at their shelter, she changed into a clean bathing suit and cover-up, hoping it would make her feel better.

It didn't.

Her body ached from physical and emotional exhaustion. Hunger gnawed at her alongside a growing cacophony of fear swirling in her gut like a Tasmanian devil. They could survive for some time without food, Wyatt had drilled the rule of threes into her head by now, but it wasn't a pleasant thought.

She wouldn't accept all the blame for the Yeti fiasco, but she could find more food. Taking a trip out to the clearing would keep her from having a complete panic attack and provide a necessary break from Wyatt. Acting decisively, she packed the backpack with her half-filled water bottle, the Swiss army knife, and a change of socks, leaving room for anything useful or edible she found along the way.

"I'm going for food. Back in two hours," she called to Wyatt, talking around the lump still lodged in her throat. She half expected him to insist on coming with her, but he barely glanced in her direction.

Threading her way through spindly curving trees, she let the calls of tropical birds and cool shade soothe her. The iguanas perched on branches, statue-like except for their eyes, which tracked her every movement. Was it the light, or were they looking at her with pity?

Close to the clearing, she found the spot where they'd located their luggage and followed roots and branches to a clump of papaya trees. As if the universe knew she needed a break, several ripe papayas were within reach. Well, within reach if she jumped and knocked them down one by one. She filled her bag with as many as would fit and continued trekking until she glimpsed the familiar patch of light illuminating trees that marked the clearing.

After she'd collected a few fresh berries and stored them in the backpack's front pouch, she took a break on a flat rock by the small pond, catching her breath. Using the knife, she cut open a papaya and devoured it. Alongside the practical fear of staying alive that rattled inside her like a rogue grenade, anxiety over letting Wyatt back into her heart mounted—seeds of doubt and distrust clouding her mind.

Only after she stopped moving did the enormity of their situation overwhelm her like a swarm of mad bees. All the fear and anger and grief she'd experienced over the past week flooded to the surface, threatening to choke her. One tear deluged into a flood, and she sobbed freely, allowing herself this small breakdown out of Wyatt's sight. She wept in frustration at being so close to happiness and rescue, only to have them cruelly ripped away. Cried over the added pain of rejection that made her want to tear her heart out of her chest and drown it in the ocean, and from the actual fear of not making it home.

What if they really were stranded here for days or weeks longer? Or worse, never made it home? What if she was forever stuck with a man who had her whole heart but didn't want it? The thought filled her with such despair she let loose an animalistic scream that reverberated off the branches of trees and scared a flock of birds into flight. She didn't care if Wyatt heard her, but this deep in the wilderness, she doubted he would.

She was all alone.

Chapter Twenty-Nine

Then

Days after sleeping with Wyatt, Piper was still flying high, an acrobat suspended in midair. Even being grounded for the weekend hadn't yanked her back down to earth. The time she'd gone without seeing Wyatt had only made her want him more. Love him more.

From up in her room, she heard Wyatt's voice downstairs. That wasn't unusual; he came by frequently, and they'd planned to go for a bike ride later that afternoon now that she was free. But amplified anger colored the voices below. When Piper walked into the kitchen, everyone stopped talking.

Irritation pinched her mom's lips. The crease in Wyatt's forehead furrowed, his eyes dark. Only her father looked like his usual self, but then again, he rarely got angry or upset.

Piper chewed her bottom lip. "Is everything okay?" No one answered her. "Wyatt, are you ready to bike into town?"

Wyatt shoved his hands deep into the pockets of his shorts and ducked his head so his tangle of brown curls hid his eyes from her. He darted a glance at her mother, who crossed her arms in response. "I forgot I have to run some errands for Molly. Sorry."

"That's okay. I'll come with you!" Piper slid the flip-flops sitting by the back door onto her feet.

Her mom stood. "Piper, have you signed up for your freshman seminar yet?"

Piper waved her away. "I will this afternoon."

Wyatt came over to the door. "You should go do that now. It's easier if I run errands myself." He nodded in her parents' direction. "I'll see you later."

Wyatt walked out the back door and down the porch steps before Piper had registered he was leaving without her. Something was up.

She ran after Wyatt, stopping him on the lawn. "Hey, what's wrong? What were you talking to my parents about?"

"Nothing important. Everything's fine." A scowl drew his face downward, betraying his statement.

"You know you can tell me anything, right?" Piper pressed.

He nodded, looking at his hands, the ground, anywhere but her. When he shut down like this, Piper knew pushing him never worked. He'd reveal anything he needed to tell her when he was ready.

"Then, at least give me a hug." She twined her arms around his neck and stepped into his warmth. For a sickening second, she thought he might not return the embrace, but his arms encircled her waist after a brief pause, drawing her in so close she couldn't breathe.

He buried his face in her neck, inhaling deeply. "You always smell so good. I never want to forget it."

"It's just my shampoo." Piper pulled back to see his face, to make him tell her what was bothering him and why he was acting so strange, but he tightened his grip.

Relaxing back into his embrace, she contented herself with listening to his heart thudding beneath her ear.

Eventually, he released her, rubbing at his eyes, but flashed his patented dimpled smile that contradicted any forlorn thoughts. "Meet me at the clubhouse after dinner?"

"Of course." She squeezed his forearms. "You promise you're okay?"

He didn't answer her directly but bent his head and kissed her. She could taste the salt of a stray tear on his lips. He kissed her like he was saying goodbye.

"I love you." Piper pressed her forehead against his, wishing she could inject her words into his body—into his soul.

"I love you, too. Always." He kissed her forehead, then pushed away and disappeared into the woods.

DINNER WITH HER parents lasted forever. The minute the dishes were put away and her parents turned their attention to the nightly news, Piper slipped out the back door. It was early evening at the peak of summer, and the moon lazily chased the sun across the sky.

The anticipation of seeing Wyatt never grew old. Usually buoyant enough to lift her off the ground, her excitement tonight was tethered by unease. Something was off, something she couldn't put her finger on, but she was confident she could kiss away Wyatt's earlier troubles. Maybe he was worried about their impending long-distance relationship. Tonight, they'd make plans for Wyatt's first trip to visit her at UNC, she decided. Having something solid on the calendar would help. Then she'd surprise him on base for his birthday in October; after that, the holidays were right around the corner.

The distance would be hard but worth it.

Wyatt was waiting in the clubhouse when she pushed open the yellow door and stepped inside.

"You're early," he said, his voice a strangled monotone. He didn't move to kiss or hug her hello.

Piper hesitated a few feet away from him. "I'm always early. What's going on?"

Wyatt looked out the window, avoiding her gaze. Piper's stomach twisted. She couldn't pinpoint what had changed, but everything felt wrong.

"Maybe we should sit," he suggested.

Piper shook her head and folded her arms to stop her hands from shaking. "Tell me what's wrong."

Wyatt picked at a loose thread on the hem of his T-shirt. When he finally looked at her, a mask had settled over his face, replacing the Wyatt she knew with a stranger. "I've been thinking about this a lot lately. There's no easy way to say this." He blew out a breath. "I think we should go back to just being friends."

The words were like a bucket of ice water dumped over her head.

"Don't get me wrong, this was a fun summer fling," he continued woodenly, "but I think we both know it won't last. I should have known better than to cross that line with you."

Piper searched his face for signs that she'd heard him wrong, but his jaw was set, his eyes defiant. Resolute in his decision. Her stomach coiled into a tight knot. She felt like he'd handed her a live grenade, and one wrong move would catapult her into oblivion.

"Where is this coming from? Did my parents say something to you?" Her throat ached. He didn't mean that. He couldn't.

He shook his head, his eyes vacant. "No, this is what I want. I think this would be best. For both of us."

"What about what I think? What I want?" Piper choked out. She rushed toward him and grabbed his hands in hers. "Are you really breaking up with me?" She hated how much her voice quavered. There was so much she wanted to vocalize, but the words wouldn't come. *You're my best friend, I love you, I'm your girl.* This couldn't be happening.

Wyatt's hands twitched but remained stiff in hers. "We're too young for a serious relationship. We should date, see other people, have fun."

Nothing sounded fun about dating other people to her, but Wyatt didn't waver.

She tried getting him to look at her, not ready to give up. "Tell me you don't love me anymore, and I'll leave." Her voice cracked.

Wyatt's eyes glistened with unleashed pain, his face contorted in anguish. "Piper," he ground out—the word a whisper. He threaded his fingers through hers and squeezed three times. Tears ran down her face, drops forming a river of hurt.

She was getting through to him. "Tell me." She grasped his hands, looking up at him pleadingly.

He leaned down, hesitating as his mouth hovered above her lips like he was torn between kissing her and turning his back.

A knock at the clubhouse door shattered the moment, and Wyatt jerked away.

"Sorry, is this a bad time?" Kiera asked, poking her head around the door.

Piper's mouth fell open, and she almost laughed out loud. It couldn't be a worse time. What was Kiera doing in her backyard, in her clubhouse? She knew Kiera and Wyatt were friendly and that Kiera was an outrageous flirt, but he couldn't possibly have invited her here. To their sacred spot.

Piper waited for Wyatt to send Kiera away, but he waved at her in greeting. "Hey, Kiera. Piper's about to leave, can you give us a few minutes?"

Kiera gave Piper a pitying smile and disappeared back outside, closing the door behind her.

"You invited her here?" Piper stumbled back from Wyatt as if stung.

Wyatt nodded and shrugged like she'd asked him if he wanted fries with a burger. When his gray eyes locked onto hers, they were as frigid and empty as a parking lot on Christmas Day.

This wasn't the Wyatt she knew. Cold, calculating. Mean and hurtful. She wanted nothing to do with this Wyatt. Her mom had been right after all.

All Piper could do was shake her head, hurt steaming out of her every pore. "Why?"

She must have looked as wild as she felt because Wyatt backed up a few more feet.

"Like I said, it's better if we both move on." Wyatt's words drove the dagger deeper.

The icy tentacles that had been working their way through Piper's veins turned to white-hot anger. It was one thing for Wyatt to break her heart, it was quite another to smash it to pieces by flaunting what "moving on" looked like.

His actions were reckless, heartless, and he knew it.

Never in a million years did she think this was how their love story would end—with Wyatt shooting arrows into her heart with every callous glare. Her pain made it hard to see straight. Or maybe that was the lurid outrage pulsating behind her eyes. How dare he tell her he loved her. Let her believe it was safe to fall in love with him, too. Talk about a future with her like it was everything he wanted and more when it had clearly been a silly summer fling to him.

"Maybe we could still be friends?" he asked haltingly, his eyes pleading. The frosty mask contorting his face dropped for a fraction of a second, and a flicker of hope flashed across his eyes.

Piper sucked in a shallow breath. Her voice trembled when she spoke. "You know what? A real friend wouldn't treat me like this." Tears coursed down her face. If she didn't get out of here soon, it would become impossible to pull herself together and leave with a hint of dignity. "I wouldn't want to be friends with you if you were the last person on this earth. In fact, I never want you to speak to me again."

She blindly found her way to the door, brushed past Kiera, and ran home, knowing if she looked back at Wyatt, it would be impossible to leave.

Wyatt didn't stop her.

He didn't call to apologize the next day. And when he left for boot camp a week later, he didn't say goodbye.

Five years of friendship and one magical summer of falling in love blew away like a wisp of smoke in a hurricane.

Chapter Thirty

Now

When her well of tears ran dry, Piper splashed water on her face and wiped her eyes with the hem of her beach cover-up. Drawing in a shaky breath, she forced herself to stand. From here on out, she would be strong. She had to be. This island adventure had taught her one thing—she was braver than she'd thought. More resilient. She'd survived a plane crash and six nights on an island so far. As a teenager, she'd survived her first heartbreak, and she could endure another.

Their night together could be blamed on a combination of desperation, lousy judgment, and booze. It didn't have to mean she was still in love with Wyatt after all these years. She needed to get a grip, tuck away her rebellious feelings of love, and hold it together until they made it home. Then she could go back to normal—back to never talking to Wyatt again. That idea nearly brought a fresh round of tears to the surface, but Piper commanded them away with a choked breath.

As she hiked back to the beach, a drizzle bloomed into thick drops, gusty winds tilting the rain sideways. Spiky torrents hit her from all sides. Great. As if she needed a physical reminder of the emotional pain she was walking back to.

Despite the rainstorm, Wyatt remained on the beach where she'd left him, still staring at the sea. She handed him a papaya and his knife.

"Eat this. I don't care if you don't want to." She may be pissed at him, her ego wounded, but that didn't mean she wanted him starving to death.

He flicked his gaze up at her, his eyes stormy. Raindrops beaded on his curls, dripping off his face. Dried blood caked the side of his calf, his hurt leg swollen to twice the size of the other. Mechanically, he cut the fruit open, took a bite, and gulped it down. If he noticed her blotchy face and swollen eyes, he said nothing. Had he been crying, too? Or was that the rain streaking his face, making his nose red?

Piper pushed wet hair out of her face. "Are you going to stay out here in the rain?"

The furrow between Wyatt's eyes deepened. "I need to keep watch."

With the wind and rain continuing to whip and wail, a search and rescue mission was likely on hold, but Piper didn't bother pointing that out. Wyatt could make his own decisions. A part of her wanted to pull him in from the storm and kiss him back to her, but she'd promised herself she'd stay strong, resolute, in her new boundaries. Boundaries that Wyatt had agreed with wholeheartedly.

It wasn't lost on her he'd rather sit in a storm alone than with her in their dry shelter.

There was nothing she could do except wait.

PIPER TRIED NAPPING, but her mind was wound too tight to relax. She passed the time by counting the veins in the leaves thatched above her, listening to the rain running off the trees, and trying to reach someone, anyone, on the radio. When the storm subsided a few hours later, the sky remained overcast, clouds hanging low and gray, hiding the sun and matching her solemn mood.

Wyatt's lone figure by the water was the first thing Piper saw when she sat up. He hadn't moved, but high tide had lured the water closer. A glittering row of crushed seashells drew a perfect outline of where the ocean had risen. Palm leaves and seaweed littered the beach. The waves loomed choppy and rough, but the air was still. The sound of an airplane approaching would be clear as a bell.

Instead, only silence filled the beach.

Piper clicked the radio on, but no matter how many times she repeated their call for help, no one responded. Her voice came out hoarse from her earlier meltdown; deep despair hardened her stomach. The weight of their situation, stark and insurmountable, sat on her chest like an elephant, making it hard to breathe deeply.

As much as she hated how vulnerable and lost she felt with Wyatt, it was worse to be alone in these dark feelings. Padding across the damp beach, she sat down beside him without a word. Together they watched the waves roll in, and the clouds sail by.

Though he sat close enough to touch, she missed him. Missed their once easy closeness that for a brief second had been re-ignited. Missed his laughter, his kiss. Under different circumstances, would they be skinny-dipping in the water or lying naked in their shelter right now? The appealing daydream hurt her heart. Piper's fingers yearned to smooth over his shoulders, her mouth to feel his lips opening over hers.

Wyatt cleared his throat. "That plane isn't coming back."

Piper suppressed her echoing hopelessness. "You don't know that." Her voice sounded thin. Unnaturally high. "They could still come."

"I'm so sorry, Piper. It's my fault. I should've known they wouldn't be able to see us over the rocks and trees. The second we heard something, I should have climbed the cliff and fired that flare." He bowed his head. "Instead, I waited like an idiot. And now we're stuck here."

A lightbulb went off in her head. Piper should have seen this coming—Wyatt shouldering an undue amount of blame and guilt. He'd always treated the problems of the world around him like they were his alone to fix. The knots in her stomach loosened a fraction of an inch as she considered the possibility that Wyatt wasn't angry at her, but upset with himself instead. That his earlier reaction could have been more about self-loathing than anything to do with Piper.

"You know that's not true. Without you, I wouldn't know how to shoot a flare gun, and I'm not climbing up the cliffside. Are you blaming me for those things?" She studied his drawn face, wary of a repeat of this morning's harsh conversation.

Wyatt's eyes were red-rimmed, his cheeks sunken like a collapsing jack-o'-lantern. "It's my fault we crashed here. I wanted to make it right. To save us."

"This isn't all on you, you know. We're in this together."

Wyatt pulled his legs up to his chest, wrapped his arms around them, and turned away from her, effectively ending the conversation.

Annoyance flared in Piper's veins like flames. She'd thought they were becoming a team, partners in this disaster they'd found themselves in, but Wyatt had withdrawn into his well-worn loner shell, shutting her out, acting like he was solely responsible for everything that happened on this island. He'd shut her out of his heart, too. Not that she needed another reminder.

Piper hurled a nearby rock into the ocean and stood to leave, unable to bear the torture of his silent treatment, when Wyatt spoke.

"My mom loved the ocean."

She froze. His mom had always been an off-limits subject. Before she could think of something to say, Wyatt continued.

"The closest beach was about four hours away, and we couldn't afford a hotel. But sometimes, she'd wake me before the sun came up and we'd drive out and spend the day by the water, eating peanut butter sandwiches she'd packed and drinking soda from a vending machine. Then we'd drive back at night, sunburned and sandy."

Piper settled herself back on the sand slowly so as not to distract him.

"She was different by the water. Freer somehow. Like she could let go of the demons that held her and enjoy life. Enjoy being my mom." Wyatt stared out over the water like he was watching a movie of memories. "It's the only time she ever talked about my dad, too. Told me how he taught her to swim in the ocean and gave me my first taste of ice cream when he thought she wasn't looking."

Piper smiled at the image. "Your dad sounds awesome. And I'm glad you have those memories of your mom."

Wyatt rested his chin on the tops of his knees. "Me, too. I've been thinking about her a lot since we've been here. Both of them, actually. Wondering if they're here with me somehow. If that's how we've survived everything so far."

Unexpected tears wet Piper's eyes, and she rubbed them away before Wyatt could notice. "I'm sorry about your mom, Wyatt. Molly told me when she passed last year, and I sent flowers and a card. I'm not sure if you got them, though. I know you guys had a difficult relationship, but I also know how much you loved her." Piper couldn't imagine losing one of her parents, let alone both of them.

"I wish I'd been able to help more. My deployment was hard on her, and she never got back on her feet after her stint in jail." Grief and guilt stained Wyatt's voice. His shoulders slumped, his gaze still searching for something beyond the horizon.

"You weren't responsible for her actions. You were the kid, and she was the mom." If only there were something more profound she could say to take away his pain.

"It doesn't matter. She needed me. She had a tough life, getting pregnant with me young, then losing the love of her life and raising me on my own. I don't think she ever recovered from my dad's death." Wyatt poured a handful of sand out like an hourglass through his fist. "I'd like to think I was a bright spot in her life, at least I tried to be. Maybe if I'd stayed in Mason or come home more, things would have turned out differently. Maybe she'd still be here."

"You can't think like that. She wanted you to go off and live your life. She was so proud of you. I remember that letter she wrote you when you graduated high school, saying that a picture of you in your cap and gown was her most cherished possession."

"That's a pretty sad prized possession."

"No, it's not," Piper insisted. "You made her happy by doing more than she could with her life."

Wyatt continued staring out over the waves. When he spoke again, his voice was as coarse as sand. "I got your flowers and your card. You were the only one who knew even half of what was happening with my mom, so it meant a lot." He took a deep breath and finally looked at her. Piper swam in the pools of his eyes. "I know I didn't deserve your sympathy, but I really appreciated it. More than you know."

He placed his hand over hers in the sand, covering it completely, and squeezed. Piper's throat felt too full of rocks to speak. She twisted her hand so their palms met and laced her fingers in his, marveling at how, after everything that had happened, it was still a perfect fit.

A key sliding into a lock with a staccato click.

They sat in silence, hands locked together as if that were the only thing keeping them from falling apart as the sky darkened. Maybe it was.

As the shadows grew longer, the sun closing out the day, Wyatt turned to her, his mouth curling to one side. "We should probably check the radio again."

Piper nodded and pulled her hand from his. Pushing himself upright, Wyatt stretched his arms above his head and rolled out his neck with a series of cracks. He walked only a few feet before grabbing a palm tree trunk for support, grunting in pain.

Piper jumped up and stood nearby. "Is it your leg?"

He shook his head. "My foot must have fallen asleep from sitting for so long. Or maybe it's a cramp." He staggered forward unsteadily, heavily favoring his unscathed leg.

Reflexively, Piper's hand shot out to support him, but she stopped herself and hovered alongside him as he hobbled toward their shelter. Yesterday she wouldn't have thought twice about ducking under his shoulder and sliding her arm around his waist, but that was before they'd decided everything between them was a mistake best forgotten.

"Can I help?" she asked when he paused and took another pained breath.

A sheen of sweat glistened on his upper lip, and his hands trembled. "No, no, I'm fine."

"No offense, Wyatt, but if this is you fine, I'd hate seeing you wounded."

He grunted and continued limping forward. Once he made it to their shelter, he gingerly took a seat and leaned back against the closest tree, mopping his brow with the sleeve of his T-shirt. "Do we have any more Advil?"

"I thought you said your leg was fine?" Piper lifted her brows in challenge.

His nostrils flared. "Okay, okay, maybe it's bothering me. Is that what you want to hear?"

She checked their first aid kit's remains, returning with the rest of their bandages. "We're out of Advil, but let me rebandage your cut at least."

He shook his head with a sharp "no," then held out his hand for the supplies. "I can do it. I don't want to ruin your appetite."

"Wyatt, it's not like I'm headed to an all-you-can-eat buffet." His macho attitude was exasperating.

"I know, but I can handle it. Speaking of food, though, do we have any more?"

It was a blatant attempt to keep her away from his injury, but he'd barely eaten in the last twenty-four hours, so she got up and dug a water bottle and a handful of berries out of her bag. Browbeating him into accepting help would be as useless as trying to catch water with a tennis racket.

When she returned, Wyatt had already changed his bandage and pulled on a pair of loose gray sweatpants. He could physically hide his injury, but it didn't dissuade Piper.

"I know you don't want to listen to me, but as the medical professional of this beach, I want you to elevate your leg for a few hours."

To her surprise, tears shimmered in Wyatt's eyes. "I know, but I feel fucking useless. I should keep watch. Do something! How does my lying around help our situation?"

About as much as him moping on the beach, Piper wanted to point out, but she bit her tongue. "I'll take over rescue watch. I bet you'll feel better after a few hours of rest."

His brow unfurled slightly. "Maybe. And maybe I can catch some crabs or something later."

"I think you should focus more on resting and less on hunting our dinner. Come on, lie back, and let's get your leg up." She dragged her suitcase under the canopy and helped Wyatt maneuver his bad leg onto it.

Satisfied that he would rest, at least for the time being, she ducked back out of their shelter. "I'll be out here keeping watch if you need me."

He propped himself up onto his elbows. "Hey, Piper."

She turned back.

"I'm sorry I was such a jerk this morning about the plane. I promise you, we will get off this island."

She nodded her acknowledgment, appreciating the sentiment but acutely aware he wasn't apologizing for agreeing they should never have slept together.

Chapter Thirty-One

Now

At some point in the middle of the night—knowing a plane wouldn't see them in the dark—Piper crawled back into their shelter to sleep. A few hours later, faint strands of daylight streamed in through the trees, waking the world, and her, with its touch. Less than twenty-four hours ago, she'd woken up to Wyatt's good morning kisses, his arms wrapped around her. Now she opened her eyes to his back, Wyatt curled as far away from her as possible in the small space. The sharp contrast gave her vertigo, her head spinning from their fast fallout.

Wyatt's gentle snoring made it impossible to forget he was here—to shake loose the memory of his hands gliding over her naked body, his lips nibbling her neck.

Suddenly she couldn't take a full breath and felt trapped, like the thatched roof of their canopy hut was closing in on her. She needed space. Needed to think and regroup.

Slinking out to the shoreline, Piper gulped in the salty, dewy air with relief as she began walking along the stretch of beach headed away from the cliffside. As the sun crested the horizon, it painted the water in shimmering shades of pink and fiery orange, casting a soft glow over the sand. The night sky faded away like a healing bruise.

How long would she do this dance? Tiptoeing around Wyatt like he hadn't cracked her heart wide, like a crowbar prying open a locked door. Ignoring how her heart leaped every time he beamed that dimpled smile at her. Pretending like he didn't have the power to devastate her, make her blood run cold, with cutting words.

Piper walked until the sandy beach gave way to a thicket of reeds and brambles, and their base camp was no longer visible. Piles of black seaweed blocked her path as the shoreline met a narrow point of land. The vast expanse of the ocean rippled before her in unending waves, making her feel like the last person on earth.

But she wasn't the last person and she wasn't here alone.

Despite the complicated double helix of love and pain that bound her to Wyatt, Piper couldn't fathom being stranded with anyone else. Wouldn't want to be despite everything. No matter what, their destinies were intertwined—connected. They'd found their way back to each other once before. Maybe they could again.

A seed of hope blossomed deep in Piper's soul. Spending time with Wyatt this past week had healed the fissures crisscrossing her heart like battle scars, his presence filling the cracks like flowers growing through broken pavement. She understood him better now. Understood why he'd rejected her before and recognized deep in her bones that every action he took was to protect her, even if it meant denying their love—a twisted logic born out of his fear of not being good enough for her. Maybe it was up to her to be brave enough for both of them and push through her fear of heartbreak.

Maybe it wasn't too late for them.

Maybe they were just getting started.

The relentless sun had reddened her neck and shoulders, a steady reminder of the passage of time. How long had she stood out on this narrow point of shore, lost in thought? It was time to face Wyatt and confront their uncertain future together. With a deep breath, she turned and began the journey back, her heart fluttering with anticipation and hope. She steeled herself for the conversation ahead but was determined to see it through, to find a way to make things work between them.

They would figure it out—together.

WHEN SHE RETURNED to their shelter, Wyatt was still asleep, one arm thrown back over his head. His long black eyelashes rested against his cheeks, his parted lips full, his expression peaceful—no traces of the pain that had marred it earlier. Her sleeping warrior.

His curls, encouraged by the moisture in the air, swirled across his forehead in perfect spirals. Unable to resist, she brushed one back, then cupped his cheek. Her hand prickled like it was on fire at the touch. Or was that his skin? Experimenting, she touched his forehead with the back of her hand. An anchor dropped in her stomach. His skin was damp and fiery, his breath too shallow. He groaned, shivering despite his high body temperature.

Something was very wrong.

Piper knelt and rolled up his sweatpants to inspect his left leg. The stench that hit her as soon as she peeled back his bandage immediately told her the cut was infected.

"Shit," she cursed out loud. Why hadn't she paid more attention? She should've forced Wyatt into a proper examination of his cut. Should have known he'd play the martyr. An infection could be dangerous, especially if it got into his bloodstream. If she got some fluids into him, she might be able to turn this around. Acting fast, she ducked out of the shelter, leaving his side only long enough to grab a water bottle and hurry back.

"Wyatt! Wyatt, wake up!" She shook his shoulders, frantic.

He blinked at her, bewildered. "Piper? What are you doing here?"

"I need you to drink some water. Can you sit up?"

Wyatt took her hand, his cold and clammy in hers. "I can't believe you're here with me. I've waited so long for this." His soft words slurred together.

"Of course I'm here." Piper tugged on his arm, coaxing him upright. She expected him to fight her, but he sat up like a rag doll. His heart beat like a jackhammer under his shirt, his eyes were glassy.

"Drink this." Piper pressed the water bottle into his hand.

He nodded and dutifully took a few gulps of water. "Piper, what's wrong? You look sad." His childlike tone sounded eerie and far away, like he was in a dream.

"I'm going to change your bandage. Can you hold still for me?"

He nodded again.

Holding her breath, she washed and redressed his wound as best she could with what remained of their first aid kit. He winced in pain but otherwise said nothing. The lack of questions or teasing alarmed Piper most of all. He must have known his cut wasn't healing properly and had hidden it from her. How else had it gotten so bad?

Hot tears pricked the backs of her eyes. "I'm going to go get us some more water. Wait right here." Piper stood to avoid Wyatt seeing her cry.

"Don't leave me, please." He grabbed her hand, stopping her. "I love you. Do you know that?" His panicked eyes burned into hers, wet and feverish. "You have to know. Please don't go."

Piper gripped his hand helplessly, too overcome by her flood of anxiety to respond. Did Wyatt even realize what he was saying or to whom he was saying it? "Wy, I'm not leaving. I'll be back in two seconds. I promise."

She pried her hand out of his and rushed to their food supply, commanding herself to breathe. They had enough water to get them through a few more days and plenty of berries. Thank goodness she'd gone to the clearing yesterday because she didn't think she could leave Wyatt alone in this state. Dread swelled in her stomach. They'd been fortunate to survive this far, but their luck had officially run out.

"Piper, wait for me!" Wyatt's voice rang out behind her. True to form, he hadn't listened to her and had somehow dragged himself to a standing position. He took a few unsteady lurches forward, smiling blankly ahead.

Then everything moved in slow motion.

On his next step, Wyatt's legs buckled beneath him, his eyes rolled back into his head, and his whole body collapsed onto the sand with a sickening thud.

"Wyatt!" Piper ran to his side.

It felt like hours had passed before she reached him. When she sank onto the sand and shook him, his eyes fluttered open a few times, unfocused.

Think, Piper, think.

Wyatt was likely in the early stages of sepsis. The combination of a deep cut and a weakened immune system from poor nutrition over the past week could be lethal. He needed treatment with serious antibiotics, but that wasn't an option here. With shaking hands, she checked the skin around his cut. It didn't look like the infection had spread to his bloodstream, so there was no reason to tie a tourniquet around his leg or do anything drastic.

Not yet, at least—it was only a matter of time.

Piper dumped out the first aid kit, searching for something that might help. Finding nothing, she turned to their luggage, pawing through it like a rabid animal looking for scraps. Everything was useless. The best she could do was roll Wyatt onto his back, prop a T-shirt under his head, and hold his hand while talking to him, trying to keep him awake. All the while swallowing back tears.

After a few moments of blinking at her, his eyes closed completely, and his body went limp.

Tears coursed down Piper's face. "Wyatt, wake up!" She shook him again. "You promised we were getting off this island together. You promised!"

Grabbing the radio, Piper changed stations blindly through her tears, stabbing at buttons and praying for a response. On every channel, she heard only static but repeated the urgency of their situation.

"If anyone can hear me, we need help. This is Piper Adams. I'm with Wyatt Brooks, and we crashed on this island a week ago. Wyatt's hurt, and we need help now."

She spoke variations of the message over and over again until her voice grew hoarse—until the radio's batteries died alongside her dwindling hope. Throwing the useless piece of garbage into the sand, she howled a desperate cry into the wind.

This nightmare could not be happening.

Time crept as Wyatt lay shivering in the hot sand, unaware of his surroundings, slipping in and out of consciousness. Piper lay her head on his chest and sobbed. Disappointed in herself for not being able to help him more, for not being the star medical student everyone expected her to be. Terrified at the idea of losing Wyatt, at the thought of making it through even one day on this island without him here—let alone go on with any part of her life without him.

And furious she hadn't told him how much she cared about him when she had the chance.

What a cruel twist of fate. To get Wyatt back in her life only to face losing him again—this time permanently. What had she done in a past life to deserve this ironic torture?

"Please stay with me, Wyatt," she whispered. "If we make it home, I promise we won't go years without talking ever again."

She wanted so much more out of life if they made it home. He'd been the one to help her realize she'd been living her life out of fear of disappointing others instead of making herself happy.

Now that she saw it, she couldn't see anything else. And she couldn't imagine going home—if that was still possible—without Wyatt.

A guttural sob burst loose from her chest. "We're both getting off this island, Wy. I want a life, no, I need a life that includes you. Don't you dare leave me. Not again. You owe me, Wyatt."

Mentally scanning through options, she categorized everything she could do to get them out of this situation. She'd remake their SOS sign in the sand, keep watch by the water with their flare gun ready to flag help down, or swim into the ocean to find help if she needed to.

When her tears dried up, she comforted herself by listening to Wyatt's heartbeat. As long as it thumped in his chest, he was still here with her. She still had hope.

Over the rhythm of his heartbeat, a new sound filled her ears. Something droning above the continuous crash of the ocean waves. Piper lifted her head and searched the horizon. Maybe it was her fragile mental state, but she thought she spotted a flash of silver over the water.

Was it possible? Could it be a plane? If so, she needed to get a flare up to the top of the seaside cliff—fast.

Piper scrambled into action. Only a slim chance existed that the plane was flying in their direction, but she couldn't let this opportunity pass. She grabbed the flare gun and tucked it into her back pocket. Setting a bottle of water down by Wyatt, she kissed him on the cheek before racing toward the cliff as fast as she could, kicking up sand in her wake like a racehorse gaining the lead.

When she reached the base of the rocky cliff face moments later, the hum of the plane's engine was clear and insistent—and coming their way. She hadn't imagined it. Somehow the cliffside looked steeper than she remembered, but she inhaled deeply, gritted her teeth, and climbed, refusing to let the unrelenting voice of fear scare her away.

She concentrated instead on getting help for Wyatt, on getting them both off this island once and for all. There wasn't time to be careful, and the jagged rocks pierced her skin with every precarious move upward. Her hands were slick with blood by the time she hauled herself onto the flat top surface. The small plane had roared past while she climbed, growing smaller in the opposite direction with every second.

Moving fast, Piper hoisted the flare gun, positioning herself as Wyatt had taught her. She pulled the trigger. The flare rocketed into the sky and exploded in a satisfying burst of orange light. The bright flare seemed impossible to miss, but she wasn't sure the pilot would notice something in the plane's wake. She aimed and fired again, betting everything they had on this last chance.

They had to see it.

She waited a minute. Then another—holding her breath as the plane continued its steady flight until she couldn't hear or see it anymore. Despair filled her lungs, forcing the air out, and she collapsed onto the ground, the fight leaving her body.

"Come back! Come back!" she yelled at the sky, her body limp, her mind numb, and her hands throbbing.

She'd failed.

And it may have cost Wyatt his life.

It could have been hours or minutes that Piper lay curled in a fetal position, but eventually, the steady whir of a helicopter thrummed in her ears. She stood and shaded her eyes to see better, certain she'd imagined the sound. But sure enough, a red-and-white chopper went from a speck in the distance to hovering right overhead.

"Please move back," boomed a voice from the helicopter. "We're going to land."

Piper stepped backward into the tree line as the copter landed like a bumblebee on the small flat surface overlooking the water.

A spry dark-haired woman dressed in an EMT or maybe a Coast Guard uniform hopped out and came toward her. Piper backed away, shocked by the sight of another human in front of her after days of seeing only Wyatt.

"Piper Adams?"

Piper nodded, tears stinging her eyes at the sound of her name.

"My name is Rosie. We spoke on the radio. Are you alone? Where's Wyatt?"

Finding her voice, Piper spoke in a rush. "He's down on the beach in rough shape. I think he has an infection. I couldn't get him to wake up." Her voice broke, and tears swallowed her words. "You have to help him."

"How are you? Are you hurt?"

"I'm fine! You need to go help Wyatt. Please!" *Why weren't they moving faster?*

Rosie said something into the radio on her vest. "Okay, Piper. I need you to get in the helicopter and show us where your friend is so we can get you both home."

Piper climbed into the helicopter and screwed her eyes shut as they lifted off the ground, silently repeating the lyrics to "Ain't No Mountain High Enough" to quell her nerves. While Piper directed the pilot toward the beach where Wyatt lay, a man dressed in a medic uniform with pale skin and a kind smile cleaned and bandaged her hands. It surprised her to see they were stained with blood. None of this felt real.

Wyatt remained crumpled in the sand by their shelter. When the helicopter landed, Piper jumped out to rush to his side, but Rosie stopped her, telling her it would be faster if she stayed out of their way and let the medics do their job. It took ten agonizing minutes for the two medics to carry and load Wyatt into the aircraft, stretching him out on the floor. He was still unconscious, his skin waxy, his lips a horrible gray. The male medic inserted an IV into his vein—hopefully flooding his body with antibiotics and fluids.

"He cut himself right there." Piper pointed to the bandage on his leg. The medic nodded and flushed out the cut with real antiseptic. The sting of it should have been excruciating, but Wyatt didn't even twitch.

"How is he?" Piper asked, wringing her hands.

"He needs medical attention." Rosie's voice was grim. "You could probably use some fluids, too, but we'll be at the hospital in less than an hour. I want you to drink this whole water bottle and eat this protein bar before we get there." She handed her the items, but for once, Piper wasn't hungry.

As they lifted off, Piper took in their temporary home one last time. The firepit where they drank prosecco and toasted their gratitude, the palm tree beach perches where so many conversations had taken place, the green thatched shelter with a bridesmaid dress bed where they'd made love—their life for the past week. All fading away under cover of clouds.

Once in the air, Piper unbuckled her seat belt and slid down to the floor, propping Wyatt's head in her lap.

"Ma'am, please get back in your seat," Rosie ordered.

Piper shook her head, not bothering to stop her tears from falling. Nothing would make her leave his side. Rosie must have seen the haunted look in Piper's eyes because she let her sit in peace.

"We're going home. Hang on a little longer." She stroked his hair, repeatedly whispering in his ear, "Please, Wyatt. Please."

When they landed, the medics rushed Wyatt out and loaded him into an aircraft with hospital markings. Piper hurled herself after him, trying to climb on board, too, but firm hands stopped her once again.

"Where are you taking him?" she demanded, not ready to let him out of her sight.

"We've landed in the Bahamas. They're going to stabilize him and airlift him to the hospital in Miami right now. We'll board another flight shortly and take you to the same hospital."

An awful wail filled the air. Piper wondered if it might be a siren or something in the plane's engine. It wasn't until a medic approached her like she was a wild animal that she realized the sound was coming from her.

"You're going to feel a small prick. Okay, Piper? This will help."

Piper welcomed the darkness that followed.

Chapter Thirty-Two

Now

A steady machine beep pulsated in her bones, footsteps squeaked up and down an echoing hallway like excited mice, and voices shouted urgent commands over intercoms, jarring her awake.

Everything was too loud—that was Piper's first thought. Her second was that cement covered her body, her limbs pinned to the bed with its weight. She lifted an arm experimentally, but the tug of an IV line snaking out of her wrist stopped her. The line tethered her to a cold and sterile room, worlds away from her sunlit beach with salty air. Panic rose inside her, her growing anxiety matched by the increasing volume of a beeping machine by her head.

A young Black woman with a pretty face and a chipper smile wearing medical scrubs popped her head into the room. "I see our patient is awake!" she said, a little too brightly. "How are you feeling?"

"Wyatt?" was all Piper could choke out as memories of their rescue resurfaced like a developing Polaroid picture, faint at first, then sharpening into stark focus. The image of Wyatt's limp and lifeless body forever imprinted on her mind with indelible ink.

"That's the man they rescued you with, right? He's here. He's recovering." The nurse consulted the clipboard in her hands. "I need you to take a deep breath and tell me your pain level."

Her whole body sagged with relief. "Is he going to be okay?" She needed to know.

The nurse frowned at the monitor by her bed beeping alarmingly. "I'm afraid I can't disclose his medical information to you, but he is under the care of our best doctors."

"When can I see him?"

"Let's talk about that after we get you back to full health. Now I'm going to give you something to help you sleep. Your parents should be here when you wake up. My name's Layla if you need anything." Layla attached a new IV bag to the pole beside Piper's bed. The cold liquid stung through her veins as her eyes grew too heavy to keep open.

"PIPER?"

She woke to the sound of her mother's voice, shrill and hysterical but so familiar she wanted to cry. Her eyelids felt pinned down, her mouth sewn shut.

"Shh, don't wake her. She's sleeping," her dad's calm voice soothed.

Piper concentrated on opening her eyes, taking in her parents sitting by her bedside. Her dad's hair was grayer than she remembered, the wrinkles around her mom's eyes etched deeper than before. Had they always looked this breakable? Deep love for them and their familiar faces overwhelmed her.

Her mom flew to her side. "Oh, baby! You're awake. You're safe!"

"How are you feeling? Does anything hurt?" Her dad snapped into doctor mode.

The cuts on her hands still stung from a heavy antiseptic scrubbing, but Piper didn't want to talk about her injuries. "It's so, so good to see y'all. You have no idea." She blinked back tears. "How long have I been here? How long were we on the island?"

"We got the call yesterday afternoon that they'd found you, and we jumped on the first flight to Miami." Her dad checked the

IV bag by her bed. "You've been sleeping all night. They said you were in shock and gave you some strong sedatives that should wear off right about now."

That explained why she was so groggy.

"I can't believe you're okay. That we got you back!" her mom said, tears in her eyes. "It should have been sooner, but they paused the search when a tropical storm rolled through. Something about protocol."

Piper would have laughed if she had the energy. Her mom must have raised hell while she was missing. She still couldn't believe she'd made it off the island. They were safe. She stretched her arms out toward her parents, and they wrapped her in a tight, messy hug.

They were clinging to one another when a doctor with a long face and white mustache walked in wearing a lab coat.

He scanned the clipboard hanging on her door. "It's good to see you awake, Ms. Adams."

"When can we take her home, Dr. Koester?" her dad asked, standing.

"The cut on her head could have used stitches, she's malnourished and dehydrated with a few scrapes and bruises, but otherwise, she's fine. After another day of monitoring, assuming she continues gaining weight and all her tests clear, she'll be discharged and continue recovering under your care at home." He placed the clipboard back on its peg and smiled at her parents. "Your daughter is very lucky to be alive. Both of them are."

Piper perked up at this news. "Does that mean that Wyatt will go home soon, too?"

The doctor frowned. "Wyatt's condition is much more serious."

"What does that mean?" Piper didn't appreciate his cryptic tone.

"I'm afraid I can't say much about his medical condition, but I assure you he is being well taken care of."

That answer was wholly unsatisfying. It killed her he was in the same building, but she couldn't see him.

"Thank you, Doctor." Her mom took Piper's hand and patted it in between hers. "I've already set up an appointment with a plastic surgeon back home to see what they can do to make your scar less noticeable. So don't worry about that."

Piper touched the puckered mark on her forehead, feeling protective of her battle wound. It was a reminder of what she'd been through—what she'd overcome.

A different nurse bustled in and announced that visiting hours were over while she changed the bag for Piper's IV drip again. Whatever was in it made Piper driftless, like she was floating outside of her body, but it wasn't enough to shake her deep worry. Rationally she knew that the hospital was the best place for Wyatt to receive the care he needed, but she couldn't shake the image of him lying unconscious in the sand.

Through a haze, she said goodbye to her tearful parents, exchanging a flurry of "I love yous."

Then she was alone once again.

ALLIE BURST INTO tears the second she walked into Piper's room the next morning. "Oh my gosh, it's really you. You're alive!"

"Come here and hug me," Piper commanded.

Allie threw herself into Piper's arms, her face blotchy from crying. Piper reciprocated the embrace with equal intensity.

"How are you?" Allie asked, still squeezing her. "That's a stupid question, but I don't know the proper etiquette to greet your best friend who's been cosplaying Brooke Shields in *Blue Lagoon* for seven days."

Piper chuckled. "Fair enough. I'm dehydrated, a little sunburned, and a lot banged up, but otherwise great."

"I've been worried sick about you. I haven't slept. You can't imagine how grateful I am that you're in front of me. That you made it home!"

Piper pulled Allie in even tighter. "You and me both."

Allie released her and sat up, taking one of Piper's hands in her own, her expression somber. Piper's stomach churned. Did she have bad news about Wyatt's condition?

"Piper, I'm so, so sorry. If I hadn't insisted that you get on that plane with Wyatt, you never would've crashed. I can't imagine how scary that must have been. Please know how sorry I am; I will spend the rest of my life making up for it."

Piper suppressed her grin. She'd missed Allie's over-the-top theatrics. "Stop it. I would have done anything to get to your wedding, and I hate that I missed it."

Allie nodded. "I hate that, too. I almost didn't go through with it. I had no second thoughts about marrying Oliver, but I couldn't imagine standing up there without you by my side. I didn't want that to be the memory of my wedding day."

"I'm glad you did it, even if it was hard. I would feel even worse if this whole disaster ruined your wedding."

"Everyone kept telling me that. That you'd want me to do it, but I didn't want to without you. It was awful." Allie paused, shaking off the dark memory. "Oliver was so understanding, though. He left the decision up to me, and in the end, I cried through the entire ceremony. Our photos are a complete disaster, but now he's stuck with me."

"He's a lucky man. I can't wait to see these photos."

"I'll make it up to him one of these days."

"I'm sure you will." Piper wiggled her eyebrows at Allie, who punched her arm lightly.

"I called and left you a voicemail before I walked down the aisle." Allie hugged a pillow to her lap. "Gave a play-by-play of the day's events to your voicemail like a crazy person, but it helped a little. Let me believe you would call me back as soon as you could." Her voice broke on the last word.

"Oh, Allie." Piper squeezed her friend's hand.

"Ugh, I promised myself we wouldn't cry." Allie wiped a tear off her face. "We should be celebrating. Oliver and I have already decided we're having a big anniversary party next year so we can properly celebrate with you. And redo the photos."

"As long as no planes or beaches are involved, I'm in." Piper grinned through watery eyes.

"I promise. We'll serve all your and Wyatt's favorite foods. You two will be the guests of honor." She frowned. "Unless you still hate him with a fiery passion?"

Hearing Wyatt's name made her stomach lurch. "For the record, I never *hated* Wyatt. I was just hurt by him."

"Hmm, I recall you making us buy a voodoo doll to inflict pain and suffering on him during our trip to New Orleans less than two years ago."

"Oh, God!" Piper covered her face with her hands. "I'd forgotten about that. That was petty of me. Looks like karma came back to bite me, huh?"

"I don't know." Allie pursed her lips. "I think it's pretty good karma that you both survived, so you must be doing something right."

"Speaking of, have you seen him yet? They won't give me any details on his condition, and it's driving me crazy." Piper couldn't hide her angst.

Allie nodded. "I just came from his room. You're the medical expert, not me, but from what I can gather, he was in full septic shock when he arrived at the hospital, and it took a while to get under control. The doctors said he likely wouldn't have made it if he hadn't gotten treatment when he did."

Piper shuddered. "But they think he'll pull through, right?" Wyatt not making it was intolerable. He had to be okay.

"That's what they're telling us. He had a rough day yesterday, but he's healing fast and through the worst of it. They have him on enough medication to tranquilize a horse, but they moved him out of intensive care. And if all goes well, he'll come to Cedar Falls in a few days and stay with my mom until he's one hundred percent better."

Piper let out a long breath. Thank God Wyatt was going to be okay. A tear leaked down her face, followed by another.

Allie tugged her close for another hug. "He's going to be fine, don't cry. Wyatt's a tough cookie. You know that."

"I know." Piper brushed her tears away. "But seeing him so sick and lifeless was one of the worst moments of my life. I've never been more scared."

Allie sucked in her cheeks. "I can't imagine. He's lucky you were there. You saved him."

"We saved each other." The corner of Piper's mouth tilted upward in a half smile.

"So, does this mean you and Wyatt are friends again?" Allie asked, one eyebrow cocked. "Can we go back to the way it used to be?"

"I'm not sure if we'll ever be able to go back to the good old days, but yeah, we're friends again."

Allie sat back and scrutinized Piper. "Friends or something more?"

Piper covered her eyes with a hand, avoiding Allie's penetrating gaze, but couldn't stop the hot flush from crawling up her neck and face.

"I knew it! Something happened on the island, didn't it?" She pried Piper's hand off her eyes. "Tell me!"

"Maybe there was a moment between us," Piper relented, giving in like an overplayed Jenga tower. "But being on the island was like being in an alternate universe where only the two of us existed, and we didn't know if we would make it back home. It's like it doesn't count toward real life, you know?"

Allie studied her. "Do you want it to count?"

Piper's stomach dropped like a free-falling elevator at the question. Her immediate instinct was yes, which terrified her. She raised one shoulder. "I'm scared to want anything with Wyatt."

A tight knot formed in her stomach from expressing her worst fear.

"Before you count him out completely, maybe give him a chance."

Piper threw Allie a side-eyed glare. "Why are you suddenly Team Wyatt? He dropped out of your life, too, remember?"

"I will always and forever be a loyal Team Piper member." Allie raised her hands in defense. "You know that. But I also know that Wyatt hasn't had the easiest of paths in life. I know he regrets how he left things with you—with all of us. Plus, he's family, and I love him like a brother, even if I've wanted to strangle him more than hug him these past few years." Allie patted Piper's knee. "There's nothing like almost losing someone to make you realize how much they matter to you and how the past isn't nearly as important as the present."

Piper nodded. "You're right." She knew that feeling all too well. "Now, enough Wyatt talk. Let me tell you how your bridesmaid dress may have saved our lives."

Chapter Thirty-Three

Now

For all the good that came with being rescued—a soft bed, a hot shower, something to eat other than papaya and seaweed—Piper would give it all back to be sitting beside Wyatt on their beach again. Okay, maybe not all of it, but being apart from Wyatt after spending so much time together left her feeling like a ship at sea, adrift and directionless.

Her doctor had promised a morning discharge, so Piper's eyes snapped open the second a ray of sunlight lasered through her blinds. After shooing her parents back to their hotel room last night, insisting they get some proper sleep before making the long drive home to Cedar Falls, North Carolina, Piper woke to an empty room. She'd agreed to stay with them for the rest of the summer, giving her enough time to fully recover per doctor's orders. Flying home would have been the faster option but Piper couldn't stomach the thought of getting on a plane anytime soon, so her parents had rented a car for the trip.

Was Wyatt waking up alone as well? He'd been on her mind constantly, as persistent as the machines humming in her room. She was determined not to leave the hospital without seeing him or confirming that he was truly all right. She needed to replace the last memory of medics loading him onto an emergency flight, his body drained of life. Needed to touch him again, feel his heart pulsing in his chest. This was her chance to check on him—before visiting hours started and the hospital came to life.

Piper cinched her hospital gown and tiptoed into the hallway to find Wyatt's room. How big could this hospital be?

"Miss Piper, you should be in bed, not wandering the halls at this hour." Layla, Piper's favorite nurse, appeared out of nowhere and kindly scolded her.

"I'm looking for Wyatt Brooks's room. Have they moved him to this floor? I need to see him."

Soft crinkles formed by Layla's eyes, a smile lighting her face. Everyone at the hospital, maybe even in America, knew their miraculous survival story. "He's not supposed to have guests until nine A.M., but if someone happened to wander into room 4004, they might find him. You didn't hear it from me, though."

"How is he? Really. Everyone keeps telling me he will be fine, but he was so out of it when—" Piper's voice broke, preventing her last words from escaping.

"His body's been through a lot, but he's already doing much better," Layla assured her. "Now, I better see you in your room when I come by in an hour."

"Yes, ma'am. Thank you!" Piper hurried down the hall before Layla could change her mind.

Finding his room a few doors down, Piper tiptoed in, easing the door shut behind her. Wyatt was asleep, wires snaking from his body to machines monitoring his vitals. Thick bandages covered his left leg, his cheekbones protruded too prominently, and a deep maroon darkened the smudges under his eyes.

But he was alive.

Piper sagged with relief against the door, her anxiety easing with every rise and fall of his breath. She slipped into the chair beside his bed. Up close, his beard was thick, his hair still shaggy and mussed. He looked like the teenage version of Wyatt—the one Piper had unflinchingly given her heart to—superimposed on top of Island Wyatt, the man who'd kept her alive and earned her trust back. Now Hospital Wyatt lay in front of her, a miracle to be alive at all. All versions of him crashed together like a Russian doll, each one swallowed by the next.

In that instant, Piper knew she loved them all.

Almost losing Wyatt for good had been far worse than the pain of high school heartbreak. It made risking her heart again more bearable—especially compared to the alternative of never seeing Wyatt again. Somehow, after all these years, they'd been pulled back to each other, and Piper wasn't willing or ready for the universe to push them apart again.

As if he sensed her presence, Wyatt turned his head in her direction, curls falling across his face. Piper brushed the tendrils away, then cupped his cheek like she'd done the last time she'd seen him. His skin was cool to the touch, a vast difference from his previous burning flesh, the realization giving her lungs more room to breathe.

"Piper?" Wyatt asked, his voice hoarse.

Was he awake? His eyes were closed. Maybe another nightmare held him in its grip. She leaned forward and whispered into his ear. "It's me. It's Piper. We got off the island, Wy. We did it."

She slid her hand onto his chest, over his heart, feeling the dependable heartbeat there. His hand covered hers, holding it captive. His eyelashes fluttered open, and his luminous gray eyes found hers. Piper clasped his hand in hers, her chest tight and breathless, leaning into the flow of heightened energy coursing through her.

She'd missed this, missed him.

Everything she wanted to say caught in her throat and poured out as tears instead.

"Piper," Wyatt rasped, then tugged her hand upward, pulling her against him, crushing her to his chest with his free arm. Careful not to disturb his bad leg, she climbed onto the tiny hospital bed and curved against him, mindful of the attached wires. All her fear and worry melted away as she breathed in his warm, clean scent. He kissed the top of her head, cradling her against his chest. His arms couldn't wrap around her tight enough.

"I feel like I haven't been able to breathe until right now. Now that you're here." He exhaled loudly. "I can't believe you're here. That we made it home."

She twined her arms around his neck, pulling herself as close to him as possible, savoring the thrill of hearing his heart beating a little too fast under her ear. It was proof that he was alive. That they'd made it. It hadn't felt real for her either until right now, now that they were together.

"I know exactly what you mean," she murmured into his neck.

Tears spilled down Wyatt's face, dampening her cheek, and she kissed one away without thinking twice. He turned, his mouth poised over hers. Goose bumps rippled across her body, and she lifted her face and met his. The salt of their tears mingled as his lips brushed hers, reminding her of the briny ocean and sea air—of where they'd been and what they'd gone through together.

His kiss was slow and deliberate, achingly sweet.

A reunion.

A homecoming.

A thank-you to the universe that they could experience this moment together.

Once their lips connected, Piper knew it would take a team of doctors to pull her away. His tongue skated over hers, languid and soft, as if he were reminding himself what she tasted like, slowly wading back in. But before long, she deepened the kiss, his mouth locked on hers, hot and furious, drinking her in like he couldn't get enough.

The intensity made the room spin, and she clung to Wyatt, melting into his arms, tangling her tongue against his, grabbing fistfuls of his hair. Only the crescendo of the surrounding machines caused them to pull back.

"Damn machines are making it very hard to play it cool right now," Wyatt complained. "We should take it easy unless we want them sending me back to the ICU."

Piper giggled. God, it felt good laughing with Wyatt. "Good thing I already know how uncool you are," she teased.

But she didn't need a team of doctors rushing in either, so she kissed him one more time before forcing herself to put a few inches of space between them. Luckily, the tiny bed didn't allow for much more distance.

She pushed his hair back and studied him. "How are you? You look much better than the last time I saw you."

"I feel much better, too. You look great." He brushed his thumb over her scar, and Piper tensed. Was it as awful looking as her mother had suggested? "We've got matching battle scars." Wyatt grinned. "But mine is way more badass."

Piper beamed back. "I'll let you have that one, but only because you almost died on me." Joking about that awful moment with Wyatt made processing the trauma easier and helped put it in the past.

"Speaking of, they told me you climbed up the cliffside and flagged down rescue." Wyatt lifted one of her scarred hands and kissed her bandaged palm. "You saved us. You're my hero."

"We saved each other." Her heart thundered as she lay ensnared in the gaze of his sexy gray eyes. Eyes that she had thought she might never see again. "But I'm still mad at you."

Wyatt frowned. "Still? I thought you'd forgiven me for ghosting you and acting like an idiot after the plane fiasco."

"No, not that." Piper shifted herself upright, tucking her legs under her chin. "You lied to me—about your cut. You told me it was fine and wouldn't let me look at your bandages because you knew it had gotten worse."

Wyatt leaned back against his pillows. "And what would you have done if you'd known the truth?"

"I don't know. Something! I do have a few years of medical training under my belt. Maybe I could have stopped it from getting as bad as it did if you'd let me in instead of shutting me out."

Angry tears sprang to her eyes. She'd been mostly kidding when she'd said she was still mad, but the words had unleashed true resentment toward Wyatt over his brush with death. Probably because it was becoming more apparent with every passing moment exactly how much she loved him.

"I didn't want you to worry." His mouth twisted to one side, and his eyes dampened with regret.

Piper wiped tears off her cheek with the back of her hand. "When are you going to get it through your head, you don't have to go through everything alone. I'm here. For the good parts and the bad. All of it."

She gripped his arm, emphasizing her point. "Wyatt, when I think about what could have happened if a plane hadn't been flying nearby or if I'd fallen climbing up those rocks. Or if we hadn't gotten to the hospital in time." She shuddered.

"I'm sorry I scared you. And I'm sorry I'm a slow learner. I promise I'm working on it." He reached for her hands, lacing his fingers through hers, pushing their palms together. "Can we blame the fever and call this a fresh start? I promise I won't keep any more secrets from you."

She searched his face and saw only sincerity shining back. "A fresh start sounds perfect."

He flashed his dimples in a patented Wyatt smile, making her stomach contract and heart sing. Using his hands as leverage, she lowered herself for a kiss. He squeezed her hands tight and kissed her back thoroughly enough to make the machines beep in protest again. She couldn't wait until they were out of this hospital and in a proper bed.

Reluctantly, Piper pushed herself back up, away from Wyatt's tempting mouth. He looked out the hospital window, running a hand along his scruffy jaw as if collecting his thoughts. When he turned back to her, his brows were knit, his eyes serious.

After a few steadying breaths, he took her hand again. "Piper, everything that happened on the island meant something to me. Well, not the parts where I was scared and tired and harsh, but the parts where I got to spend time with my best friend. To laugh with you, hold you again . . . kiss you." A blush darkened his cheeks. "I'm so damn grateful we made it off that island, but it will all be for nothing if I don't ask you for a second chance." A tear escaped down his face, and he smiled at her shakily. "For real this time."

Piper sucked in a breath, light-headed with how fast her heart raced, grateful she wasn't hooked up to any hospital machines herself right now. Otherwise, they would've given away her pure elation coupled with the crushing fear of getting hurt again—two trains racing toward each other on the same track.

She gnawed on the inside of her cheek. "I want that, Wyatt. It's all I've been thinking about . . . but I'm scared."

Wyatt tightened his hold on her hand, his thumb tracing comforting circles over her knuckles. "I understand that. Believe me, I'm terrified, too. But I'm even more afraid of not telling you how much I care about you. Because I do, Piper. I've always loved you. And I'm in love with you now. I'm sorry for all the years I wasted doubting myself, doubting us." His eyes glittered with unshed tears, pools of sincere love and admiration.

He loved her. He always had. As she listened to his words, Piper's eyes filled with hot tears mirroring Wyatt's. His confession was everything she'd ever wanted to hear. Now it was her turn to let him know she loved him, too, that she'd never stopped.

"I—" She swallowed hard. Old fears squashed the words like a bug in her throat. "Wyatt, you're—" she tried again, but a loud rapping on the door interrupted her.

Chapter Thirty-Four

Now

B arbara, Piper's mother, bustled into the room as if she owned the hospital, overdressed in a lavender sundress and gold slingbacks.

"Piper, there you are! You know, disappearing from your hospital room after a week missing is not a nice trick to play on your dear old mom."

Layla trailed behind Barbara rolling a wheelchair and offered Piper an apologetic smile. So much for the strict visiting hours. Piper lurched away from Wyatt so fast it gave her whiplash, an old force of habit. Was it obvious they'd been making out? And if so, why did she care so much if her mom knew that?

As gracefully as possible, she slipped into the chair by Wyatt's bed and smoothed her hair around her face, strategically covering her scar. Barbara's lips pinched together, but she said nothing about Piper's flushed face or Wyatt's rumpled bedsheets.

"I didn't disappear. Layla knew where I was." Piper winced in Layla's direction. She hadn't meant to throw the nurse under the bus, but she felt like a teenager caught sneaking out of the house and didn't want to be grounded. "I wanted to see Wyatt before we left."

Barbara nodded at Wyatt like she was making his acquaintance for the first time. "Wyatt, it's good seeing you awake. I ran into Molly downstairs in the coffee shop, and she said you're doing well?"

"That's what they tell me," he said politely, but his eyes were as hard as concrete. "I'm stuck here for another day or two, though."

She nodded. "Dr. Adams and I wish you a speedy recovery, and I told Molly I'd drop off a casserole when you get home. I assume you'll be staying with her for a few days once you get back on your feet?"

Why was her mom being so dismissive of Wyatt? She probably blamed him for the plane crash, for scarring her only daughter's perfect face.

"Yes, ma'am, and thank you," Wyatt confirmed.

Barbara turned her attention back to Piper. "Piper, you're officially discharged. Are you ready to go home?"

That question had never been more loaded. There was nowhere Piper would rather be than nestled back at her childhood home—except in Wyatt's hospital bed with him right now.

"Yeah, home sounds great, but can I meet you out front? Wyatt and I were in the middle of a conversation." Possibly the most important conversation of her life.

Barbara lifted one perfectly groomed eyebrow. "Honey, your father's already gone to get the car. We should leave now to make it home before dark."

Piper glanced at the clock on the wall. There was plenty of time to make the eight-hour drive during daylight. "What's the rush? Can't we wait a few more minutes?"

Her mom sighed. "You know your father gets cranky when he has to wait. And I'm planning a special dinner for you tomorrow night, so I need to get back to prepare for it." Food was her mother's answer to everything.

"I don't need anything fancy, Mom."

"This was going to be a surprise, but you know I'm terrible at keeping secrets. Tag and his parents are flying in tomorrow to visit, so it's only polite that we host them with a nice meal. You know he's been so worried about you." She turned to Layla, who stood in the doorway. "Tag is Piper's boyfriend," she explained. "They're both studying to be doctors. Isn't that the sweetest thing?"

Next to her, Wyatt stiffened, his hands clenched into fists. The vein in Piper's head throbbed. So that explained her mother's bad attitude. She still had her heart set on the possibility of Piper becoming a Sinclair one day.

"Mom, Tag and I—" Piper began explaining that Tag wasn't her boyfriend, that Wyatt was the one she wanted sitting at her family's dining room table, but her mother chattered on like she hadn't heard her.

"Oh, that reminds me. I already booked us mani-pedis tomorrow morning." Barbara looked Piper up and down. "Maybe we'll make a whole spa day of it. Get a haircut, too. So, like I said, we need to be on our way." She snapped her fingers at Layla like she was a bellhop, gesturing for her to push the wheelchair toward Piper.

"Mom," she tried again. "I just need five minutes."

Her mother's bullying tactics may have worked on her once, but Piper refused to be railroaded anymore. Not after everything she'd endured.

Barbara huffed and crossed her arms, not backing down. "Piper, please. Your father and I haven't slept in days. I'm worried about his health and I'm desperate to change into clothes that don't smell like a hospital."

Exhaustion darkened Piper's mind like a shadow, sweeping over her. She'd been prepared to stand up to her mother but hadn't braced for a guilt trip. Fresh remorse over the agony her parents must have experienced in her absence colored her mood and made the prospect of picking a fight untenable.

"It's okay, Piper." Wyatt interrupted her inner turmoil in a flat monotone that was far from reassuring. "You should go." His eyes glittered dark and dangerous.

Piper froze in place, like a butterfly pinned under a glass frame. She wanted to stay. Wanted to kick her mom out of the room and tell Wyatt the depth of her feelings for him. But her head hurt, and her stomach churned with unease. Maybe she wasn't in the best shape to have this serious conversation with Wyatt, anyway. Waiting would be better. Or maybe she was still too much of a coward to defend what she wanted.

Piper faced Wyatt, willing him to read her facial expression, understand that Tag meant nothing to her, and see she wasn't ready to say goodbye and leave this hospital room. To recognize her deep love for him etched on her face, but Wyatt fixed his stare on the door, his jaw clenched shut.

She curled her fingers around his wrist and squeezed. "I'll call you when I can and see you soon. Promise."

His gaze flashed down at her fingers braceleted around his arm, his hand still locked into a fist, but he said nothing.

She and Wyatt had waited years to be together—they could wait a few more days, right? She would see him in person soon, when he returned to Cedar Falls, where she'd be waiting for him, and they would start their next adventures together then. It would all be okay.

It had to be.

Barbara cleared her throat, and Piper grudgingly let Layla help her into the wheelchair. She looked back at Wyatt as Layla rolled her from the room, but he'd already closed his eyes.

PIPER SLEPT MOST of the eight-hour drive home, partly because sleep had evaded her for days but mostly because she wasn't ready to answer a million questions about her time on the island. Plus, Wyatt's love bomb still had her reeling, along with sweeping shame over chickening out about sharing her own feelings. She soothed her shame spiral by imagining everything she would say to Wyatt as soon as they could talk. Because now that they'd made it home in one piece, time had to be on their side. Right?

She'd expected to luxuriate in her bed, but now, hours after coming home, the pinching ache of missing Wyatt kept her wide awake. She missed the curve of his body around hers, how his eyes glinted silver when he looked at her, and his ability to make her smile, even in the worst situations. Thinking about him made every inch of her skin tingle—alert and pulsating like a drug addict undergoing detox.

The long, restless night left her ill-prepared to deal with the force that was her mother on a mission. The second Piper appeared in the kitchen, still wiping sleep from her eyes, her mom pounced.

Barbara wore an apron with French hens in chef hats and a manic smile that suggested she'd already had more than three cups of coffee.

"Piper, you're awake! Come sit. I made all your favorites." She loaded up a plate with eggs, bacon, grits, and a stack of pancakes and set it in front of Piper.

Her dad sat at the table, a medical journal open beside him. They both watched as Piper took a small bite of the scrambled eggs.

"How is everything? Do you need me to reheat anything?" her mom asked.

Piper savored the buttery taste of eggs. "No, it's great. Best thing I've had to eat in days." She'd meant it as a joke, but her mom blanched.

"Aren't you guys going to eat breakfast, too?" Piper frowned at their empty place mats.

"Oh, we already ate." Tears misted her dad's eyes. "We've been up for a while. It was hard to sleep last night knowing you would be here when we woke up."

"It's better than Christmas morning." Her mom dabbed the

corners of her eyes with a napkin. She squeezed Piper's arm, then, as if that contact wasn't enough for her, stood and wrapped her arms around Piper's shoulders. Her dad jumped up and joined the family hug.

Gratitude that she could even hug her parents again filled her soul, but everything about this moment was surreal. How many times had she eaten breakfast at this table? Only now, it was a brand-new experience that cast Piper as a stranger in her own home. Like walking into class on the first day of school when you know you belong but don't yet know everyone's name or where to sit. She struggled to articulate the overwhelming feeling of being present physically while her mind remained trapped in survival mode. So she remained quiet and hugged them back. A deep rumble in her stomach saved her from having to speak.

"My goodness, we're stopping you from eating your first real meal!" Her mom sat back down, aghast.

"We stopped at Subway on the way home," Piper reminded her.

Barbara wrinkled her nose. "Like I said, your first real meal."

Piper took a bite of pancakes, the sweet syrup bathing her tongue. Her parents continued watching her like she was the season finale of their favorite TV show, so she followed up the pancake with a bite of everything else on her plate until the hungry rumbling in her stomach became a distant memory.

"The Sinclair family will be here around five o'clock, and dinner's at six," her mom said, getting down to business. "I know you only have clothes from high school here, but don't worry, I already placed a Nordstrom order for some more options, including some dresses for tonight, and new makeup, that we can pick up on our way home from the nail salon."

Piper's stomach flipped like the pancakes she'd just consumed. She'd forgotten about Tag's impending arrival, probably because readjusting to reality had completely preoccupied her mind.

"Mom, Tag and I aren't in a serious relationship. We've been on a few dates, that's it. Don't you think it's kind of weird that he's flying down here?"

Her mom waved her concern away like a puff of smoke. "Nonsense! The Sinclairs have been family friends of ours for years. And Tag adores you. I know you've been through a lot and are probably still processing, but I think you'll be excited to see him once he arrives. This will be a good thing, you'll see." She scooted her chair back and stood as if the matter were settled. "Now go wash your hands and get changed so we can get you ready for tonight."

Maybe clearing the air with Tag in person would be better, less awkward than a phone call or text, especially if he was already on his way down. Because their parents were so close, he would be in her life one way or another, so she might as well do what she could to salvage a friendship, even if her mother would be disappointed that's all it would ever be. Besides, based on experience, nothing would stop the Barbara locomotive once it was chugging down the tracks.

Chapter Thirty-Five

Now

Tag and his parents, Cindy and Martin, arrived promptly at five, the women complimenting each other on their outfits and the men exchanging hearty handshakes. The hard lump in Piper's stomach had grown since that morning, and now, after greeting Tag with a chaste kiss on the cheek, it swelled like a papaya pit sprouting roots deep in her gut.

Tag fidgeted with the buttons on his shirt collar, not quite meeting her gaze. "You look great," he told her as they moved into the sitting room, where Piper's mom was doling out wine in oversize goblets. "I wasn't sure what to expect after, you know, but you still look like you. How are you doing?"

Piper looked down at her manicured nails, past her Tory Burch dress, to her shiny new heels. Had Tag been expecting a sea monster in her place? She'd let her mother straighten her sun-bleached hair and pick out her outfit, but Piper hardly recognized herself.

She felt like a fraud—Island Piper pretending to be Perfectly Put Together Piper.

"I'm not sure," she answered, even though his question had been the kind where the correct response was saying, "Thank you, I'm doing great," with a smile plastered on her face no matter the truth lurking underneath.

"I guess that's expected, right?" He accepted a glass of wine and downed half in a few noisy gulps.

Piper shrugged, raised her glass, and followed his lead. She was pretty sure there wasn't a precedent for what qualified as normal after being stranded on an island with the former love of your life turned current, but wine seemed like a good starting place.

Before they could get drunk off Kim Crawford Chardonnay, Barbara ushered everyone into the dining room to enjoy her famous pot roast. Piper placed her napkin in her lap, surreptitiously wiping the sweat from her palms. Sitting at the formal dining room table with her parents' wedding china was like returning from vacation and getting behind the car wheel for the first time in a while: foreign and uncomfortable.

"A toast," Barbara said once everyone had settled around the table. She raised her glass. "To the Sinclairs for being so kind to make the trip to see us after this extraordinary situation. And to Piper, my baby girl, we are so, so grateful to have you home with us again. We love you so much."

"Cheers!" Her dad lifted his wineglass in agreement. "We love you, Pipsqueak."

Piper placed her hand over her heart. "I love you guys, too. And I'm so glad to be home."

Everyone clinked their glasses together and dug into the meal.

Maybe this dinner wouldn't be so bad after all. Tag didn't seem as intent on making her his girlfriend as he'd been before, and she loved her mother's pot roast. Relaxing, Piper let the rhythm of small talk and forks scraping on plates wash over her, trying to remember her former social skills.

"Dinner is amazing, Mrs. Adams," Tag said, taking a second helping.

She waved him away. "Please, call me Barbara. We're practically family." She'd never offered Wyatt that same invitation. "You know," she continued, turning to Mrs. Sinclair, her eyes sparkling, "if all goes well between these two, we could have a family full of doctors."

Piper went rigid, her mouth too full of food to set her mom straight. How on earth had she leaped to marriage when Piper had told her things with Tag weren't serious just this morning? It was even crazier considering she'd caught Piper in bed with Wyatt the day before. Or maybe that was exactly why her mother was hyperfocused on sealing the deal with Tag. Wyatt had never been good enough according to her mother's impossible standards.

"We would be delighted to have Piper as a daughter-in-law." Mrs. Sinclair smiled. "And I always thought our Cape Cod home would be the perfect wedding venue."

Piper kicked Tag under the table, prodding him to say something, anything, to stop this madness, but he only shrugged helplessly.

Barbara nodded. "A New England wedding sounds lovely."

The women clinked their glasses together conspiratorially while Piper took a swig of Chardonnay to wash her food down faster. The wine only made her choke, panic rising in her throat. Next to her, Tag sputtered in nervous laughter, or maybe his pot roast had also gone down the wrong way. Piper rubbed her temples, trying to erase the throbbing building behind her eyes.

"Speaking of doctors, I have some good news," her dad announced, oblivious to Piper's distress. "The dean of Emory School of Medicine personally called earlier this morning. She said they're open to working with you, Piper, and supporting you however you need. Whether that's starting late or getting more resources. You should call them and discuss the best next steps whenever you feel up to it."

"Oh, that is such a relief!" Her mom clapped her hands together. "Now you won't waste any more time."

Time. Funny how the meaning of that word had changed entirely. On the island, time had been measured by life-or-death consequences. How long until they ran out of food? Until they were rescued? Now she'd been given the gift of time and the freedom to pursue her dreams. Dedicating the next six years to training for a profession that didn't ignite any passion within her would be an unworthy use of that gift.

"That's great, Dad. Thank you." Piper gritted her teeth, concentrating on making her smile reach her eyes. Anxiety swirled in her stomach, and the pounding in her head increased its tempo.

"Piper, if you decide to do your residency in Boston, you're welcome to stay at our town house up there," Mr. Sinclair offered between forkfuls of green beans.

Her mom smiled. "Oh, that would be perfect. Isn't that perfect, Piper?"

Perfect Piper.

That's who she'd always been.

She'd spent years chasing after a life her parents deemed perfect, but the pressure to live up to someone else's standards had shattered her. Fractured her beyond repair. Her old life no longer fit, like a sweater shrunk in the dryer. There was no going back.

Wyatt's words from the island lit her mind like a billboard: Life is short, and you only get one, so you might as well live it on your terms. A tidal wave had been building inside her all day, and it finally reached its peak, ready to crash back to earth. Piper placed her fork down and closed her eyes, summoning courage through a deep breath. There was no good way to do this, so she dove in headfirst.

"I'm not going back to school this fall."

Silence filled the room, drowning out the lighthearted small talk.

Her parents exchanged a worried glance before her father spoke, his brows furrowed in confusion. "We can discuss the benefits of taking a term off, but I don't think you want to lose any momentum."

"I'm not talking about taking a term off. I'm talking about not finishing medical school," Piper said, her voice growing in conviction. "I gave it a shot; I really did. But I don't care about medicine the way you do, Dad. Your eyes light up when you discuss the latest medical breakthroughs and your patients. Mine glaze over."

The rush of saying the words aloud nearly matched the adrenaline spike from scaling that cliffside days earlier. What had taken her so long to find the courage to share her truth?

Her mom's eyes grew large. Her fork fell onto her plate with a sharp clang. "Piper, this has been your dream since you were a little girl! You can't just throw it away because something bad happened to you."

Piper shook her head. "It may have been my childhood dream, but only because you told me what to dream. It isn't my dream anymore. It hasn't been for a while. And as hard and as scary as it was to crash on that beach, I think it may have been one of the best things to ever happen to me."

"Talk to her, Henry!" Her mom threw her napkin on the table and implored Piper's father. "She's making a huge mistake."

"I don't think I am, Mom, but either way, it's my mistake to make."

Around her, Mr. and Mrs. Sinclair busied themselves clearing their plates while Tag drained his second glass of wine. Ripping off the metaphorical medical school Band-Aid had been deeply satisfying, if not slightly terrifying. Might as well risk it all and set the record straight about Tag, too.

"And speaking of making my own decisions, I told you before, but you weren't listening. Tag and I are not together." Words spilled out of Piper's mouth, unstoppable now that she was on a roll. If she'd known it would feel this good to stand up to her mother, she would have done it years ago. "He's a great guy. Kind, considerate, and smart, but we definitely are *not* getting married. Sorry to burst your Cape Cod wedding visions."

"Piper," her mom hissed. "We'll talk about this after our guests leave. You're being very rude."

Tag stared down at his wineglass as if hoping it would refill itself.

Piper crossed her arms and leaned back in her chair. "How am I being rude? Because I'm not saying or doing what *you* want? We can talk later, but I'm not changing my mind." Her heart pounded so hard under her dress she thought it might propel her right out of the room.

Her mom's nostrils flared. "I think you should excuse yourself from the table." Her voice was scarily calm.

Piper jutted out her chin and met her mother's gaze. "I'd love to."

Scraping her chair away from the table, she wiped her mouth delicately with her napkin and stalked out the back door to the porch, not looking behind to see the destruction left in her wake.

Once outside, she leaned over the porch railing and filled her lungs with fresh air as her heart rate slowed. As the adrenaline drained from her limbs, panic set in. What had she done? She may have almost died in a plane crash, but that wouldn't stop her mom from absolutely murdering her.

Maybe she should hide in the clubhouse.

Or run away.

Sinking onto the porch steps, Piper tilted her head back and let the balmy summer breeze soothe her nerves. She wished Wyatt were here reminding her of her strength—encouraging her to be brave. Then she remembered her mother's actions had indirectly caused her breakup with Wyatt all those years ago, and a new source of determination flooded her veins. For too long, she'd been the perfect daughter, bending over backward to fulfill her parents' expectations. But at what cost? She'd sacrificed her own happiness, stifled her own desires, and lost the love of her life, all in the name of pleasing them.

Even though Piper knew her parents loved her and were only doing what they thought was best, they'd been wrong. They didn't know everything, and they certainly didn't know everything about her, which she had to admit was partially her fault. She'd have to introduce them to the real Piper, the Piper with opinions and dreams of her own, and see what happened. Either way, she was prepared to deal with the consequences. She still cared about her parents' opinions, but no longer enough to sacrifice herself at the altar of their expectations. No one, especially not her mother, would dictate her actions, push her around, or decide what was best for her ever again.

The screen door creaked open behind her. She expected to see her father coming after her, but Tag's stocky frame cast a shadow.

"Did they send you after me?" She squinted up at him.

"I volunteered. I needed a break from the awkward small talk happening inside. Is it okay if I sit with you?"

Piper nodded and scooted over to make space for him on the step. He pulled his meticulously pleated pants up at the thighs and sat beside her.

"Tag, I'm really sorry about all of that." Piper winced. "I didn't mean to drag you into my family mess. That's not how I meant to handle things with us."

He shrugged. "It's okay."

"No, it's not. You didn't deserve that. You've been wonderful to me, and my parents love you."

"But you don't," he stated simply.

She shook her head. "I'm sorry."

"Don't be." A tiny smile graced his face. "We're on the same page, and I had a feeling this was coming. I told my parents you weren't my girlfriend and that coming down here was overkill, but they didn't listen."

"Yeah, I can relate to that." Piper rolled her eyes.

"Does your dinner dumping have anything to do with the guy stranded with you? I heard on CNN that you two were high school sweethearts." He sounded more curious than accusatory.

"Yes and no." Piper blew out her breath. "I think it's more about finally doing what's best for me instead of what others think, but I'll admit that seeing Wyatt again may have pushed me to that conclusion faster."

He nodded in understanding. "I hope everything works out with you two, then."

Tag always knew the right thing to say. His impeccable manners used to put Piper on edge, but now she felt only gratitude for his ability to remain unfailingly polite, even during a breakup.

"I hope so, too," she whispered.

Tag didn't press her for conversation as he twisted his silver watchband back and forth with a soft click, click, click.

"How bad is it in there?" Piper asked after a few minutes.

"Well, I've never seen your mother's face turn that shade of purple, but now she's dishing out dessert like nothing happened."

"That sounds about right."

"Don't worry about it too much. I don't know if you've noticed, but everyone's pretty stoked you're alive. I think you have a free pass right now."

Piper barked out a laugh. "You don't know my mother."

"That's true. She can be a little . . . intense."

"You mean terrifying?"

"You said it, not me." Tag grinned. "I should go. I'm sure my parents are ready to make an escape." He stood, straightening his shirt. "Are you coming in?"

She shook her head. "I'm not quite ready to face my mom's wrath."

"I get it. Then I guess this is goodbye. For now, at least."

Piper rose. "Thanks for coming down here, Tag. And for being a good friend. You're going to make some girl so happy one day." She settled into one last hug before he headed inside.

Twenty minutes later, her dad poked his head out. "The coast is clear, kiddo. I've never seen a group of people eat strawberry shortcake so fast."

"I'm sorry I ruined dinner." Piper followed him into the kitchen. "How upset is Mom?"

"Give your mother some time. She'll come around."

She raised a skeptical eyebrow. "We'll see. Are you mad at me, too?"

"I could never be anything but proud of you, Pipsqueak. Of course, I'd love for you to take on the family business, but all I want is for you to be happy." He crushed her into a hug.

Piper hugged her dad back hard, his acceptance meaning more to her now than ever. At least one of her parents had taken the news well.

"Oh, before I forget. I got you a new phone." He picked up a still shrink-wrapped white box from the counter and handed it to her. "They said once you log in, all of your contacts and anything saved to the cloud, whatever magical place that is, will come back, but if you have any issues, we can go back to the Apple store."

Piper thanked her dad with a kiss on the cheek and rushed up to her room. An eternity had passed since she'd last spoken to Wyatt, and she couldn't wait to hear his voice—and finally confess her love.

Chapter Thirty-Six

Now

Unlike some parents, Piper's had opted to keep her bedroom exactly as it was when she went to college. Pictures from high school dances and football games smiled in frames on her nightstand. Academic awards and her high school diploma hung on display, and her collection of well-loved books filled floor-to-ceiling shelves along an entire wall. Even the stuffed bear she'd had since birth sat jauntily on her bed atop a Carolina blue–striped comforter. Piper had once loved returning to her frozen-in-time haven, but now she felt like a stranger, an out-of-place guest in her home.

Nothing had changed since her last visit home. Except her.

And because of that, everything was different.

She hated upsetting her mom, but Piper couldn't remember the last time she'd felt freer—more excited about her life. Her confession had wiped the slate clean, leaving a blank canvas to rewrite her story. No more awful medical lectures she didn't care about. No more late nights with the cadaver. No more feeling empty on dates with Tag.

Though the small matter of figuring out what to do with the rest of her life terrified her, an immense sense of freedom and joy from no longer being shackled to any obligations dwarfed any fears.

Seven days had changed everything.

As soon as she'd set up her phone, her contacts having imported from the cloud as promised, Piper found Wyatt's name and pressed call with a shaky hand. She'd blocked him ages ago but had kept his number to screen his calls, although she'd never needed to. It had been years since his name had flashed across her phone screen, and seeing it teleported her to the anxious teenage thrill calling him had always elicited.

When the call went straight to voicemail, she followed up with a text, letting him know she was home, had a phone, and would love to talk when he had a chance. She added a heart emoji for extra measure.

Next, she dialed Allie, who picked up right away.

"How are you? How's Wyatt?" Piper asked in a rush.

"Ha! At least you masked your reason for calling by asking about me first. I'm fine, and Wyatt's doing great. Everyone at the hospital is impressed by how quickly he's bounced back. He's coming home tomorrow."

"He is? Oh, thank goodness." Piper let out a breath.

"I'm surprised he didn't tell you himself. He got a phone yesterday," Allie mused. "I'm headed to the airport now to fly home to Cedar Falls, and my mom and Wyatt should fly in tomorrow night."

Piper's heart sank like a stone in water. She'd called Wyatt the second she got her hands on a phone. Why hadn't he done the same? Was it possible he thought she and Tag were actually dating? Or had he changed his mind about her already?

"If you talk to Wyatt, can you tell him to call me?" She hoped her voice didn't sound as distraught as she felt.

"Sure. Hey, let's all get together Tuesday night at Charlie's Diner, okay? Ethan's flying into town that morning, and we're long overdue for a Lonely Only reunion."

Piper enthusiastically agreed and signed off with Allie, already feeling like Tuesday was too far away when in reality, two more days in her parents' air-conditioned home was nothing compared to the long, hot days on the beach. She caught up with Ethan next, solidifying plans and assuring him she was not too sick of the taste of prickly pears to enjoy a margarita with him in the future.

She tried Wyatt again and was about to leave another voicemail when her mom knocked on her door.

"Do you have a minute to talk?" her mom asked, walking into the room.

It wasn't really a question, but Piper nodded, sitting up straighter against her bed's headboard. Her whole body tensed, preparing for a fight.

"I'm worried about you, Piper." Her mom perched on the edge of the bed, clasping her hands in her lap. "I'm not sure who that was at dinner tonight, but it wasn't my daughter. I've never seen you behave that way."

"I'm sorry I ruined dinner, Mom. But I'm not sorry about anything I said." Piper concentrated on keeping her breath even.

Barbara pressed her lips together. "I wonder if you'll feel different after you settle in more. This could all be in response to the trauma you've been through. Understandably, you're confused."

"I won't feel different." Piper shook her head, confident. "And I'm not confused. I have more clarity now than ever about what I want out of life and who I want to spend my time with."

Her mom stared up at a spot on the ceiling. "I still don't understand what happened between you and Tag. You two seemed so perfect together." She looked back at Piper with a deep frown. "I hope you come to your senses before it's too late."

Her mother wasn't even putting herself in Piper's shoes. Exasperation bubbled in Piper's gut before erupting like a volcano. "Mom, enough!" She threw her hands up in the air. "Maybe I don't want perfect. Maybe I want something messy and honest and real."

Her mom shook her head. "I don't think you know what you're saying."

When Piper was growing up, her mother had always had all the right answers, and Piper had been all too willing to follow her lead, but not anymore.

"I know about your conversation with Wyatt." Piper folded her arms tight across her chest and jutted her chin out. "Before he left for boot camp. I know you tried to keep us apart."

"Is that what this is about?" Her mom shook her head with a laugh. "Piper, you were a heartsick teenager about to ruin your life over a boy who—"

"A boy who what?" Piper interrupted, her eyes flashing. "Loved me? Was my best friend?"

"Sweetheart." Her mom grabbed her hand, but Piper pulled it out of her grasp.

Barbara's eyes narrowed. "Say what you want, but I knew that boy would be trouble for you, and I was right. Because of him, you were on a plane that crashed in the middle of nowhere, and we almost lost you!" Her mom's voice broke, but she blinked back tears.

"*That* boy is now a grown man, and he has a name," Piper said through clenched teeth, but she put an arm on her mom's shoulder to comfort her. "Wyatt's one of the best guys I know. He loves me for who I am, and he believes in me. What happened to us was not his fault, and I'm not certain I would have survived without him. Why do you always think the worst of him?"

Her mom took a steadying breath and smoothed her palms along her pants. "I don't think the worst of him. It's never been about Wyatt, but your relationship in high school was way too serious. What kind of mother would I be if I let you throw away college or your career before you even started? I was just trying to protect you."

Piper's nostrils flared. "And now?"

Her mother opened, then closed her mouth.

"I think you're threatened that Wyatt's given me the strength to believe in myself. To follow my own path instead of yours."

"I'm sorry you feel that way." Her mom stood. "I disagree with your decisions, but I don't want to fight with you. I know I'm not always the easiest person to talk to, so I came here to give you this." She pulled a business card out of her back pocket and handed it to Piper.

Piper plucked the card from her mother's grasp like it was an explosive. It read DR. LINDA BARRETT, LICENSED COUNSELOR. She arched an eyebrow at her mom.

"Several of the ladies in Junior League recommend her. She's supposed to be the best for this sort of thing."

Piper wasn't sure if "this sort of thing" referred to surviving a traumatic event or rebelling against your mother, but she wasn't opposed to talking to a therapist. There were many ways doing so would help her process everything she'd been through, but she knew with absolute certainty that she was making the right choices for herself.

Finally.

"I'll set up an appointment." Piper extended the tiniest of olive branches to her mom.

Her mom paused on her way out and looked over her shoulder. "Piper, you're my whole life. Everything I do is because I want the best for you."

Piper sighed but resisted the guilt trip. "I know, Mom, but it's time for me to decide what's best now."

Her mom nodded, her brow still furrowed, and closed the door to Piper's room behind her.

Though there'd been no real winner in the conversation, Piper felt victorious, bulletproof. Superman standing on railroad tracks, unflinching, while a silver train barreled toward him.

She'd been polite and hadn't let her emotions get the best of her while standing her ground.

Her mother no longer intimidated her. Perhaps, for the first time, Piper saw her mother as she truly was—an imperfect person just trying her best. Taking her mom down from the pedestal Piper had placed her on years ago relieved some of the pressure she'd put on herself to live up to Barbara's high standards. With some distance, Piper recognized her mother's opinions were just that—her own. Piper didn't need to take them on anymore.

To distract herself from overthinking their conversation, Piper paced the length of her bedroom, inspecting old photos and trailing her fingers over the worn spines of her childhood book collection. She pulled out her well-loved copy of *The Return of the Queen* and breathed in the comforting musty scent. She'd missed this—being surrounded by the fictional worlds she'd spent so much of her childhood exploring.

From atop her collection of special-edition Narnia books, she picked up the tattered notebook she used to meticulously track which books she'd lent to friends (mostly Wyatt at a certain point), when they'd been "checked out," and when they'd been returned. Opening it up, she frowned at the last entry. According to her notes, Wyatt still had her copy of *The Silver Battle*.

Flipping through the worn pages, she ran a finger over the pen indentations that detailed the long-running relationship between her and Wyatt and their mutual love of fantasy stories. Pages and pages of shared adventures, hours spent discussing the nuances of world building and arguing over their favorite characters. She hoped their own story wasn't over yet.

Something slipped from the pages and bounced off her foot. Her old Cedar Falls library card. Picking it up, Piper smoothed her thumb over the worn piece of plastic that had once been her most prized possession. Her gateway to adventure. Did library cards expire? Moving to the bed and propping herself up against the headboard, she pulled out her phone and scrolled to the library's website. Using the digits on the back of her library card, she logged in and found her account still active, with a detailed history of books she'd checked out over the years.

An event announcement popped up for a retirement celebration for her favorite librarian. She clicked the link. In the large photo at the top, Mrs. Koh still had the same kind eyes and salt-and-pepper hair Piper remembered. She scanned the page, smiling at the flood of memories coming back to her.

After 40 years of exceptional service, it's time to bid farewell to our esteemed Library Director, Mrs. Koh! Please join us for a special retirement celebration to honor her remarkable career. Mrs. Koh earned both a B.A. in Communications and her Master of Library Science from the University of North Carolina, and has been the guiding light of our library, bringing knowledge, passion, and dedication to every aspect of her work.

Piper knew that librarians weren't volunteers, but she'd never given much thought to what actually went into becoming one. Opening a new browser, she searched "How to become a librarian," an idea taking shape in her mind. In her soul. Her research quickly revealed that an ALA-accredited master's in library science was the essential requirement. When she opened a new tab to explore options, the program at the University of Denver popped up first.

Piper tapped further, taking in pictures of a welcoming campus with redbrick buildings and lush green trees, and before she knew it, she'd fallen down a rabbit hole reading course descriptions for their master's in library and information science degree. The two-year program was no joke, including classes such as

Cataloging & Classification and Information Literacy, but every description she read resonated with her so much she felt foolish for not having contemplated this career path earlier. It made such complete sense. Like the answer had been there all along, but she'd been blind to it.

Was she really even considering this? Did she even want to go back to school again? To study information technology and organization? So she could sit in a library all day and help patrons discover their new favorite author?

Yes. Yes, she did.

The answer erupted from deep within her like a volcano, flowing freely. Not because she felt obligated to please someone else, but because something inside her resonated with the idea. Or at least, resonated enough to want to explore the possibility. She may not be ready to dive headfirst into a totally new career, but for the first time in ages, she felt a spark of excitement when thinking about what the future might bring.

As clear as glass, she could picture herself going to school in Denver, studying at the library, then coming home to Wyatt in the evenings, cooking meals together, walking his dog, and drinking wine on the porch under the stars. The more she envisioned the possibility of that life, the more she wanted it.

Now she just needed Wyatt to call her back.

Chapter Thirty-Seven

Now

Adjusting to her regular life came in fits and starts. Although Piper's sunburn had faded, fireworks of freckles still covered her nose and cheeks. Her scar glowed pink, a constant reminder of her brush with death. Sometimes Piper felt like she'd never left her childhood home, and other times the claustrophobia of four walls forced her to run outside and gasp in breath after breath of sunshine and summer air until her heartbeat returned to its normal rhythm. She yearned for the sound of the waves at night and the salty scent that had lingered for days in her hair, now rinsed clean.

Adding to Piper's recovery roller coaster was the fact that the one person who might understand this specific brand of anxiety was giving her the silent treatment. Over the past few days, she'd reached out to Wyatt enough times to have her committed, but she was past the point of playing it cool. She'd even marched over to the McLaughlins' house the day he'd returned, only to be told by a sympathetic Molly that he was sleeping.

But what frustrated her most was how much she missed him. He played in her mind like an always-on radio, a constant buzz, alternating stations between missing and worrying about him— and wondering if he was thinking about her. Puzzling over why he'd shut her out. Not hearing from him reminded her of those dark days after he'd coldly closed the door on their love. Even knowing now why he'd behaved that way as a teenager, his current silence made her uneasy. Piper felt like she was climbing a ladder whose rungs kept breaking beneath her feet.

Had he meant it in that hospital room when he told her he loved her? That felt like a million years ago now instead of mere days. Maybe it had been the painkillers talking, and now that he was on the mend and back to reality, he no longer felt the same way. She tried to rein in her restless, galloping thoughts, but they'd already run away like a Chincoteague pony. She needed to see his face, look into his eyes, and know if his love burned bright or if the ocean had swallowed it like it had their Yeti.

By Tuesday, the day of their Lonely Onlys reunion, Piper's whole body was strung taut with nerves. Her desperation to see Wyatt, talk to him, and hug him once more left her jittery. But instead of Wyatt's dark curls, it was Ethan's shock of blond hair Piper spotted when she pulled her dad's Buick into the Charlie's Diner parking lot.

Ethan didn't wait for her to get out of the car. Striding over, he opened her door and yanked her out into one of his signature bear hugs.

"I can't believe you're here!" Piper cried into his ear.

"I can't believe *you're* here and not fish food." Ethan pulled back to look her up and down, then squeezed her again.

Allie bounded over from the other side of the parking lot and piled into the hug. "We've been way overdue for a Piper sandwich."

"Is Wyatt coming?" Ethan asked when they pulled apart.

"I haven't heard from him." Piper heard the slight catch in her voice but hoped the others hadn't.

Allie shot a glance at Piper, her face drawn in concern. "Wyatt told me he needed to take care of a few things and couldn't make it, but I'm sure we can talk him into something another time."

This casual rejection stung more than Piper expected, but she collected herself with a few deep breaths, not wanting her increasingly bad mood over Wyatt's absence to darken the joy of this reunion with her friends.

Ethan shrugged. Not much could dull his sunshine. "More fries for us. Wyatt's missing out! Come on, let's go eat."

The threesome settled into their favorite corner booth and studied the oversize menu, even though it hadn't changed in years. Everything listed made Piper's mouth water.

Once they'd ordered more food than was reasonable for one meal, Ethan focused on Piper. "So, quick life update: I got a job promotion, and things with Jack are going great. You'll have to meet him sometime soon. He reminds me of you."

"I can't wait." Piper grinned. Seeing her friends in love was the best feeling in the world.

"And Allie got married," Ethan continued, "so what I want to know is, what's new with you, Piper? I've missed you! Fill us in on your life."

"Oh, I'm sorry. Surviving a plane crash wasn't enough to keep you interested?" Piper laughed. The amount of change in her world these past few weeks was dizzying. "Hmm, where do I begin? I basically blew up my life. I officially broke up with Tag even though we were never together. And quit med school, too."

"What?" Allie gasped. "Piper, that's huge! How did your parents take the news?"

"My dad was cool, but my mom is teetering on the brink of a full nervous breakdown."

Allie cringed and patted Piper's arm. "I'm proud of you. I know that couldn't have been easy."

Their food arrived: plate after plate of French fries, burgers, mozzarella sticks that smelled like heaven, and large frothy glasses of Coca-Cola.

Ethan pulled a plate of greasy fries to him. "Wasn't Tag the hot doctor? What went wrong there?"

"Nothing went wrong. Tag's great. It's just that—" Piper bit her lip. She lowered her voice to a whisper. "He's not Wyatt." She shielded her face with her hands, elbows still on the table, waiting for the inevitable response from her friends.

Ethan whipped his head up, almost choking on a fry. "Wait, wait, wait. Are you telling me there's a chance for Wiper to get back together? I shipped you guys so hard back in high school."

Piper groaned into her hands, then looked at her friends. "I don't know. I think I may have messed it up somehow. He's not answering any of my calls. And now I'm not sure if it's such a good idea for us to get back together. You remember how bad our breakup was." She curled her lip. "What's that saying, 'Fool me once, shame on you, fool me twice, shame on me'? I don't know if my heart can take a breakup round two."

Ethan pouted and pushed the mozzarella sticks in her direction.

"Speak of the devil," Allie said in a stage whisper.

Piper whirled around, expecting to see Wyatt walking through the door, but Kiera Gomez entered and stood by the front counter, waiting for a to-go order. She didn't look as intimidating as she used to. Still gorgeous but softer. Muted. Or maybe it was Piper who'd changed.

Piper scooted down in the booth, attempting to hide, but Kiera acknowledged them with a friendly wave. Great. On top of her unease over not speaking to Wyatt in days, the last thing Piper wanted was a face-to-face reminder of her high school heartbreak.

"Excuse me," Piper said to her friends and escaped to the bathroom, hoping to hide out until Kiera picked up her order and left.

But when she came out of the stall, Kiera was standing by the sink.

"Hi, Piper." Kiera twisted the ends of her long black hair around her finger. "I heard about the plane crash, and I've been thinking of you. I'm so relieved you're okay. You and Wyatt." She

smiled, revealing a row of pearly white teeth. "But I wasn't surprised to hear you were together—I always knew you two were
endgame."

"Oh, we aren't together," Piper corrected, her heart constricting at the statement. *You saw to that*, she thought as she busied
herself washing her hands to avoid eye contact.

Kiera swayed on her feet. "I'm sorry, I assumed. My brother,
Donovan, served with him and told me he kept a picture of you
by his bed for years."

Piper turned off the water and met Kiera's gaze in the mirror. Unshed tears stung the backs of her eyes. Even after they'd
parted ways, Wyatt had kept her picture close by?

"I didn't know that," Piper whispered, turning around. "We
hadn't talked in years, not since that day in the clubhouse . . .
when I found out about you. Until we ended up on that island
together."

"*What?*" Kiera's jaw dropped open. "That doesn't make any
sense. If I had any idea that would happen, I never would have
agreed to his stupid request."

Piper folded her arms protectively across her chest. "What request? What are you talking about?"

"I thought Wyatt would have told you by now." Kiera knitted
her brows in confusion. "Piper, nothing happened between us.
I owed Wyatt a favor for agreeing to look out for my brother at
base camp, and he asked me to make it look like you had caught
us meeting for a date. It was all part of Wyatt's plan to get you to
accept the breakup since he knew he wouldn't be able to easily
let you go. I think he needed me as a backup, so he'd actually go
through with it." She bit her lip. "But it was all an act, I swear."

Piper leaned back against the sink, trying to catch her breath
as the information washed over her. The story matched Wyatt's
version of their breakup, and looking into Kiera's wide brown
eyes, she believed her. The revelation knocked her off balance.

All this time, she hadn't underestimated the depth of their love. It hadn't been an afterthought or fleeting, like a passing cloud or fading sunset. It had been real then, which meant it could be real now.

A teardrop slid down her cheek, shortly followed by another.

Kiera frowned at Piper's teary response. "I thought you guys might break up for a few weeks tops. I never imagined it would be permanent. You were always so in sync and you were the only girl he ever looked at. I was supremely jealous of you in high school."

Piper choked out a laugh through her tears. That felt harder to believe.

"Maybe I shouldn't be telling you all this now." Kiera's frown deepened. "If surviving a plane crash wasn't fate screaming at you loud enough to be together, I'm not sure I can make much of a difference. You should know the truth, though. I'm so sorry if I caused you any pain."

"It's okay," Piper said, and she meant it, finally letting go of the past. "Thanks for telling me." She pulled Kiera into an impulsive hug before walking out of the bathroom. Kiera wasn't her enemy. She'd never been.

When Piper slipped back into the diner booth, tears still dampened her face.

"What happened in there?" Allie asked, alarmed. "Do I need to go beat Kiera up?" She stood as if to follow through on her threat.

"No, sit." Piper tugged her back down. "Everything's fine. More than fine." She quickly filled her friends in on what she'd learned from Kiera, along with the real reason behind their breakup.

When Piper finished, Allie threw back her head in a peal of laughter.

"What?" Piper failed to see the humor in the situation.

"It's just that my cousin would've taken a bullet for you. It never made sense how he broke up with you or moved on so quickly.

But ending things thinking he was doing the right thing is the most Wyatt thing ever."

When Allie put it like that, Piper had to laugh, too. It *was* such a Wyatt thing to play the martyr, assume he wasn't good enough, and remove himself from the situation. Piper was mad at herself that she hadn't seen through the whole thing from the start.

"So, to recap," Ethan said, pointing a fry at Piper. "You're no longer dating Tag. You might be in love with Wyatt. He never meant to break your heart, and maybe he's always been in love with you?"

Piper nodded, her eyes shining. "I'm definitely in love with Wyatt." The words dove off her tongue like Olympians into water, performing a routine they'd perfected endlessly. Her entire body buzzed with euphoria.

"Yes! I knew it." Ethan punched his fist into the air. "Wiper forever."

He and Allie exchanged a high five.

"I never signed off on that couple's name," Piper grumbled halfheartedly, but she couldn't wipe the smile off her face.

"This calls for a round of milkshakes." Ethan flagged their waitress down and ordered for the group.

"We can't celebrate yet." Piper's elation burst like a bubble. "Wyatt won't return my calls or answer my texts. We may be over before we even start again. I don't know what else to do."

"Are you fucking kidding me?" Allie's face darkened. "You two survived a week together on a remote island and worked through your issues, but you're letting technology stand in your way?"

Piper's mouth dropped open at Allie's passionate response, but Allie continued, holding out her hand, palm up. "Let me see your phone."

Piper did as she asked, watching as Allie scrolled through her contacts and double-clicked the screen.

"I knew it. You have him blocked." Allie pressed a few more

buttons and handed the phone back to Piper, grinning like a Box-car Child who'd just solved the biggest mystery of the summer. "My guess is he blocked you, too, and y'all have been screaming into the void this entire time."

Could it be as simple as that? If it was, she needed to find Wyatt. Now.

Behind the counter, their waitress placed cherries on top of their milkshakes.

"Wanda, I'm going to need mine to go," Piper called out. "Can you make that two? One's for Wyatt."

Ethan cheered.

Wanda gave her a thumbs-up and set two shakes in to-go cups on the counter a moment later. "Tell Wyatt the extra cherries are from me," she said with a wink. "And these have been paid for by Kiera Gomez."

"I need to go." Piper slung her purse onto her shoulder and snagged one more fry. "Wish me luck, y'all."

"Wait, fists in first." Ethan held his hand out in a tight fist over the center of the table.

Piper didn't have time for this, but Allie stuck her fist on Ethan's and looked up at her expectantly.

"Fine." Piper stacked one fist on top, then the other in the same order.

"Love wins on three," Ethan ordered. "One, two, three. Love wins!"

"Love wins," Piper repeated. She clasped each of their hands before grabbing the milkshakes and heading home.

Home to Wyatt.

Chapter Thirty-Eight

Now

Piper's phone pinged halfway through her drive home, and a voicemail notification popped up. How had she missed a call? She didn't recognize the number but pressed play.

"Hey, it's me." Wyatt's deep vibrato poured through the speakers, nearly causing her to rear-end the car in front of her. "It's Wyatt. I'm calling from Molly's new number because I don't think my messages are getting through. I'm calling because . . ." He paused, sucking in a winded breath. "I miss you, Piper. I can't sleep without you. I wake up in the middle of the night not knowing where I am and reach for you, but you aren't there. You're the first thing I think of each morning, and I dream about you every night. I'm going crazy over here not talking to you. If you're happy with Tag, I'll support you. I'll be happy for you. But I can't lose you in my life. Not again."

His voice cracked, and he gathered himself. "So, if you only have room for me as a friend, I hope I've earned that spot back. And if you have room for more, well, I'd very much like to discuss that, too." He took another pained breath, and she could picture him running his fingers through his hair like he did when agitated.

Piper's throat tightened. She missed him deeply and not just in a "we've been through major trauma together" kind of way. She craved his company and ached for his touch. She missed his dimpled smile, easy laughter—even his know-it-all survival tips. Hearing his voice without being able to hold him was a bittersweet reminder of the distance between them. Like tasting sea salt without feeling the crash of ocean waves. Her emotions swirled like stormy waters, and she almost missed the end of his message.

"Sorry, this is getting rambly and weird, but I'm at the clubhouse right now. Being out here in the woods helps me think and keeps me calm. It's where I've been sleeping at night since I got back." He took another stuttering breath. "Anyway, I'm heading to the airport in a few hours, but I'd love to see you. I need to see you. If you get this, please come find me."

Her heart almost stopped beating. The airport! Was he going back to Denver already? She hadn't had enough time to set things straight, to tell him she loved him. Twice now, he'd been brave enough to share his inner thoughts, his deepest feelings with her, and she had yet to return the favor. Timing had never been their strong suit, but this felt ironically unfair.

At a red light, Piper checked when he'd left the message. Over two hours ago. He must have called when she was getting ready for dinner, and she'd ignored the unknown number. Pressing her foot down harder on the gas, she urged the car to speed home, hoping against hope she wasn't too late.

She pulled into her driveway with a screech, grabbed the milkshakes, and ran toward the clubhouse. Bursting into the tiny house like a wild animal, out of breath, her hair windblown, she called out for him. "Wyatt?"

No response.

The clubhouse was empty.

Piper set the sweating milkshake cups on the wooden table. The last time she'd been to the clubhouse was over a year ago for a glamping-themed celebration of Allie's engagement. The twinkle lights they'd strung for the party still glowed, though not all the bulbs worked. Faint evening light streamed in through the windows, lighting the room like the inside of a honey jar. On the far side of the clubhouse floor, someone, likely Wyatt, had arranged an assortment of sleeping bags, blankets, and pillows—a comfier re-creation of their island sleeping arrangements.

Sinking to the floor, Piper settled into the pile of pillows and leaned back against the wall, cursing herself for being too late. For not paying attention to her voicemails. For blocking Wyatt all those years ago.

She tried calling, then texting Wyatt to let him know she was at the clubhouse, but both call and text went unanswered. Maybe she could still stop him at the airport?

Next, she texted Molly. Hey! Do you know what time Wyatt's flight was?

He's on his way home now came Molly's swift reply.

So, that was it. At this very moment, Wyatt was flying home to Denver and away from her without so much as a goodbye.

Piper didn't bother wiping away the tears spilling down her face. Why hadn't she told Wyatt she loved him when given the chance? She'd been so worried about saying the wrong thing or getting hurt that she'd frozen.

Eight years ago, she'd given up on their relationship, but she wasn't that scared little girl anymore. Heartbreak and rejection no longer frightened her. Now she only feared not living her life to the fullest, not taking the kinds of risks that mattered—and losing Wyatt.

This couldn't be the end.

Drying her eyes, Piper formulated a new plan, determined not to let miscommunication and bad timing tear them apart again. Maybe she could get on a plane for Wyatt. The mere idea of flying made her stomach burn, but sitting idle and doing nothing was unbearable. According to the airline's website, the next flight to

Denver left in two hours. If she hurried, she could arrive there by late tonight.

Piper stood and took a long, frothy pull of her milkshake, the sweet drink spreading liquid courage to her nerves.

She could do this.

Securing her hair into a high ponytail, she opened the clubhouse door to face this next challenge, but an animal moving at breathtaking speed knocked her to the floor.

Something wet and warm licked her face.

From the ground, Piper blinked.

A shaggy black dog with a teddy bear face nudged a green, chewed-up stuffed animal toward her with his nose, whining softly. He wanted to play.

Piper pushed herself up to sit, still catching her breath. The dog resembled a real-life version of the cartoon Goofy, with floppy black ears and a big dumb grin. Most of his fur was dark, but he had a white ruffled bib of curls on his chest and tufts of white hair between his toes. She scratched behind his ears, searching for a collar or identification, but found none.

"Where did *you* come from?"

The dog settled at her feet, his head resting on his stuffed animal toy, looking up at her balefully. Judging from his full belly and shiny coat, this was someone's pet, not a wild animal coming to eat her. Good thing, because that would have been a very tragic ending after her already pathetic evening.

"Badger!" a voice shouted from outside. A familiar voice that sent butterflies scattering in all directions deep in her stomach.

A voice she loved.

Piper wiped the mascara from under her tearstained eyes, certain she must be dreaming. A moment later, Wyatt's broad frame filled the clubhouse door. Even though his Wranglers and fitted white shirt were wrinkled, his eyes haunted, and his hair disheveled, Wyatt was the most welcome sight she'd ever seen—sunshine piercing through the clouds on a rainy day.

All she wanted was to bury herself in his warm pine scent and feel the scratch of his beard against her cheek. To press her lips against his and forget all the pain and confusion they'd ever caused each other, but everything left unspoken between them prevented her from running to him.

Wyatt snapped his fingers, and Badger jumped up to sit beside him. "Sorry about Badger. He has a hard time with boundaries." He smoothed his bedhead hair and gifted her with a shy smile. "I was hoping you'd be here."

Slowly, Piper stood, brushing the wrinkles out of her dress.

"I'm here. But what are *you* doing here?" Her brain whirled.

Wyatt remained in the doorway, shifting his weight from one foot to the other. "Molly said you were looking for me? I would have called, but my phone died. I keep forgetting to charge it."

"Yeah, I was. I got you a milkshake." Piper nodded at the Charlie's Diner cup on the table between them—an easier explanation than everything she needed to tell him.

Wyatt walked closer and gave the milkshake a sniff. "As long as it's not papaya flavored, I'll drink it."

"It's Oreo. Extra cherries."

He took a sip. "My favorite."

"I know."

He caught her gaze, pulling her underwater until she was drowning in his silver eyes.

"I got your message." Piper took a tentative step in his direction. "You said you were going to the airport. Shouldn't you be in Denver right now?"

He groaned, realization dawning on his face. "No! I went to the airport to pick up Badger. A friend of mine flew him out because I've missed him so much."

Badger barked from his corner like he knew he was the topic of conversation.

"Oh, my God. We really can't keep up with one another!" Piper burst into chaotic laughter, happy relief coursing through her like cool water on a burn.

Wyatt's mouth tugged up in a half smile, but his eyes remained guarded, uncertain. "Did you listen to the rest of my message?" A tremor tinged his words.

His nerves gave her strength.

"I did. I also left you several voicemails, but I don't think you got them."

"I didn't." Wyatt stepped forward until he stood within arm's length of her. "What did they say?"

Piper inhaled shakily. This was it. The moment she'd been waiting for. Her chance to lay it all on the table.

She lifted her face, capturing his gaze. "They said, I'm sorry I left the hospital the way I did. I should have made it clear Tag's not my boyfriend. He never was, and my mom knows that now. I said, sometimes I wish we were still on the island because then I'd get to wake up next to you." Words poured out of her like a waterfall now. "I left a message saying I hate falling asleep without saying good night to you. I can't stop thinking about you. I miss you. You're my best friend, and I need you—"

Wyatt cut her off before she could finish, closing the gap between them with a single stride. Putting a hand behind her head, he pulled her roughly toward him until his open mouth joined hers. The shock of his hot lips on hers jolted every fiber of her being.

Brought her back to life.

His tongue tangled with hers, spelling out his love for her without words, his mouth moving over hers with the same uncontrollable longing she'd been holding on to for what felt like a lifetime. Kissing Wyatt mended her wounded ego and bruised heart. Every kiss pulled her deeper in love.

Piper wove her fingers through Wyatt's thick hair, tugging him closer, straining to press her entire length against his. He responded by clasping his hands under her butt and hiking her up so their faces aligned. Emboldened by this new access to his lips, Piper wrapped her legs around him like a pretzel, crushing herself to him, deepening their kiss. She could stay like this all night and planned to, but first, there was so much she needed to say.

Pulling back, she rested her forehead on his, their noses touching. "Wait, wait. I still need to tell you something."

A flash of fear passed over Wyatt's face, and he set her down.

Piper twined her fingers through one of his hands and stroked his cheek with her other hand, wanting to wipe the doubt from his brow. Swallowing hard, she made herself look at him before she spoke. "I need to tell you I love you. That I'm *in* love with you."

Though they were terrifying to say out loud, it was a relief to release words that had been frolicking in her heart for days, years, yearning to burst free.

Wyatt's grin split his face, dimples beaming on full display.

"Come here," he murmured, pulling her back to him and kissing her, unrushed and deliberate. Then he crushed her to his chest, burying his face in her hair. She hugged him back, breathing deeply, wondering if she had ever been this happy in her whole life.

"I love you, too," he whispered in her ear, sending a shiver down Piper's spine. "Always have."

His affirmation set her soul on fire. She lifted her face and found his lips again. Her whole body buzzed like she was filled with champagne fizz and might float away on a cloud of happiness. Only Wyatt's lips on her cheeks, her neck, and her mouth kept her anchored to earth.

Wyatt had Piper's dress off before she'd even unbuckled his

belt. She tugged at his pants while he pulled off his T-shirt and tossed it to the side, not looking where he threw it. His gaze locked on hers, a hunter staring down his prey. The second he kicked his shoes off, he scooped Piper up and laid her on the pile of blankets on the floor.

"Thank God I dragged these out here," he said, more to himself than to Piper as he kissed his way from the curve of her neck to the valley between her breasts.

"It is a step up from sleeping on a bridesmaid dress." She sighed happily as his mouth teased one breast, then the other.

Wyatt continued kissing down her stomach, past her belly button, to the part of her that ached most for his touch. "What I have planned for you does not involve sleep."

Piper choked out a strangled "good" before losing herself under Wyatt's roguish mouth until she begged him for more.

For all of him.

She pulled on his hair, yanking him back up until he hovered over her.

"I love you," she told him again, running her hands over his shoulders and down his back, then back into his hair, coaxing him closer.

He stilled, staring deep into her eyes. "I love you, too."

Was he remembering their first time in this exact location the way she was? It was unbelievable how far they'd come from that moment, how much had changed, and how deep their love had grown.

Then he was moving inside her, and Piper couldn't think about anything but the feel of Wyatt deep within her. Time stood still, sunlight waning, shadows stretching across the wooden floor. Once again, they were on an island of their own, the world melting away around them. Piper could see the boy he'd been, the man he'd grown into, and the guy she wanted to spend the rest of her life with all at once.

She loved every one of them.

When they parted, Wyatt drew a blanket over them and held her against his chest, kissing the top of her head.

From his corner, Badger barked loudly, demanding some of the attention for himself. Wyatt whistled, and Badger trotted over, tail wagging.

Piper turned in Wyatt's arms to rub Badger's furry stomach as he sprawled before her. "I can see why you missed him. He's awfully cute."

"Don't let him fool you. He's a troublemaker."

"Kind of like someone else I know," she teased.

He laughed into her hair.

Badger nosed his chewed-up stuffed animal closer to Piper and whined.

"He wants you to play, but once you start, he'll never leave you alone," Wyatt warned. "He takes that thing with him everywhere."

Piper indulged Badger by throwing the toy to the corner of the clubhouse, laughing as he retrieved it in several bounds and carried it back, panting eagerly. "What is it?"

"Well, it was a frog, but he's chewed it beyond recognition. Damn dog stole it from me the day I adopted him."

Piper examined the shredded stuffed animal more closely, recognizing the shape of its worn-out eyes. Warmth tickled her rib cage. "Wait, is this the frog you won from the state fair?"

He kissed her temple, his hand snaking around her stomach to tug her closer. "It's the frog *you* won and gave to me. That thing's been to literal war and back without a scratch and look at it now. I can't blame Badger, though. It acted as my lucky charm for many years, and now it's his."

Piper tossed the toy for Badger again and twisted in Wyatt's arms, facing him. Cupping his face, she looked at him in awe, her eyes prickling with happy tears. "You kept it all this time?"

He swallowed thickly and nodded, arms tightening around her. "Even when we were apart, I never stopped thinking about you. You were always with me."

Piper melted into his kiss, blown away by how much Wyatt truly loved her. Had always loved her. All this time, she'd felt blindsided by him, but maybe she'd just been blind. Because here in this moment, lying in his embrace, cocooned in his warmth and on fire from his kisses, there was no other way to interpret how he felt about her. They were meant to be together, and no matter what challenges lay ahead, they would face them side by side.

Piper lifted her gaze to him. "So, am I your girlfriend again?"

"No." Wyatt laughed at the frown on Piper's face. He tilted her chin up for another kiss. "You're my everything."

Piper smiled against his lips and burrowed into the nook on his chest, carved for her alone. She could get used to that.

"So, I have some news." She kissed his chest above his heart. "I quit med school. Officially. I'm not jumping into anything right away, but I'm considering studying to be a librarian, and there happens to be a great program out west."

"Piper, that's amazing! You would be an awesome librarian. Congrats. How far west are we talking? Close to Colorado?" He held up crossed fingers.

"Very close. It's in Denver. I thought I might check out the campus and see if I could make a life there."

Wyatt grinned. "I could help with that."

"I was hoping you would."

"So, it's settled. As soon as I'm cleared from physical therapy, you, Badger, and I will road-trip to Denver."

She angled her face to kiss him. "That sounds perfect."

"Maybe we can detour and visit my uncle and cousins in Tennessee."

Piper sat up. "Really? You reached out to them?"

"I did, and they want to meet me. But I'd love company if you're up for the adventure."

"I'm not sure I trust your definition of adventure, but that sounds like something I can handle." There was no way she'd miss meeting Wyatt's extended family.

Piper groaned. "Speaking of family, I should let my parents know where I am so they don't call the National Guard." She shimmied back into her dress before texting her parents.

"What are your parents going to think about this?" Wyatt frowned, following her lead and sitting up, pulling on his boxers and T-shirt. "About you and me."

"It doesn't matter. It's my life, not theirs." Piper sat cross-legged in front of him.

Wyatt bit his lip, still looking worried. "I've spent the last eight years doing everything I can to become someone worthy of you. To prove I'm good enough to call you my girl. All I ever wanted was to be the kind of man that you're proud to be with. And I want your parents to be proud, too."

She placed her hands on his shoulders. "You are more than worthy. You always have been." She wished he could see himself the way she saw him. Strong, brave, kind. Exceptional.

When he wouldn't meet her gaze, she climbed into his lap and wrapped her legs and arms around him, so he had nowhere else to look but at her. "Anyone who can't see how wonderful you are is an idiot. And that includes my parents. No one will tell me what I should be or who I should be with. And I want to be with you."

His eyes swirled with a brewing storm of emotions, and his Adam's apple bobbed.

She kissed his cheek, nose, then the corner of his lips, forcing him to acknowledge her words. "You're the best guy I know, and I'm so lucky to be loved by you."

"We're both pretty lucky," he agreed, capturing her lips in a kiss.

"The luckiest."

Wyatt withdrew, his expression growing serious. "Hey, can I ask you something important?"

"Anything." A million terrible scenarios raced through her head.

"How does *The Wrong Duke* end? It's been keeping me up at night."

Piper dissolved into laughter and smacked his arm. "I thought you hated that book."

"I don't hate it!" he protested. "I need to know if Lady Arrieta and the Duke figure it out."

"They do. It ends happily ever after."

Wyatt beamed, dimples flashing. "I like the sound of that."

"Me, too," Piper said, sealing her words with a kiss.

Epilogue

Six Months Later

Snow crunched under her boots as Piper wound through the trees along the path leading to the clubhouse. Fluffy white flakes danced like a shaken snow globe, kissing her nose and settling on her coat. There was nothing like the magic of the first snow in the South, especially when it coincided with the holidays.

The clubhouse was easy to spot among the bare trees, lit up within an inch of its life in soft white icicle lights. A green fir wreath adorned the door, and jolly red bows hung from the windows. Inside the clubhouse, Christmas décor made it look like the home of one of Santa's elves.

It was the day before Christmas Eve, and Ethan had called an emergency meeting of the Lonely Onlys for 6:00 P.M. sharp. At 5:50, Piper arrived first. Being back in the clubhouse was like pulling on her favorite worn sweatshirt—cozy, comfortable, and nostalgic.

Wyatt walked in a few minutes later, stomping his feet and shaking snow out of his springy dark hair. He spotted Piper and broke into a dimpled smile that made her glow as warm as a southern summer day despite the mini snowstorm raging outside. Badger trotted in behind him and ran up to Piper, who leaned down to ruffle his fur and let him lick her face.

Wyatt shrugged his jacket off, revealing a gray Henley that matched his eyes. "I guess I should get used to Badger getting the first kiss these days," he grumbled, hanging his jacket on the back of a chair and moving toward her. "Hey, stranger."

"Hey, yourself." Being in the clubhouse with Wyatt always had a dizzying effect on her. "It's been too long."

"I know. I've missed you." He brushed a melted snowflake off Piper's cheek.

She grinned up at him and pulled his face down to meet her lips, their cold noses warming from the scorching kiss. "I missed you more."

"Barf. Get a room!" Allie walked into the clubhouse with Oliver.

Wyatt gave Allie a playful middle finger and continued kissing Piper.

"Didn't you guys just see each other?" Allie complained. "I used to think you two getting back together would be amazing, but I'm changing my mind."

Since road-tripping to Colorado, Piper had never left. After taking one MLIS class this fall and loving it, she would start a full load in the spring. She and Wyatt took Badger hiking every warm weekend and read by the fire when the nights grew cold.

Piper playfully nudged Wyatt away and hugged her friend. "In our defense, we slept in separate rooms while visiting Wyatt's relatives in Tennessee."

Since reaching out to his relatives, Wyatt had steadily built a relationship with his newfound family through regular video calls with his uncle Andrew and cousins Darren and Rory, who were only a few years younger than Wyatt. The initial in-person meeting had been awkward for less than thirty seconds before everyone embraced and cried and welcomed Wyatt back into the family, thrilled to be reconnected to the nephew and cousin they thought they'd lost forever. They'd welcomed Piper, too, and the time they'd spent making holiday memories this week would not be their last.

Sandra, his paternal grandmother, still had the Christmas stocking she'd knitted for Wyatt when he was a baby and hung it proudly on the mantel. Piper thought her heart would overflow with gratitude that Wyatt had found another piece of himself in the world to call his own.

"Plus, we stayed separately at our respective houses last night, too." Wyatt embraced Allie and Oliver.

Allie unwound her scarf from her neck. "Speaking of, how is it with your mom since being back, Piper?"

Piper shrugged. "We're still adjusting to all the changes, but I think the distance and space apart have been good for us. Time will tell."

Her parents had flown out to Denver for a visit a few months ago, and Piper had been incredibly nervous initially, but her mom had been on her best behavior. It turned out Wyatt was a skilled cook, having learned a few things in the army, and they'd found common ground in the kitchen. They wouldn't all send out a family Christmas card together anytime soon, but it was a start.

"If the clubhouse had heat, I'd insist Piper stay out here with me. I'm not sure how many more nights I can go apart." Wyatt bent his head to kiss Piper again.

"Maybe I'll have to sneak in through your window tonight." She kissed him back.

"Wait until he knocks you up, and nothing fits, and you have morning sickness all day long." Allie rubbed her small baby bump while glaring at Oliver, who raised his hands in mock surrender. "Then see how much you miss him."

"For the record, I still miss you anytime you're gone," Oliver said sweetly.

Allie rolled her eyes but kissed his cheek. "And that's how this baby happened in the first place."

As hard as she pretended to be upset, Allie glowed with pride.

Her steadfast adoration of Oliver was obvious, and the two would be awesome parents.

"I still can't believe you're having a baby!" Piper shook her head in amazement, caressing Allie's bump. "I'm so excited to spoil this little one."

Ethan poked his blond head through the doorway. "Is everyone here?"

"We're here!" Allie assured him. "What's all the fuss? Why the emergency meeting?"

Ethan strode in, holding Jack's hand, beaming like a fool.

"We're engaged!" He held up his hand, where a simple silver band with a tiny diamond sparkled. Jack showed off a matching one with an equally sparkling smile.

The room exploded in cheers of congratulations and applause, everyone surrounding them with hugs and pats on the back.

"Welcome to the family, Jack." Piper wiped a tear from her cheek. Ethan had never looked more relaxed and at peace than beside Jack.

"Thanks, guys. It didn't feel official until we all celebrated together." Ethan produced a bottle of Veuve Clicquot from his bag, a sparkling seltzer for Allie, and several plastic cups. He filled their cups and passed them out.

"To Jack and Ethan!" Allie declared, and everyone toasted and took a sip.

Jack and Ethan kissed as Wyatt whistled loudly among a chorus of "aaws."

"Y'all are next," Allie whispered to Piper, nodding in Wyatt's direction.

"I know." Piper smiled. "But we aren't in a rush."

They'd had many long talks in front of a crackling fire about the future and what they both wanted out of life. In all versions of their daydreaming, they were together, married, and surrounded by children—the inevitable part, the guarantee, the promise. Everything else was wide open, an adventure to explore together, and they were more than happy to focus on the present moment, living life to the fullest.

Oliver leaned over to share a private joke with Allie. She looked down at her bump, then up to Oliver with a mischievous wink. By the door, Jack and Ethan compared rings, twisting and turning them to admire how they twinkled in the light. Piper laced her fingers through Wyatt's and smiled up at him. He brushed a quick kiss on her lips, tugging her closer.

The tiny room overflowed with love, thick as honey. Surrounded by the Lonely Onlys—her favorite people in the world—each of whom was standing next to their favorite person—Piper couldn't imagine a better feeling than the warmth and love coursing through her body. And best of all, she had her best friend and the love of her life all wrapped up in one.

Piper cleared her throat to get everyone's attention. "Hey, guys, I think we need a new group name."

Allie raised a curious eyebrow.

"I mean, look at us." Piper held up her and Wyatt's interlocked hands and gestured at the couples standing close to each other. "We're not exactly Lonely Onlys anymore."

Ethan nodded, wrapping his arm around Jack's shoulders. "Piper's right. We're more like the Lucky Ones."

Piper nodded. "It doesn't rhyme, and it's super cheesy, but I like it."

Allie raised her cup. "To the Lucky Ones."

"The Lucky Ones," everyone echoed, clinking glasses.

Ethan poured more champagne as the celebration continued.

Wyatt squeezed Piper's hand. "The luckiest," he said so low only she could hear. She lifted onto her tiptoes, wrapping her arms around his neck, and pulled his face close to hers. Wyatt captured her mouth with a searing kiss, locking his arms around her waist.

Ignoring their friends' "oohs" and "aahs," Piper kissed him back, thanking the universe for luck, lifelong friends, and love.

And second chances.

Acknowledgments

The acknowledgments have always been one of my favorite parts of a book, so it's surreal to write my very own. The act of writing is often a solitary experience (especially when drafting during a pandemic) but creating a book and putting it out into the world takes a village—and I'm lucky to have the very best villagers in mine.

Tessa Woodward and Madelyn Blaney, my editors extraordinaire, thank you for your immediate belief in Piper and Wyatt's story. I'm still pinching myself that I get to work with not one but two smart, thoughtful, and wildly talented editors. And to the entire team at Avon and HarperCollins, I'm so fortunate *Crash Landing* found a home here.

My agent, Cathie Hedrick-Armstrong, thank you for your unwavering support and many editing checklists. You are the best agent mom and cheerleader, and you've made me a stronger writer.

A huge thank you to my Kiss Pitch mentors, coauthors Erin Rose ("the Katies"). I'm so grateful you picked me. Your edits, support, advice, and friendship are the reasons why this book exists. I'm blown away by your talent and thrilled we are agent sibs. Thank you doesn't feel like enough!

And, of course, to my fellow Kiss Pitches. I feel so lucky to be part of this talented group of writers. Your camaraderie and support mean the world to me. To my writing Discord groups—SM 2.0, the Tortured Writers Department, the

Kitchen Party, and 2025 Debuts—you've been a wealth of knowledge and my safe place throughout this journey.

Alex Sunshine, the first (and only) person to read the original version of this story. Thank you, thank you, thank you for seeing the diamond beneath my messy draft and encouraging me to make those first massive revisions that ultimately led to this!

To Emily Wood, my critique partner and now dear friend. The moment we started writing together, everything changed for the better, and now here we are with debut novels like we dreamed. We did it! Thank you for the many writing sprints, *Schitt's Creek* and *Ted Lasso* GIFs, and endless hours spent on Zoom discussing books, television, publishing, and sometimes writing. Your thoughtful edits and clever ideas are woven into the fabric of this story.

To Jessica Hartung, my creative genius bestie, for being part of my writing journey from the beginning. Thank you for being a sounding board, helping me brainstorm plot points, and for encouraging (and sometimes demanding) me to keep going.

To Evelyn Koh and Mary Riddle, thank you for instantly jumping on board with enthusiastic support when I announced I was writing a book and for reading multiple versions. I'm so grateful for our monthly dinners and book swaps.

To my other early readers, I appreciate your feedback and enthusiasm so much: Ryan Huckabee, Gina Dean, Aunt Linda, Aunt Barb, Holly Pike, Ava Watson, Marie Schow, Shiran Lugashi, Shayna Becker, and Vienna Veltman.

Thank you to my mom and dad for their endless support and for being nothing like Piper's parents! To my sister, Carrie Simpson, for being my co-manifester PR queen, and for giving me two perfect angel nieces.

And to John, my love, who didn't want a shout-out because he doesn't want to "take credit" for my writing, but has provided endless support throughout this publishing roller coaster, dreamed big with me, and celebrated every milestone. If I had to pick, I'd choose to be stranded on a desert island with you.

To every single other person who has encouraged me and my writing, including the Hill Friend Fam, my Raleigh Girls, the Best Team Eva, Cameron, and the Between the Tropes book club. Y'all are simply the best!

A shout-out to the Bookstagramers, BookTokers, librarians, book reviewers, and booksellers for loving stories and getting them into readers' hands. You are the real heroes.

And most of all, to you, dear reader. My dream of publishing a book would not be possible without every single one of you who bought, borrowed, listened to, or downloaded this book. I am forever grateful.

About the Author

Annie McQuaid lives in North Carolina and works as a marketing director for an education technology company. When she's not putting her characters in life-or-death situations, you can find her visiting the beach, blasting Taylor Swift, tackling her never-ending TBR, or spending time with her adorable nieces. *Crash Landing* is her debut novel.